WINNER OF
DUNDEE INTERNATIONAL BOOK PRIZE

Judging panel:

Neil Gaiman
Kirsty Lang
Scott Pack
Stuart Kelly
Felicity Blunt

The Dundee International Book Prize has been running for 14 years and provides a chance for debut authors to have their voices heard. The prize is £10,000 and a publishing deal with Cargo. It is supported by the University of Dundee, Dundee, One City, Many Discoveries Campaign and Apex Hotels. For more information about the prize please visit www.dundeebookprize.com.

Praise for *The Other Ida*

"A brilliant debut. Fresh, lyrical, fearless, and very funny."

~Emma Jane Unsworth

"A brilliant first novel about the ultimate dysfunctional family. Truly original and exciting – a must-read."

~ Viv Groskop

"A fine debut from an exciting new voice in fiction."

~Scott Pack

"*The Other Ida* is a wild, exuberant ride through booze, Bournemouth, family, funerals, soul-searching and sisterhood. It's singular, inventive, warm and deeply affecting."

~ Beatrice Hitchman

"Ida will 'always do what needed to be done for fun and adventures and art.' Relish her story and Amy Mason's sensuous writing. Both have a dazzling spark and a delightful bite. I love this book. It is a winner."

~Tiffany Murray

THE OTHER IDA

Amy Mason

Cargo Publishing

The Other Ida
Amy Mason
First Published in 2014
Published by Cargo Publishing
SC376700
Copyright © Amy Mason 2014

ISBN 978-1-908885-24-1

Printed and Bound by Bell & Bain in Scotland
Typeset by Cargo Publishing
Cover design by Kaajal Modi
Cover photography by Michael Gallacher

www.cargopublishing.com
www.dundeebookprize.com
www.dundee.com

Also available as:
Kindle Ebook
EPUB Ebook

For my family and Stef

Chapter one

Standing up to her knees in the sea, Ida spread her long arms wide against the freezing wind.

"The sky is bruised and low," she shouted, over the shrieks of the gulls above.

It was still very early and the sky was marbled with colours she'd hate on her bedroom walls – princess pink, vein violet, fairy-wing grey – while the usually soupy sea sparkled with the greens and golds of a fish's tail. Far to her right, at Sandbanks, the silhouettes of houses had been transformed into dragon's teeth and treasure.

She sucked hard on her cigarette and turned towards the smudged black line of Bournemouth Pier. They could go there afterwards and muck about on the empty rides. It would be properly scary with no one about.

"The sky is bruised and low," she said again. "The gulls swoop and squeal their secret songs, there is nobody else around."

"It's ready, Ida – it's on," came a small, strained voice from the beach.

The wind was blowing her hair across her face, but through it Ida could just make out the figure of her sister. Alice was holding the ancient square black Standard 8 high with both hands and visibly shivering in her nightie.

Ida squeezed her eyes shut, prayed quickly for inspiration, and dropped her damp cigarette butt into the sea.

"Here I am," she roared. "This is my home now. I have given up my ugly shoes and my cardie – given up the trappings of modern life."

She pulled at her hair.

"See the seaweed of my hair, my iridescent limbs flailing," she said, flailing them.

She grabbed her new breasts.

"My breasts are jelly fish... my eyes are giant pearls." She opened them wide. "I am the sea. My breath is the slow creep of the tide. I am at peace."

Flinging her arms into the air, she fell back, the icy water a rock against her skull. But she had done it. She would always do what needed to be done for fun and adventures and art.

She stood up and waded towards the beach, her mother's blue kimono heavy against her skin.

Alice looked like she was going to cry and jiggled one arm around wildly. But she had filmed it. And that was all Ida cared about. She was sure she looked fantastic.

"There you go, nothing to it. Do what I did – remember the lines from the play but add in your own stuff too."

Ida's hands were stiff with cold and she could hardly hold the old cine-camera, but her determination to make Alice do what she'd just done was so strong that she couldn't give up.

"Right in it, Ida? What about my grommets?"

"Fuck your grommets – think of Joan of Arc. And you don't have to put your head under. Or put your head under but put your fingers in your ears."

Alice walked forwards slowly, tucking her hair behind her ears again and again. She was wearing one of Ida's nightdresses and it was far too big for her; against the enormous sky she looked like a toddler. She put one foot in and pulled it straight out.

"It's freezing! God."

"Do it," said Ida.

The filming plan had been fully formed when Ida had woken up that morning, as if it had been shoved right into her brain while she'd slept. She imagined Our Lady, or someone else magical, leaning over her bed in the night and whispering *make a film on the beach, Ida, it'll be fantastic*. And she'd done what they'd said, of course.

Alice had stayed quiet as she was lifted from her bed, crusty eyed and floppy with sleep, denied even her jacket and shoes. Then she'd followed on her battered pink Raleigh as they headed through the chine, while in front Ida peddled like crazy on her rusty red shopper, their mother's kimono brushing the spokes.

The pine trees smelled so strong in the damp, early morning that Ida could taste them. Beside her the stream whispered as she rode – *go girls, go go go!* – while in the distance gulls made inky shapes against the fading moon.

"Drown or burn?" Ida had asked as they rode up the hill, wobbling over branches and through patches of mud.

"Drown, I reckon," said Alice, panting.

"Shag Peter Green or Daniel Sears?" Ida asked.

"Ummmm."

"Neither. You're nine. Kill Ma or Me?"

"Errr, Ma, I suppose."

"Right answer," said Ida as they got to the top. "Now take your hands off the bars. Don't be a wuss."

As they'd gone over the brow of the hill they'd stopped peddling – their legs out, their hair glowing under the brightening sky, the icy wind against their skin making them hard and reckless and wonderful.

"This is how I want to go!" Ida had roared as they flew towards the beach. "Gliding down a hill then BAM, hit by a truck or something. Perfect."

Alice stood at the water's edge with her arms out, her fingertips touching the horizon. Slowly, wincing, she started to walk in. "I'm in the sea," she shouted back half-heartedly, close to tears.

"You're a poet aren't you, Alice? Be a bloody poet." I am lying, Ida thought, she is a scientist, or something else boring.

"I am as cold as ice, as a dead person, a fish," said Alice, drowned out almost entirely by the sound of the birds above. "The sea is salty and grey like my tears, the sand is yellowish like my skin... and... and..." she started to sob.

Ida almost wanted to hug her. She left the camera by the bikes, waded into the sea and grabbed her sister's shoulders, staring into her eyes before pushing down, hard.

Alice's knees buckled and she slipped sideways into the water, her silent open mouth the last thing to disappear beneath the waves.

Ida knelt and held her sister there, pressing her hair and face as Alice began to struggle.

There was a sharp pain in Ida's palm and she pulled her hand away, amazed to see deep teeth marks filling quickly with blood as the small girl emerged, her hair covering her face, panting violently and clawing at the sea as though it was earth.

Chapter two

Ida woke up with her leg over her boyfriend's naked thigh and instantly felt the bare mattress with her palm. Dry. She had recently developed the terrible habit of wetting herself when drunk. Still, there was a haze of what felt like embarrassment, and it was only when she lit a cigarette that she remembered what Terri had said on the phone the night before. Her mother had finally died.

She walked across to the sink to pee, pulling down her shorts and hopping up onto the kitchen unit, which creaked beneath the weight of her. Ida was used to the creaks and had tried to prepare herself for the day it would actually collapse. She mouthed the words to herself as she sat with her legs dangling.

"Mum's dead. Ma is dead. My mother, Bridie, is dead."

The ceilings were low in Ida's new bedsit and she hunched her shoulders instinctively as she walked back over to Elliot, despite the three-inch gap between the plaster and her head. The floor slanted to the right making her feel even wobblier than the hangover would have done on its own. Although it was morning it was very dark – Ida's room had once been the roof space and the tiny window was almost entirely covered by the sign outside that read 'rooms to let, DSS no problem'.

Ida sat on her bed. The room was pretty empty, she didn't have much stuff, but what she did have was brightly coloured – a rainbow of scarves hung from her wardrobe door, while the wardrobe itself remained empty apart from some tissues and books on the bottom slats. Her clothes were on the floor – floral Crimpolene dresses, stretched out t-shirts with holes in them and white stains under the armpits, hand-knitted jumpers that had belonged to old boyfriends, a couple of stringy, ill-fitting bras. At the end of the bed stood her huge red motorcycle boots.

Canvases lined the room, new ones facing outwards, ones she

had painted on against the wall to hide her shame. For a while she'd liked painting and still had a cardboard box full of art stuff on the shelves by the door, tubes of oils and acrylics mixed in together with gold pens and stiff brushes and broken pencils.

They were pictures of her flat, or self-portraits sometimes, her hair piled high on her head and wrapped in a scarf, her big bottom lip hanging in an expression of artistic disinterest. She didn't do much of that sort of thing now.

"Hello, yes, I'm the daughter of the late Bridie Adair," she said quietly to herself. Would they make a documentary about her mother? Would she get asked to be in it? That would be bloody brilliant.

Perhaps, even better, she'd find things in the house, important things about the play, and write a book about her mother or even make a documentary of her very own. She'd become a millionaire, maybe. Or a thousandaire at least. She hoped it happened before the millennium came and the whole world fell apart.

On Ida's bed lay a bare duvet, and a yellow sheet – translucent with age – was crumpled up into a ball. The mattress was stained with dark shapes that had only bothered her the first time she'd slept on it.

By her pillow was a cabinet where important things were kept – her collections of pills, her ashtray and her fags, tampons, bottles, some books.

The opposite wall was covered with floor-to-ceiling cupboards. Inside were three melamine kitchen units, their green doors bloated and cracked with damp. On the scratched work surface was a two ring electric hob, a kettle, a toaster and a minuscule fridge. Apart from some bits of dry spaghetti a previous inhabitant had left, the units were empty. Ida ate from Halal Fried Chicken around the corner – *burger, chips and coke only £1.50!* – and empty polystyrene takeaway boxes lay all over the floor. Elliot was appalled and had promised to cook her a meal. In four-ish years he hadn't yet.

Out of the room and to the right was the bathroom and loo, and Ida could hear the grunts of the man who lived downstairs as he took his morning shit. The toilet was filthy, the ripped lino streaked and stained with years-old piss and the dust on the cistern so thick you could cover your hand in it, which was why Ida used the sink. Fingers crossed it would hold out on her.

"Yeah, it's been a difficult time. But at least she's at peace now," Ida mumbled, practicing.

Elliot yawned, put his hand up her t-shirt, and rested it on her stomach.

"Fuck," she said.

He opened his eyes and reached over her for his packet of fags.

Ida looked at the faint, ugly marks on the inside of his forearm, a reminder of his recurrent and worrying habit, before catching herself, and moving her eyes to his face. "I'm going to have to go fucking home," she said.

Ida threw the paper onto the floor of the coach and then picked it up again, skimming the piece quickly, muttering to herself and sighing loudly as the teenage boy in the next seat eyed her suspiciously.

In the photo they'd printed she looked beautiful – younger than Ida was now, solemn-faced with shiny dark hair and a thick, straight fringe. She was looking straight into the camera, stern and committed, as though she was acting a part.

> Bridie Adair, the controversial playwright who has died aged 57 from liver cancer, was a major figure in the boundary-pushing British theatre world of the 1960s.
>
> Nudity, bad language and honest discussions of sex were hallmarks of her contemporaries' work but it was her strange and haunting depiction of young, working class, Irish women in her debut, *Ida*, which was truly ground-breaking.

The play, written when Adair was just 25, builds to a shocking and tragic conclusion. Adair's writing was influenced by Greek tragedy and in a 1970 interview she said: "I was sick of men's problems being treated with gravity and respect. I wanted to imagine a universe where the supposedly domestic troubles of supposedly ordinary women could be the subject for high drama."

Critic Martin Boyd wrote, in 1972, "Ida is more than the name of a girl. It is something not quite concrete, a feeling or emotion. Perhaps a name for that peculiar, wild spirit that working-class women sometimes possess."

The play's premiere at The Royal Court Theatre in 1967 – in breach of the licensing decision by the Lord Chamberlain – is held up by many as being the final blow to cultural censorship in this country.

The surrounding controversy propelled the play and its glamorous author to brief, unlikely fame, with a subsequent film starring Anna DeCosta. The film differed in many ways to the play and was a modest commercial, if not critical, success.

'Ida is more than the name of a girl. It is something not quite concrete, a feeling or emotion. Perhaps a name for that peculiar, wild spirit that working-class women sometimes possess'. What a load of snobby, sexist bollocks.

Ida folded the paper, bit out the sentence and wiped it on the back of the seat in front of her. With a sigh, the track-suited teenage boy to her left stood up and headed towards the front of the coach, evidently deciding that even the woman with the crying child was better than this. "Fuck this mad bitch," he said loudly as he walked away and people turned to look as Ida laughed, lifting her filthy bare feet and legs onto the now spare seat and turning her back to the wet window. She flattened the paper out on her legs to read the final few paragraphs.

> Adair briefly worked as an actress before marrying television critic Bryan Irons in 1962. She gave birth to her first daughter, Ida, in 1969 with Alice following in 1973. Of her first child's name she said: "I spent two days after the birth deciding what to call her before she let out such an almighty yell that I knew she was Ida after all".
>
> Christened Brigid Catherine, Adair was born in London to Irish parents, and was an only child. Her mother died shortly after childbirth and her father worked as an engineer before succumbing to cancer when Bridie was 16.
>
> Adair struggled throughout her life with alcoholism and depression and Ida remains her only major work. She is survived by her former husband Bryan Irons, and her daughters Ida and Alice.
>
> Bridie Adair, born 12th January 1942, died May 2nd 1999.

Ida closed her eyes and began to shred the paper into strips, dropping them onto the floor. No one had a clue what the play was about, not really, but people had tried to work it out. Ida had been curious when she was little, she still had some ideas. But now, who cared? The woman was dead after all and the play was over thirty years old.

Against the top of her neck the sharp cold of the glass was delicious, and even the water trickling down her back felt better than the numbing heat and stench of the bus.

She woke herself up with a loud snore as they neared Bournemouth, confused for a second about where she was. A woman looked over with disgust and Ida grinned back, tempted to shout that her mother had died. She would leave it – after all, things could be worse. She had downed a mug of whisky with four diazepam and was feeling cushioned and light. As so often in time of supposed tragedy, Ida gleaned enormous comfort from being warm, dry and drunk. Things were rarely as bad as people said.

At the bus station she marched past the rest of the passengers, carrying a Tesco bag with her things in it while the others dragged their luggage through the spit and rubbish that littered the ground.

It was exactly the same as it had been years before – a wide concrete lip over a pawn shop, filthy public loos, a cut-price bookshop and an overpriced sandwich place. In the corner, near the photo booth, a small gang of teenagers stood drinking White Lightning and smoking, the same group, she could have sworn, who'd hung-out there forever. She was still woozy with pills and drink but walked fast with a clear aim in mind.

She'd planned the route she'd take. On the coach she hadn't been able to help going over and over it in her head. She wanted to avoid the beach, to keep to the main streets, and it was about forty minutes she thought if she went down the High Street and took a left through Westbourne, straight to the end of her mother's road.

She couldn't help but notice things. The weird 'American Golf Centre' was still there, druggies in the car park were still there, and the old church, where someone in her family – her dad's aunt Gill maybe? – was supposed to have got married: that was still there too.

Some things were different though. There was an Asda so big it looked like a minor airport, and her beloved, smelly Hothouse – the only club that would let her in when she was thirteen – had been renamed Extreme. But it kind of felt the same. The area by the train station, the nasty bit of town, had the same flat, grey feeling she remembered from when she was young. Bournemouth had always felt grey, actually. It was like all the colour had been used up on the end-of-pier rides and the ugly bedding plants on roundabouts. The rest of the town had to do without.

She headed into the centre and felt a hot rush of anxiety as she realised she may well bump into someone she knew. And what if they'd seen the paper? The thought of their sympathy – their thinly veiled nosiness – made her wish she at least had the cash for a cab.

A flock of seagulls appeared above her and she froze before she heard them call, bracing herself and closing her eyes. They shrieked as they swooped and she bent forwards, her mouth and eyes shut tight, noticing a strange scratch of memory at the back of her throat as though she had just woken and, for a split second, remembered some extraordinary dream.

It had been an unusual day, she thought, she was bound to feel a bit odd. The sky was turning dark and she dug her fingertips into her palms as she walked. It would be okay. She was sure she'd be relieved, rather than angry or afraid, when she finally reached the house.

At first Ida wasn't certain she was on the right road. The corner house, where Mad Harry used to live, its windows covered in newspaper, had been knocked down and in its place stood a block of cream coloured flats. It was the same all along, the 1930s houses that had stood in vast, tree-filled gardens, had been demolished and replaced by glass-fronted towers looking out towards the sea and filling every inch of space.

But not her ma's. As she neared the house she saw the familiar crumbling wall and the overgrown oak tree that she had swung on as a child.

And yes, it looked the same. Not smaller as she thought it might, but as big and unnerving as ever. A steep path led up to the wide white house, which peered over the woods and towards the sea through its mean slits of windows. The pointing was still crumbling and Ida remembered an earnest builder who – so many years before – had told her mother the house wouldn't last the year.

She ran her fingers along the wall and unlatched the gate. A curled, dead squirrel lay at the edge of the path, and she booted it into a bush.

Above her the curtains were closed and the rooms looked dark, but Ida was sure someone must be in, forgetting for a moment that it was her mother who was always at home, and her mother was no longer there.

With her head bowed she climbed the uneven steps, hammered like a bailiff at the chipped black door, and turned to see the lights on the water.

Behind her she heard the slow creak of the lock and held her breath despite herself.

Chapter three

Despite feeling sick Ida had been singing 'Daisy Daisy' to her sister for what felt like hours. Normally there'd be someone else in the car – Uta, sometimes their mother – to calm Alice down if she was upset, but today there was only Da, and he was busy driving.

Ma was somewhere behind them in her little car, the roof down probably, putting on lipstick and smoking while people hooted their horns. Ida hoped she wouldn't crash or get arrested. She'd done both those things before.

On Ida's lap lay two *Observer Spotter's Guides*, *Cats* and *Lizards*, bad choices for a journey that had mainly involved straight, fast roads. She wished she has bought *Cows* or *Trees* instead – she'd seen lots of them.

"Well, your books are all packed," Da said when she had realised her mistake. "You can't have them until we get there. Try to go to sleep."

Instead she looked through the back window at the van that was following them. The two fat removal men sat in the front and Ida was annoyed that they'd be able to read her books if they wanted to, although at the moment they just seemed to be smoking.

Da was humming songs she didn't recognise. On the dashboard lay the cine-camera, ready to catch their expressions when they first saw the house. He was in a good mood, the best mood he'd been in since Christmas. Ida couldn't tell him that she felt ill.

From where she sat she could see the thin bit of hair at the back of his head, the collar of his pink shirt, and his hands tapping the steering wheel. He was wearing the tan leather driving gloves that Ida liked to smell.

"Wanker," he shouted, as a red car pulled out in front of them.

Ida had never heard the word before but liked the sound of it and mouthed it to herself. Alice, who had been dropping off to sleep, started to cry again.

"Nearly there sweetheart," their father said, grabbing at the map that lay open on the seat next to him.

Ida knew that her parents hadn't seen the house, except in photographs, although Da had sent his secretary to have a look. She'd told them they couldn't move in, not until the builders and cleaners had been, but Ma wouldn't talk about it and Da got so annoyed he made them move down straight away.

Bridie didn't want to move at all but they were moving anyway because 'a change is as good as a rest,' Da said. Ida didn't like resting (especially not when Uta made her lie down after lunch). She hoped this change would be better than that.

She imagined the house to be like Miss Havisham's, which she'd seen in a film, and felt scared but excited too. Mostly she was excited about the mice, and planned to put some in a box and keep them as pets. She could imagine her mother sitting in the dark, her dress ripped up like Miss Havisham's was. But what about Da? She tried hard to imagine all his pairs of shiny shoes lined up together on a dusty floor.

Alice was still crying, and kicking now too. She was lying next to Ida on the back seat, twisting and turning, the tell-tale signs she was about to throw a fit. Ida started to sing a song about tigers' feet she'd heard in the playground.

"Not pop music, Ida, please," her father said. Ida was confused. Pop music was about love, not tigers, wasn't it? If that was pop music was 'Old MacDonald' pop music too?

"Sing 'Daisy' again," he said.

But she suddenly couldn't, there was water in her mouth and her tummy felt odd. She put her hand over her lips, but her stomach jumped and sick came through the gaps between her fingers. It went all over her kilt, right down her legs and into her patent shoes. She tried hard to be quiet.

Alice stopped crying. "What's happ'ning Ida? What's happ'ning Ida? Sing 'Daisy' Ida," she said over and over again.

"What's that smell?" Da asked and glanced at them over his shoulder. "Jesus."

Ida could see her sicky face reflected in his sunglasses.

"Sorry," she said.

He took a red handkerchief from his pocket and thrust it back at her. "Here, darling. God. Don't let your mother see you like that."

Ida brushed the worst of it onto the floor, wiped her mouth, and stuffed the hankie in the ashtray while her father lit a cigarette. He was either angry or nervous, she couldn't quite tell which.

Although it was sunny it felt cool and dark in the car. They were kind of in the woods even though there were houses about.

"We're here," he said as they turned sharply into a driveway, gravel crunching under the wheels.

Normally Ida would be desperate to escape after a long drive but something made her sit and wait. She looked out of the window and saw trees everywhere, with some steep stone steps leading up to a house.

Da walked round to the door and pulled it open. "Come on then sweetheart, what are you waiting for?"

She climbed out. There were bushes either side of the narrow path, so overgrown that even skinny Ida couldn't imagine a way through.

"You'll have fun playing in there, won't you?" said Da.

He sounded happy, and Ida nodded although she felt scared. Dead things and monsters, she bet they were everywhere.

The house was enormous and totally flat, with lots of small windows. Their real house, their house in London, had decorations on it, stone bits over the windows, but this one was as smooth as a piece of paper.

"Is this a hospital?" Ida asked.

"This is our new house – you know that. Are you coming down with something?" He touched Ida's head to feel for a temperature.

"But it looks like an advent calendar."

She was serious but her father laughed loudly.

"It's 1920s," he said. "You'd better like it. And please don't let on to your mother if you don't. That's the last thing we need."

He switched on the camera and started filming as the van drove up to the house.

Ida shuffled from foot to foot. Now she needed a wee.

"Look," he said and pointed towards some birds flying overhead.

"Pigeons?" she asked.

"Seagulls."

"Up, up," said Alice, holding her arms out to Ida.

The van stopped and the two men jumped out and opened the doors at the back.

"Ready girls? Follow me," said Da, running halfway up the steep steps then turning round to shoot them with the camera. "There's a surprise at the top I hear."

Ida held Alice's hand and helped her up to the front door.

"Now turn around," he said.

They did as they were told.

"Glorious," he said. He sounded as though he'd opened a present.

Ida felt sick again. From where they stood they could see over the houses and all the pine trees, right down to the sea. Only it didn't look like the seaside sea in Brighton, it looked like something horrible, everything big and grey and mean. She could see the wind, pushing everything in the same direction, all the trees and the boats and the people.

"Ten minutes through the woods and we'll be at the beach. Marvellous, eh?" he said.

She couldn't speak. Tears hurt her eyes and throat until she couldn't stop herself and let them out with a loud sob.

"My goodness, you funny little thing. Let's go inside," he said as he fumbled with the key.

Ida didn't like this house. She didn't like the garden or the scary woods or the horrid view. She was glad that after the summer she could go back to London and see all her friends and her cat. She thought about that and tried to be brave.

"Voila," said her da.

They followed him into the dim hall as he patted the wall to find a switch. "What an adventure. God, it smells funny." There was a scuttling noise and he whooped. "Say it, Ida! Say it!"

Ida knew what he meant – their favourite line from *The Railway Children*. "It's only the ratttssss," she said in a hissy voice and he laughed as he walked to the end of the corridor and switched on a light.

They were in a long hall with a staircase at the end. From the ceiling hung a glass lampshade, all black inside with dust and dead flies. The rose-patterned wallpaper was peeling in places. Near Ida's head some naughty child had drawn a picture of a dog with a green crayon.

"Look Da," Ida said, but he'd gone into another room.

"So through here is the kitchen," he shouted. "Bloody hell, it hasn't been touched since 1950." He ran out and up the stairs. "Okay girls. Let's choose your rooms," he called down to them.

"Come on, Alice," Ida said.

Alice went first up the bare wooden stairs. Ida noticed her bottom was wet, her nappy had soaked through her trousers.

"Be careful, Ally," she said, patting her sister's hair. "There might be splinters."

He met them at the top. "I've worked it all out girls. I'm going at the back, your mother can go over there, and you two are next to each other." He pointed to the left. "Ally baby, you have the little one, Ida, the big one is for you."

Alice sat down. Her face was red and she was rubbing her eyes which meant she was tired.

Ida felt she shouldn't ask, but she needed to – she'd waited all day long.

"When's Uta coming, Da?"

He touched her hair. "Try not to think about her. You've this marvellous house to play in after all."

"But who will change Ally's nappy?"

"Your mother will have to do it I suppose," he said.

He leant down to Alice and picked her up under the armpits. Alice looked bewildered.

Ida stood on the landing. She still needed a wee. Downstairs there was lots of banging and loud, deep voices as the men started to bring in the sofas and the boxes and things. How long before she could have her books and toys? Why wasn't Uta here? She turned to a door her father hadn't said was a bedroom. It was small inside, the floor made up of black and white squares. Her first thought was *good for hopscotch*, and she felt excited, before noticing the brownish loo that stood in the corner with dust all over its seat.

Round the bath was a shower curtain with red and blue fish swimming up and down it and Ida summoned her courage and pulled it back. The bath was the same as the loo, cracked and sort of brown, but at least her bottom wouldn't touch the bath. Climbing over the edge, she rolled down her knickers, and watched her pee snake through the dirt and go down the plug.

She took off all her sick-covered clothes, left them in a pile on the bathroom floor and walked across the landing to the room that Da had said would be hers.

It smelled of dust but was bigger than her room in London, with peach wallpaper and two tall windows that looked out towards the front. The carpet was soft and red and like nothing they had in their old house; it was like something a king would have. She walked into the middle and lay down. The deep pile felt lovely between her fingers and on her naked body. She wished Uta was there to read to them and sing Swedish songs, and plait their hair with her cool, white hands. Ma had said she'd gone on holiday, but when would she be back? Ida never imagined that her holiday would last all the time until they moved.

She shut her eyes. She could hear the wind outside and tried to ignore it. So this was her new house. The house Ma said was probably just for the summer. At least the carpet was nice.

From the corridor downstairs she heard the sharp sound of high heels and knew her mother had arrived.

Ida stood up, closed her bedroom door as quietly as she could, and lay back down on the floor.

Chapter four

~ 1999 ~

"Fuck me, come in then," said Alice.

Ida had forgotten her voice – shaky, high pitched, and still slightly posh. A softer version of Bridie's. It was the voice that Ida had worked so hard to drop. She turned around.

"God," Ida said.

Alice had changed. The mousy fourteen year old was now a slim woman, her wavy hair tied up into a messy bun. Her features were still small and neat, like their da's. She wasn't wearing make-up and looked clean and toned, an immaculate dark blue tracksuit revealed a slice of flat stomach. Ida pointed at it and raised her eyebrows.

"You've got those diagonal lines going down to your fanny, those muscle things – like you're in *Gladiators*."

Alice didn't laugh but put her finger to her lips and pointed upstairs to indicate someone was sleeping, beckoning Ida through the dark hallway towards her mother's study.

"What about my room?" Ida asked, unable to hide the hint of panic her voice.

"Your room?" Alice said. "It's been my room for ten years or something. You'll have to go in here." She opened the door.

"It smells different," Ida said, trying not to look around.

"No fags," said Alice, as she folded out the chair bed in the corner.

"Can I light one?"

"No."

She lit one anyway and Alice threw a cushion hard onto the floor.

"What?" Ida laughed. "It's what she would have wanted."

Alice turned, her face screwed up with irritation, her hands punching the air by her sides. She was whispering so hard her voice sounded raw as she began to chuck quilts and pillows onto the bed.

"Don't tell me what she would have wanted, don't you dare. I can't stand any of your fucking bullshit. Are you pissed? You're slurring your words and you stink, Ida. You can sleep in here, wash your clothes, or throw them away. You can take some of Mum's from the airing cupboard here. No drugs or booze in the house."

Ida laughed but she was taken aback.

"You never used to swear."

"What the fuck do you fucking expect? I've had it."

Ida smiled at her sweetly, her palms held up in mock defeat.

"Oh, fuck off, you big stupid cow," said Alice.

Ida roared with laughter. "Brilliant, Alice, you've surpassed yourself. You look like some Bournemouth High Street nightmare. Nice tracksuit by the way."

Alice took a deep breath and stepped into the doorway. "Get whatever you want from the kitchen. I can't talk to you about this today. Go to sleep, you look terrible and you're drunk." She closed the door.

Ida kicked the side of the bed. She usually loved conflict, excelled at it in fact and was angry with herself for the tracksuit thing, she'd been doing so well up 'til then. She unzipped her boots, pulled down her shiny gym shorts, took off her damp jumper and threw them all on the floor. She had no knickers on – she rarely wore them – so stood in just her falling-to-bits bra as she looked around the room, feeling her squishy curved stomach with her hand. How did you even get a stomach like Alice's? Why exactly would you want one?

In the corner, to her right, was her mother's old oak desk, piled with books and unopened post. Bills mainly, she imagined. She sat on the bed, unravelling the quilt her sister had thrown there, and took the things from her Tesco bag – a box of diazepam, Prozac, Marlboro reds, whisky, Wrigley's Extra – and put them under her pillow. Then she reached for the pills, swallowed two, lay down, and stared at the ceiling. The streetlight from outside made an orange arc against the paper, and in the unfamiliar quiet she hummed to herself. Near the window a spider spun a web, and behind him a damp patch had made the wallpaper curl, revealing the edge of a rose petal pattern and causing her throat to once again itch with the taste of something she couldn't quite place.

It was so light, the bed was so near the floor, and the birds were singing so loudly, that for a second Ida assumed she was sleeping outside. She was cold, almost naked on top of the covers, her neck hurt and she found it difficult to stand.

She picked up her cigarettes and wrapped herself in a sheet as she opened the door to the hallway and walked towards the kitchen, touching the chipped paintwork as she went. The walls were lined with pictures and photographs, dark frames from floor to ceiling, and a marble-topped table held bunches of white and yellow flowers among the dusty plants and handmade pots.

The kitchen looked like it always had, long and dim and narrow with 1950s units and a quarry-tiled floor. It seemed older of course, far more decrepit, but Ida was pleased to see her mother had relented and bought an electric kettle. She put it on and opened a cupboard, searching for coffee, and codeine, if she was lucky.

"If you're looking for pills I chucked them all away."

Alice was standing in the doorway, looking pretty and dishevelled in a fluffy pink dressing gown and a nightdress printed with teddies and hearts. The tracksuit wasn't her pyjamas then, she actually wore the tracksuit out.

"I – shit, you spoilsport, Alice." She had been going to deny it but she'd never win that way. "Do you want a coffee? I'm sorry I didn't get in touch – I didn't have any money for the phone." Her hand went to cover her mouth, aware of the cold sore on her top lip.

"Can I have soya milk, but no sugar please?" Alice said as she sat down at the kitchen table and stared outside while Ida made coffee in silence. The back garden was more overgrown than ever and wild grass reached the handle of the French doors.

"Look I can't be bothered with excuses or anything, leave it, seriously, but while you're here you can help me," Alice said.

"Okay."

"I know what you're like, you enjoy being a victim, and you'll like to say I haven't consulted you, so I want you to help me plan."

"Okay." Ida lit her cigarette on the cooker and watched as Alice went to the dresser, where a penguin Ida had made at school still sat, her tiny thumb prints all over his beak. She opened a drawer and handed Ida a brochure.

"Eco-coffins," Ida read, "awesome."

Alice sat and looked at her nails.

"It's got to be a Manchester United one. Or one of these gold Egyptian things," Ida said.

"I'm serious. It's up to you," Alice said. "I was thinking a willow one. Anyway, she wanted to go to the Catholic graveyard obviously, it'll have to be the one in Charminster, and the funeral is on Tuesday at two – Father Patrick's been so helpful. She always said she wanted to be buried as soon as possible, 'the way the Jews do it', but that was the earliest we could get. We have to sort out flowers and stuff and the wake – or whatever you call it –and who's going to stay here. I'm letting Hendon's, the funeral directors, take over most of it, I don't care how much it costs."

Ida was still reading. "Wait, we could get a plain cardboard one. It says here 'some relatives choose to personalise these coffins with meaningful messages and drawings', she would have loved that. Ha! She'd haunt us for it."

Alice put her hand over her eyes and Ida was surprised when she started laughing too. "God, imagine. We could get Terri to paint on a poem she'd written. Oh wait, Ida. You have to look at the card she sent. It's in the sitting room. She's outdone herself."

Ida put her cigarette out under the tap and sat down at the table.

Alice scrunched up her nose. "What's going on with you Ida? Honestly. You've practically got fucking dreadlocks."

Ida's hand went to her scalp and it was true, the back part of her hair was forming ropes. "You know my hair's weird, this always used to happen when I was younger."

Alice looked sceptical. "Not when you washed it."

"Oh for fuck's sake. Can we not talk about this?" She paused. "Where are you living now? Cornwall or wherever?"

"No, not for years. I moved when I left uni. I live in London. West Dulwich."

"Dull-itch," Ida laughed. "That's not London, is it?"

She noticed Alice's face. "Oh, is it really? Sorry, I don't get out much. Well, don't leave Camden much anyway. It sounds like the countryside or something."

Alice just looked at her.

"When did you get here?" Ida asked.

"I've been here for ages on-and-off – months. You didn't know that? Didn't Da tell you? Fuck me." She started to cry.

"Jesus, Alice, I didn't know," Ida said. "My phone got cut off for a bit..."

Over Alice's shoulder she was surprised to see a man standing in the kitchen doorway, a short, skinny, dark-haired man with a big wonky nose and jaw-length shaggy hair. He was wearing a navy Adidas tracksuit top and faded red boxers and hovering, seemingly unsure about whether to join them. Ida noticed a patch of wee on the front of his underpants.

"Yes, I was here when she was crawling around and screaming in agony, and I was the one who found her having a fit and bleeding from the nose the other day. If you look at the sitting room carpet you can still see the blood. There was lots of it."

"Fuck," said Ida.

"Yes, fuck," said Alice.

Ida looked up as the man walked over and touched Alice's hair. She didn't turn towards him, but instead looked straight and hard at Ida who shook her head.

"I don't know what you want me to say. It's over now I suppose," Ida said.

Alice grabbed a silver candlestick from the table as if to strike her with it and Ida raised her arm to her face, exposing a hospital band.

Alice yanked it off Ida's wrist, and Ida laughed, amazed.

"Alice, Alice, sweetheart," said the man in a soft, northern voice. He held Alice's chin in his small hand and twisted her face towards him. "Sweetheart, sweetheart," he kept saying.

Alice pushed him away, looked at Ida and held up the white band. "How long have you had this on? Months I bet. Does it make people feel sorry for you? Did you overdose? I wish you'd fucking been here, honest to God. All your self-indulgent bollocks would have gone out the bloody window," she said.

Ida was amazed at her luck. There was an audience here and Alice had proven herself, surprisingly, to be loud, angry and potentially violent. Ida looked at the man. She was still wearing only a bed sheet and let it slide down slightly, exposing her cleavage.

"I know you're upset, Alice. But you've got to understand my relationship with her wasn't like yours. She was horrible to me. I hated her. I was fifteen when I left and she didn't give a shit."

"You patronising bitch," Alice said.

Ida stood and took the man's hand. "I'm Ida," she said, "nice to meet you."

"Tom," he said, "yes, you too."

Ida had a reason to look nice, now, which outweighed even the chance to annoy her sister by wearing the clothes she'd turned up in. How'd she got him, Ida wondered, her humourless, anal sister with this scruffy, northern man?

She opened the airing cupboard in the study and was hit by the warm smell of lavender and damp. She started pulling things out – an expensive velvet dress with a tiny, tiny waist, a blue woollen skirt with a perfect, circular hole in it, lots of floral sheets, and some screwed up silk scarves. Her mother had been tall but slim-hipped like Alice and thinner still, and Ida stood at nearly six feet with big hips and breasts and thighs. Nothing was going to fit. It was only when in desperation she pulled at the top shelf that she had any luck. A pale brown tweed man's suit, crisp from some ancient pressing, beautifully made with perfect stitches. The waistcoat was too small but the jacket and trousers were fine. She found a cream thermal vest, slightly yellowed, and wore it as a t-shirt.

Now for her hair. She stood for a moment at her mother's so-called desk – the desk her mother never used – unsure whether to sit down or not. It was a dressing table really, with a dusty mirror attached to the back. She hovered, her fingers inches away from the surface, until reason took hold and with one action she pulled out the chair and sat down. As she cleaned the glass with her palm she could hear the muffled, urgent sound of her sister explaining something, or complaining about something, to Tom.

Stuck on the corner of the mirror was the typewritten quote that had always been there:

The theatre will never find itself again except by furnishing the spectator with the truthful precipitates of dreams, in which his taste for crime, his erotic obsessions, his chimeras, and his utopian sense of life and matter, even his cannibalism pour out on a level not counterfeit and illusory, but interior.

(Antonin Artaud,
'The Theatre of Cruelty: First Manifesto')

Ida hadn't understood it when she was young, but perhaps she did now.

She gazed at herself in the mirror and realised why Alice had been shocked at her appearance. Her skin was dry and sallow and there were purplish circles under her eyes, the corners crusty with black eyeliner from days before. She picked it out with her finger, and then examined the cold sore on the lip and the crusty spots that dotted her chin. Normally she wore a scarf wrapped round her head and without it her wiry dark hair was stiff and matt, unwashed for weeks now. Picking it apart proved useless and she opened a drawer, found a pair of nail scissors, and started to cut it off, first to a bob and then close to her scalp.

Long strings of hair fell onto the papers and carpet and into the drawers. She finished, chose a red silk scarf from the pile on the carpet, tied it round her head and felt cheered-up. There was a knock and she opened the door. Tom stood there smiling, dressed now in flares and a seventies cowboy-print shirt. He had an earring, a silver hoop.

"Wow," he said and nodded as though he approved. Ida gave him a wide smile. "Time for a change I thought. Is Alice okay?"

"Yes, well, kind of. It's been a difficult time. I thought – we thought – we could all go for a walk. To the beach maybe? Alice has gone for a jog, but when she gets back."

"Would the countryside be okay? Or the heath? It's pretty cool, there are snakes. I'm not a big beach fan."

"Of course." He looked relieved that she'd agreed. "That's a bloody good suit, by the way."

They listened to Radio One in the sitting room while they waited for Alice to get back, both drinking black coffee while Ida chain-smoked and talked about the songs that were playing, taking the piss or singing along while Tom nodded and made approving or disapproving noises depending on what was required. He would have liked a cigarette, Ida was pretty sure he smoked from the look of him, but she guessed he wouldn't risk it around her sister.

The room was large with long windows at the end, and one

wall was covered with packed bookshelves. In the far corner was a battered black piano no one could play and there was a TV on it, a new looking silver TV, which looked strange and out of place. On the left was a square, red brick fireplace filled with driftwood and pebbles and above it hung a huge poster that Ida couldn't avoid.

Ida by Bridie Adair it read in rounded pink writing. Underneath the text was a black line drawing of a girl, roaring, her hair becoming flames, and next to her the same girl, naked this time, the line of her bare breast continuing and forming a lily. At the bottom some heavy square black words read: *So Good, So Strong.*

"You'd never get away with that now," Tom said pointing at it. "Everything has to be rammed down people's throats these days – five stars here, an Oscar there." Tom was a film director, or rather the second assistant to one.

To the right of the poster was a large dark square outline on the paint, as though something had been moved from the spot. Ida stood and walked over to it, stroking the wall with her fingers.

"Is everything okay?" Tom asked. "Hey, give us a drag."

She handed him her fag.

"Yes, well no, it's just there used to be a painting here, of my mother," she said, looking around the area as if she might find it. "It belonged to me. It's one of the reasons I came back."

On the sideboard were more flowers and cards. She read a few until she found the one – hand painted – that had to be from Terri.

"Wow," said Ida.

"Fantastic isn't it? Your stepmum sounds like she's something else. I can't wait to meet her."

"*So as you sleep in Jesus' arms, you rest now, happy, free from harm, we've had our struggles, that is true, but dearest Bridie we'll miss you, Terri Irons '99.* She signed it. A fucking condolence card," Ida said.

"I know, that's the icing on the cake," said Tom, laughing.

"I only remember poems about cats and birthdays. She's

obviously matured as a writer since I've been gone," said Ida.

She put the card back down and moved towards the mantelpiece, where there lay a carved stone ashtray, a tortoiseshell hair clip, and a framed photo of Ida and Alice as children, grinning and frizzy haired in their boaters and school blazers.

"Fucking hell," she said, picking it up and revealing a bottle of whisky that the photo had hidden from view.

"Apparently she had hiding places all over the house," he said seriously.

Ida winced. Did he think she didn't know that? That he knew her mother better than she did?

"Well, Alice won't like that. Waste not, want not," she said as cheerfully as she could and went to put the bottle in her room.

Alice showered after her jog and came downstairs in a red high-necked sixties shift dress, blue Adidas Gazelle trainers, and a white mohair cardigan. A satchel was slung across her front, covered in colourful badges.

"Still a 'Bournemouth High Street nightmare'? Will I do?" she asked.

"It was your tracksuit..."

"Yeah, the tracksuit that I wear to do exercise – mental."

"Well, you look nice. I like your shoes," Ida said. She really did.

"Thanks," said Alice, not quite sure if Ida was taking the piss. "You've still got those boots. I couldn't believe it when you turned up."

Ida lifted her leg and showed Alice the sole. "They're on the way out. Full of holes. I did get them from a charity shop about fifteen years ago, though."

"Shall we go?" Alice asked. "We can't be long, Dad's asked us for lunch. Tom still hasn't met him."

Ida followed as Alice took Tom's hand and stepped outside.

It was a breezy day and Ida's head felt cold without the thick hair she was used to. She yawned. The house had made her tired.

They walked along the road, past flash cars, Ida increasingly impressed and disgusted by how fancy the area had become. She wouldn't mention it now, she knew she'd better not, but she wondered how much they were going to get for the house. There'd be debts, that was certain, but surely they'd each be in for a decent sum – enough for a deposit on a flat or Alice's wedding to this indie-schmindie dwarf. She wished she could feel more excited. But the truth was she felt scared. She knew she was terrible with money, she had been all her life, and that in her hands even fifty grand could be fifty quid by the end of the month.

They reached a battered Mini. Ida expected Tom to drive and was surprised when her sister walked round to the driver's side and took some keys out of her satchel.

"What, you're going to drive, Alice? You can drive?" Ida asked.

"I'm twenty-six," said Alice.

"Oh, okay. Wow," said Ida, squeezing into the back seat.

"You can't drive?" asked Tom, from the front.

"She can't even walk in a straight line," said Alice as she put on her seatbelt.

They were silent in the car, seemingly regretting the idea of the walk. Under normal circumstances Ida would have suggested the pub and it took a great deal of strength for her to swallow that suggestion each time it came to her lips. Tom drummed on his knees incessantly – something Ida was sure was driving Alice mad – and took the fact that her sister stayed quiet, politely, as an indication that their relationship was still pretty new.

The heath was not how Ida remembered it and she was almost embarrassed. Instead of the snakes she had promised Tom there were used condoms and crisp packets, power lines stretched overhead and in the distance stood a new housing estate, rows and rows of red-brick boxes and gaping black windows. It was massive, that was still true, a great dirty expanse of scrubland, reined in by a wide, humming road.

Alice and Tom held hands as they walked and Tom did seem to be enjoying himself, poking at the ground with a stick and snake-watching as they went. Ida trailed behind, kicking the earth. "I'm cold," she said. "Shall we turn round?"

They stood for a moment on the top of the hill, the breeze stinging their cheeks, while Ida struggled to light her cigarette.

"Look!" said Tom, pointing at a fox then running down the hill towards it. He was showing off, willing her, or both of the women, to laugh and follow him.

They stayed where they were. "What's he going to do? Catch it?" Alice asked, smiling.

Ida didn't laugh. "I need to ask you where the painting is, the one of Ma looking into the mirror."

"What?" asked Alice. She was still looking down at Tom, who was waving wildly, trying to get them to come down to look at something.

"You know which painting, my painting."

"You mean the Jacob Collins painting? We sold it ages ago."

"But it was mine," said Ida. "Where's the money then? I need that money."

"Okay. Right. Well, I have no idea where the money is but I certainly don't have it."

"That was mine. You knew that, Alice. That wasn't yours to sell. Fuck. I want to go home."

"Are you joking?" Alice asked.

Ida shrugged.

"Oh God, I can't believe this, as if things weren't bad enough," said Alice.

"You know he's with you because of me – my name and Ma's. You do know that, don't you?" Ida asked as Tom gave up and jogged back up the hill towards them. "I've got a boyfriend. Who loves me," Ida whispered. "If you want to think I'm jealous then don't. It's not that."

Tom reached them, panting and wrapped his arms round Alice. "Jesus, I'm unfit," he said, and then, leaning back to look at her, "is everything okay?"

Chapter five

~ 1999 ~

As she squished herself back into the car Ida realised she had no idea where they were going. The location of her father's house was one of those things she was sure she should know, but the truth was she hadn't a clue. There'd been the strange flat by the beach, but they'd have moved somewhere else by now, Ida was sure. For one thing, that stinking old Jack Russell Terri had loved so much could barely make it up all the stairs.

Ida had a sudden, unwelcome memory of Bridie meeting that dog, and screwed up her face. It must have been just before she'd left home, and she and Bridie had been walking to the shop, to get cigarettes probably, when Terri had appeared from round the corner, listening to her new Walkman and pushing the dog in some odd type of pram. Terri had been so proud of the Walkman her nephew had bought for her that she'd listened to it constantly despite only owning a single Dolly Parton tape. To Terri's credit she had taken off her headphones and extended her arms for a hug, while Bridie had frozen with her eyebrows raised.

That dog must be dead now, Ida thought. She wanted to ask Alice if Terri had bought another one, but Alice wasn't speaking very much. It was a shame as it would have been fun to make bets about the awful things Terri was bound to say, and ask, and give them for lunch.

Tom was aware of the tension and tried his best to make conversation. When that failed he fiddled with the radio for five minutes, finding static and distant French voices, until Alice tapped his wrist and he turned it off.

They drove past Ida's very first bedsit and she pointed it out to Tom. "Look, there out the window," she said as cheerfully as she could. "That's where I lived when I left home first. With this mental slag called Tina who sold hash at the pub. God – look at it."

It was clear Tom didn't know what to say as he looked at the gloomy building. The windows were all different, some brightly painted wood, some UPVC, and a broken child's go-kart lay in the drive.

"We had one room, to share. Alice came round once, didn't you? With Terri – to pick up some of my stuff. She wouldn't drink the tea I made. Said the cups were too dirty. You were what, Al, eleven?"

Alice nodded.

They passed the old-man pub where Ida had worked for a bit, and then it was the junk shop – where she'd worked when she'd first left home – still dark and empty with a badly hand-painted sign. It gave her the creeps. Both places brought back horrible memories, and she made a secret sign of the cross on her knee.

Across the road was the phone box where she'd reversed the charges every week to Terri and Da.

She tried to imagine the house they were heading to as they turned towards Poole. Square and modern, with a neat paved driveway, net curtains and a pond. There'd be an extension that Terri would have spent years planning. Ida stopped herself, realising that she was thinking in the same snobby way that her mother would have done, the way she'd always sworn not to.

They passed the green where she'd once snogged Ben Palmer, then all the way along Sandbanks Road, the houses getting bigger the further they went.

Of course they were heading to Sandbanks, the narrow spit of land jutting out into the sea, beloved by football players and eighties one-hit wonders. Their father had been born to live somewhere like this.

The huge curve of the sea took Ida by surprise. She had made this place twee in her mind, written it off as shabby and fake, but the view across the water was still wild and past a few brave windsurfers lay the dense green of Brownsea Island.

They turned off into a tree-lined road, and through black

electric gates into a wide, paved drive.

"So, we're here," said Tom as the car came to a halt. He sounded relieved.

Terri stood in front of a pebble-dashed chalet bungalow, her arms held out towards them and a tea towel dangling from one hand. Her hair was still ash blonde and blow-dried into a stiff ball, and she was wearing the same kind of thing she'd always worn – smart, pressed pale blue trousers and a polyester-satin blouse.

Ida took a deep breath and got out.

"Baby, it's been too, too long," said Terri, wiping away tears.

Ida walked over, leant down, and let herself be hugged. She was much the same as Ida remembered, thin and neat but the smell of her gave Ida a shock. She had forgotten the strong tinned-fruit sweetness of the perfume Terri wore – one of the only things in the whole wide world that truly hadn't changed.

Terri pulled away and turned towards the others. "And you must be Tom. Goodness, what long hair you've got. Couldn't you have given some to Ida? She seems to have lost hers. Come in, come in, I've made a quiche." She summoned them into the hall and locked the door behind them. "You can't be too careful these days. Some Asians moved in, on Salter Road," she told them in a loud whisper.

"Terri doesn't mean it, do you?" Alice said to Tom while looking at her stepmother's back.

"No, well, I'm sure they're perfectly nice," Terri said gazing earnestly up at Tom. "It's just when different people move in, different races and classes, it signals something about an area. What?" she asked, noticing Alice's furious face.

Ida recognised the stubborn toddler she'd known as a child. She grinned involuntarily and Terri laughed, mistakenly believing that Ida's smile signalled support.

"Oh, come on Ida, let's go and find your dad before your sister shops me to the PC police," she said.

It was extremely warm in the house and Ida took off her

jacket as they walked through the hall. The wall had a floral strip halfway up; above it were pastel stripes, below it pale pink paint. On the stripy part there were framed photos, and Ida slowed down as she recognised Terri's gormless blonde nieces and nephews, remembering how terribly she'd teased them when they were young. There were other pictures too, prints mainly, and a cross-stitched sampler that read *I like hugs and I like kisses but what I love is help with the dishes*. It was initialled *T.I.* in bright pink thread.

From the room they were heading to Ida could hear the muffled sound of the TV and then a gravelly voice. "Is that my girl here to see me?"

"Yes it is," said Tom affectionately, poking Alice in the small of the back as Terri led them into the room.

"He doesn't mean me," Alice replied crossly as Ida pushed past her to hug their da.

He was sitting in a beige chair facing an enormous television. On his lap was a cushioned tray strewn with biscuit crumbs and a glass of milk. The room was a startling mauve, filled with porcelain ornaments, and in it her father seemed terribly out of place. Against the back wall were shelves packed with his 'archive' – thousands of copies of *The Daily Mail, Radio Times* and *Readers Digest*, each containing one of the polite reviews or sycophantic interviews that were, as Bridie so often and cruelly pointed out, his hallmark.

It had been four years since Ida had seen him, but in that time he'd aged a lot.

"Here she is, Bry," Terri said with enthusiasm as Ida leant towards him. He reached awkwardly for her face and Ida was shocked to see that his arms were shaking.

"You gorgeous girl, stand back and let me look at you," he said.

Ida could hear Alice muttering to Tom in the background, trying hard to ignore their father's delight at seeing his oldest child.

Ida stepped back and flung her arms out.

"Ta da!" she said, attempting a wide smile to hide the shock on her face. He was very thin.

"Oh dear, darling, you're not a lesbian?" Bryan asked, looking her up and down from her boots to her shorn hair. Alice groaned with annoyance in the background, but Ida just laughed, walked back towards him and kissed him on the cheek.

"Would you mind if I was?" she asked.

"Not really, I suppose. The theatre was full of them."

There was a loud laugh from the telly and he grimaced, fumbling for the mute on the remote control. "Oh bugger, this noise. There we are." He took Ida's hand in his. "I'm so sorry about your ma, it's hit us hard." Ida noticed tears in his eyes.

"I'll go and make the tea," said Terri, taking the tray from his lap. As she lifted it, Ida noticed that under the milk glass and crumbs was a large photograph of a fat Jack Russell.

"Pull up a chair sweetheart, tell me everything," he said, brushing down his cardigan which looked, to Ida, as though it would have fitted a child.

"There's someone else to meet you Dad, Alice's boyfriend, Tom?" she beckoned to him from behind her and Tom stepped forwards, extending his hand.

Bryan held it weakly and craned his neck backwards to look up at Tom's face.

"What is he? Some kind of hippy?" he asked happily, pointing at Tom's hair and shirt.

Tom laughed.

"Fucking hell," said Alice wearily, to Ida's astonishment. Bryan didn't appear to hear.

"It's lovely to meet you Mr Irons, can I sit down?" Tom asked, reaching for a chair.

"Eee by gum," said Bryan, noticing Tom's accent, and Tom laughed again, politely.

They chatted about the theatre and TV while Ida sat near them and watched, letting her father roughly knead her knuckles in the way she'd hated as a child. Tom agreed with most things her father said, however controversial, and only occasionally muttered his disagreement, giving a delighted Bryan the false impression that they were having a lively debate.

Alice sat in the far corner of the room and hardly spoke, while Ida tried to laugh and join in when she could. She was pleased to have the time to look at her father properly, to get over the shock of his sudden old age.

From the waist upwards Bryan was dressed more or less as he always had been, in a pale pink shirt that had definitely cost more than all of Ida's clothes put together. Over it he wore a yellow cardigan of fine, soft wool, and round his wrist hung his gold watch. He had always worn scarves, but now a loose piece of fabric hung pathetically round his scraggy neck. It was covered in orange stains which Ida guessed had come from his breakfast eggs. At the bottom of the blanket that covered his lap Ida was surprised to see he was wearing sheepskin moccasins and above them the elastic cuff of a pair of jogging bottoms.

And his face! Bryan had been known for his pretty, small face, with its pointed girlish features and pale blue eyes. His eyes were greyer now, and the delicacy of his features was less obvious among the wrinkles and age spots that covered his skin. He had always looked like Alice, and Ida wondered whether her sister felt like she was looking, horribly, into her future. Ida realised for the first time that she would never see how her own likeness, their mother, would age.

Ida remembered the last time she had seen her father. He'd come to London for work and taken her for dinner and Ida had been so hungover she couldn't eat her salad and her fingers shook when she tried to drink her wine. Bryan, luckily, was unaware of her plight and rattled on about people he worked with who Ida couldn't remember. As he had left her at Euston he had slipped fifty pounds into her pocket and winked at her and Ida had almost cried with gratitude. What had she spent it on, she wondered? All the fifty quids she must have spent in her life – almost thirty years' worth. What a bloody waste.

They ate at a bamboo table. The chairs were hard, with plastic seat covers and the quiche was full of eggshell, but nobody minded, and Tom ate four slices and two bits of arctic roll. In the corner was an electric waterfall lit by a flickering blue lamp and Tom managed to talk about it with Terri for a good fifteen minutes. Ida was genuinely impressed.

"I've got a boyfriend, too," said Ida to the table, not that anyone had asked.

"Really? Lovely. What's he called?" asked Terri.

"Yes, what is he called?" asked Alice, looking down at her plate.

Ida couldn't tell if she was making some subtle point.

"Elliot. He's an artist and an art dealer. He lives in the East End. The East End's not like it used to be, Da, before you say anything. It's very up-and-coming now – there are loads of galleries and things. He's collected some brilliant painters."

"Well he can't make any money, not with you in that God-awful suit," said Bryan.

"I like this suit," said Ida.

"Well, it doesn't seem to like you," said Alice, looking up, and everyone, except Ida, laughed.

Even Tom was laughing and he hardly knew Ida – perhaps he wasn't as nice as she'd thought he was after all.

"Look, have you got any port, or sherry or something, I'm really thirsty," she said, cutting them off and rubbing her eyes.

Terri half stood up from the table and looked to Bryan for approval.

"Get it for her, Terri, what are you waiting for? I think we could all do with a drink," he said.

By the way she turned the wheel it was obvious that Alice was furious, and Tom knew better than to try to help.

Ida had drunk most of the bottle of port and was feeling better, whereas Alice, who had simply watched her drink, seemed to be feeling considerably worse.

By the time they reached Ashley Cross Ida couldn't bear it any more.

"Alice, if you want to say something to me, can you come out and say it? I'm sick of all this passive aggressive shit," she said.

"If there's anything passive about it it's unintentional. You're a total dick. A total, selfish dick."

Tom took a loud breath.

"Fuck this, I'm a grown woman. Can you let me out somewhere? I want to get out."

Alice carried on driving.

"Let me the fuck out of this fucking car!" Ida shouted.

"We're on a main road, I'll let you out by the snooker hall – you can walk home or go to the park. Or do whatever," said Alice, calmly.

She pulled over to the side of the road, and Tom got out, so Ida could squeeze past.

"Thank you," she said to him.

"Don't be too long," he said, bravely attempting a smile. "I'm making chilli for dinner."

"This is the last day of fucking around, by the way, we've got the flowers and all the calling to do tomorrow, and to organise the whole bloody thing," shouted Alice across the passenger seat.

Tom got in and Ida slammed shut the car door.

Ida had not had a clear aim in mind when she'd asked to leave the car, just a desire to be free of her sister and all the bad things she made her feel.

Now as she walked past the snooker hall where she'd gone so often when she was young she prayed that she wouldn't bump into anyone from school or any frumpy acquaintance of her mother's who would want to express their condolences. Why was not mentioning things frowned upon? Children and teenagers had it right. Death was embarrassing for all involved.

She knew she looked unusual in her airing-cupboard suit and

people noticed her as she walked, a group of teenage boys shouting something she couldn't understand as they overtook her on their BMXs. She smiled, reassured that she didn't fit in, and aware that this was childish.

She walked through the gate and into Poole Park. Next to the cricket pavilion, an old man sat reading the paper, and ahead of her a little blond boy was cycling his trike towards his mum. On the other side of the pitch was a boggy pond, filled with reeds and throaty, squawking Canada geese, and around its edge curved a tiny train track which Ida walked along, taking careful steps in between the metal girders.

Hearing the train coming Ida watched as it headed straight for her. It was slow and very small but the children at the front were shouting for her to get out of the way and waving their hands about in hopeful horror. What would happen, she wondered, if she lay down right here? She supposed the driver would brake, but she would like to know what would happen if he didn't. Could her body stop a whole train? She had a feeling that it probably could.

The woman tried to charge Ida for a child's ticket as well as her own and seemed taken aback that she was travelling alone. In fact, she gave the distinct impression that she did not like the cut of Ida's jib, and for some reason Ida felt compelled to thank her effusively.

Clutching the pink raffle ticket that had cost her 60p, Ida boarded the train, jamming herself into the seat that was meant for two children. It was the last train of the day and was almost empty apart from a stern-looking man wearing socks and sandals with two young boys that she supposed were his. The younger one turned round and stared at her and she waved at him and stuck out her tongue. The father smacked the boy on the knee, giving Ida a suspicious sideways glance. She put her feet up on the opposite seat and clutched the sides of the carriage.

The train began to move very slowly indeed. Ida watched two girls playing football and a mother holding up her baby's chubby fist, making him wave, his arms stiff in his coat. Ida waved back and the child giggled. She waved at the geese, the sky, and even at two teenage boys who were smoking behind a tree, and who swore back at her and spat.

As they neared the end of the track Ida noticed the ends of her fingers were tingling. For a few minutes she hoped it was the cold, but by the time the train came to a creaky halt and she had warmed her hands in her armpits, she realised that the tingling was nothing to do with the temperature. Instead, it was the alarming, magical feeling that always came when something big and surprising was about to happen.

Chapter six

~ 1975 ~

Ida hit her head on something – her wardrobe or the wall – and warm liquid began trickling from her forehead. She put out her hands and felt the pointed plastic roof of her Sindy house and the dusty top of her chest of drawers. There was no use shouting out – her parents could sleep through most things – so she fumbled for the door handle and walked out onto the landing. A light was on downstairs.

Ida bit her lip, sucked in her tears and gripped the banister, feeling her way down each step, with her eyes still almost closed. Someone was on the phone in the hall below and they sounded really cross.

Only babies were frightened. She would try not to be frightened.

She reached the bottom of the stairs and stood with her arms out, waiting for someone to notice her.

The phone clattered onto the table and she felt her da's hands around her.

"Jesus, darling, what on earth? Is it a full moon or something?"

"I don't know," she said. "I didn't wet myself."

"No you didn't, darling. Look – you must have hit your head trying to get to the loo. Want to see?" He lifted her up, took her over to the mirror and held her in front of it.

Ida's tears came all at once. The girl in the mirror was covered in blood. It was on her chin and in her hair and all over her nightie.

"Shit. I'm sorry," Bryan said, putting her down. "I didn't know you'd be scared. I thought you'd be interested."

"I am interested, Da," she said in between sobs.

He started wiping her face with his hankie. "I thought your mother was bad enough. What a night. There, a small cut, just lots of blood. You're going to be fine."

"Where is she, Da?"

"I'm not sure sweetie, I'm trying to find out. Let's clean you up and put you back to bed."

"No," Ida said. "I want to stay here." She'd never said no to Da before and she wasn't sure what he'd do.

"Alright," he said. "Why not? Do you know how to put the kettle on?"

Ida didn't know how to put the kettle on, so she'd made tea with the hot tap, and they sat drinking it – the teabags still bobbing in their cups – as they waited for the police to bring back her ma.

She wished she and Da could go out and look together, down through the woods with torches, but he said they couldn't. He said they had to stay in for Ally, but Ida knew that he was frightened. Ida certainly wasn't, she had learnt to love the woods and the dark. She was Mowgli and the chine and the beach were hers.

She had never been up this late and they were having fun. Da didn't understand the kitchen any better than she did, so together they'd made a tray of unusual, brilliant snacks – unwashed carrots, two slices of white bread, and the last bit of a tub of Neapolitan ice cream that had been re-frozen so many times it went to powder in your mouth.

The road was quiet at this time of night and any car they heard was likely to be the police. Ida knew Da was worried, but she was excited. Things were nearly always fine, and if they weren't at least it would be an adventure.

There was the sound of a distant car, and Bryan sat up to listen. It got nearer, slowed, and pulled into the drive.

He ran into the hall and unlocked the door.

Coming up the steps was her mother, wearing a blue kimono and no shoes, sandy and shivering, with two policemen holding her arms. "I wanted to make it all better, Bry. Why won't you let me?"

Ida walked over to the stairs and sat part way up, watching.

She had never seen her mother cry.

The policemen lifted and pushed her ma into the hall but she tried to run back out. Bryan held onto the kimono while all three men prised Bridie's fingers from the doorframe. They slammed the front door.

"Let me get you a drink, let me get you a drink," Bryan was saying over and over again. "If you still want to leave you can go after that."

Bridie sat on the floor with her head in her hands as she rocked backwards and forwards, wailing like a cat.

Ida's head was starting to hurt.

Chapter seven

~ 1999 ~

Despite having cooked dinner, Tom insisted on doing the washing up, while Ida helped Alice in the sitting room, rooting through Bridie's disintegrating address book and phoning people about the funeral. They hadn't mentioned the incident in the car since Ida came back to the house and Alice appeared to have got over it. In fact, she was making a list of people for Ida to call tomorrow – all the particularly boring ones who'd sent the nastiest flowers.

"We've got no family to ring," Alice said. "And hardly any friends. She pissed off everyone she ever met."

"Well, at least a few of them are coming out of the woodwork. It's horrible to say, but if it hadn't been in the paper who would have known?"

"Mrs Dewani from the offy?" They both started laughing.

"We shouldn't laugh," said Ida, "the poor cow's going to go out of business."

They laughed until their stomachs hurt and they both took deep breaths, rubbing their eyes and trying not to look at each other or they knew they'd start again.

"Will you go and help Tom?" Alice asked. "I can't do this phoning with you sitting here, I'll wet myself."

Ida nodded, grateful to be able to leave the room. Despite the occasional laughter it was depressing and boring hearing Alice on the phone, putting on her telephone voice and smiling like a twat, saying the same things again and again.

She walked into the kitchen where Tom was sweeping the floor. "You okay?" he asked. "I think I found more mouse droppings under the cupboard. I'd buy traps but Alice won't let me."

"Oh, don't worry about the mice, they've been here longer than we have. God, we're gross aren't we? Must be weird being thrown into all of this – the situation, and, you know... us."

"It is a bit odd, I've only been seeing Ally seriously for two months or something, and then to find out her Mum had died... You know I saw it in the paper before she even had a chance to tell me. I rushed down as soon as I heard. I can't imagine how hard it must be for you, being on the news so soon. It's horrible."

His face showed genuine concern and Ida realised it was years since anyone had looked at her like that.

"Thank you," she said quietly, picking up a plate to put away. She had grown up with obituaries; the hard-living friends of her parents died young more often than most. In fact, she had written her own mother's obituary so many times in her mind that seeing the actual thing wasn't much of a shock in the end. But the look he gave her was a surprise. Not pity, really. Actual sympathy, she supposed.

"I don't know. I'm surprised it hadn't happened sooner," she said, "and anyway, I mean I've never responded properly to things. I get upset about weird things, not the things I'm meant to get upset about. It's like how I've always remembered strange stuff. You know, there are certain things that happen to you that you know you're going to remember for the rest of your life."

"Like births and deaths? Or your first snog?"

"No, no, the opposite. I don't mean events, everyone remembers events, I mean certain points in time when everything suddenly stops and I think, ahhhh yes, here I am, this is me, here now, and it kind of links me to all the other points where I felt like that. You know? I don't know if this is coming out right. I mean, I had one the other day, just before Ma died. I was standing in Sainsbury's, when it started raining. That wouldn't normally be a big deal, I'm in London after all, but the way it started raining was with this massive devastating roar, y'know? It had been so sunny and then, bam! And it didn't just rain, it hailed too, and there were these winds. It was like we were on some tropical island or something. It was so weird, in London! So everyone stopped and faced the windows, and I could tell that everyone was thinking, well, this is it… this could be the end of the world. It sounds ridiculous now but I know that was what they were thinking. And we were all elated and free-feeling and smiling at each other because we were all in it together, like we were in some air raid shelter. I thought, am I going to die here? Among these people with their fat, shiny faces, and their wanky expensive shoes? If I really have to stay here, and we're the last people on Earth, would I have to have sex with one of these men to ensure the future of the human race?"

"Were they all that bad?"

"I've got unexpectedly high standards, I'll have you know. Anyway, I'm talking bollocks and I'm pissed. It's been a long day."

"Not at all, you're bloody funny," said Tom, putting away a saucepan. "You should write that story down. My mate's got this fanzine, well, more of a magazine; there are book reviews, not only music stuff, and some weird short stories. You could write something for that."

"Bah. I spend too much time drinking. Don't tell Alice I said that."

"That doesn't need to be all you do. I'm in a band. We're rubbish, but it's fun."

"Yeah, everyone's got bloody interests," Ida said, "everyone except me."

He paused. "Shit, I'm so sorry. I'm not having a go at you. I don't even know you. And your mother's just died. I'm trying so hard to keep Alice going that I forgot it's not my job to help you too."

There was something so earnest, so open about him, that Ida spontaneously squeezed his arm. "Thank you," she said.

There was a bang from the hall as the sitting room door slammed. "Right, that's it for now," Alice shouted, "I've had it, let's go to bed. Two of them say they can't come because they're 'under the weather'. Somehow I don't think they're as 'under the weather' as Ma was. I nearly pointed that out to them." She appeared in the doorway. "Leave the rest of the washing up, we can do it tomorrow."

"Sweetness, you look knackered," said Tom, stepping towards Alice, hugging her and kissing her forehead. "Let's get you upstairs."

Ida looked away.

"And Uncle Peter wasn't in," Alice said as she left. "You get to call him tomorrow."

Ida slept through her alarm.

"Shit," she said to herself.

She'd fully intended to help out this morning, to try and show that she was capable and mature. Inexplicably she felt angry with her sister, as if she'd been tricked into failure. Sitting up, she saw there was a note under the door.

Morning Ida.

Could you please do some stuff around the house? Cleaning? We're going to need to sort through Mum's things too as I want to sell the house as soon as poss. Could you make a start? Please put anything you might want to keep to one side so I have a chance to look at it too. There's a list on the back of this note of people who need to be called – their numbers are in the book.

PLEASE HELP. I'M SICK OF FIGHTING BUT I REALLY NEED HELP! Al x

Ida turned the note over.

Margot
Dianne
Julie and James
Uncle Peter

Ida sat on the sofa, flicking through her mother's address book. It was virtually incomprehensible, full of crossings-out, and Ida noticed how like her own spidery writing her mother's had been. In some places there were notes about people: 'wonderful actress' or 'total prick', making Ida laugh. Still, she held the book at a distance, as if she were holding something precious but vaguely nasty you might find in a museum. It was interesting to see all the names she didn't recognise, next to long defunct dialling codes. Who were all these people that her mother had once had a reason to call? It made her realise how little she really knew about her ma.

Ida stared at the phone. She hadn't spoken to Elliot since she'd arrived and ached for him to ring. There was no way for her to contact him – it had been months since his phone had been cut off – so all she could do was wait.

It wasn't only because she loved him so much, there was more to it than that. She was desperate to speak to someone who understood her, someone normal, who got up late and got wasted and forgot to wash their hair. She tried hard to put aside the other constant worries she felt about Elliot, that he'd take too much, or take something bad, or get beaten up for unpaid debts. She hoped somebody would have got in touch if something like that had happened.

The phone was an old fashioned one with a circular dial, and she misdialled Peter's number four times.

"054," said a young-ish man, to Ida's surprise.

"Oh, hello, can I speak to Peter please? It's Ida Irons."

"Ida! The famous Ida! I'll get him, so sorry about your mum, I'm Jonathon, his friend. One mo."

There was rustling then some distant shouts and then a deep, older voice.

"My darling, darling, fabulous thing – Princess of Bournemouth! How are you sweetheart? Crying into your wine or 'Ding Dong the Witch is Dead'?"

"Neither really."

"Oh it will come, you mark my words. Now, when do I need to come down? And where shall I stay? John's working but I'll be there. We've been praying all over the shop, me and John, and had a mass said at St. Mary's."

"It's on Tuesday. You can come down whenever though. And stay here of course, we'll find room. I can't wait to see you. Oh Peter, you couldn't just talk to me, for a bit, about any old crap? Make me laugh."

When she put down the phone she noticed a pain in her side. She decided she must be hungry and put the list on the floor. Breakfast first; the rest of the calls could wait.

For a full forty-five minutes Ida stood outside her mother's bedroom, staring at the unmade bed and rubbish-strewn floor through the foot-wide crack in the door. She couldn't go in. The thought of it made her exhausted and then panicky – it would be like cleaning her own room times fifty and she couldn't face it, not yet. She would clean the bathroom, cut the grass, vacuum the house, anything, except sorting out that room. Alice could do the sentimental stuff; she actually enjoyed sentimental stuff. She would let Alice boss her around as much as she wanted to if she would let her off the grown up jobs and give her some clear instruction. Ida was disorganised, she was scatterbrained, she was ruthless and lazy, and drunk. Why would Alice want her to sort through her mother's room? She'd be sure to do it all wrong.

But she couldn't quite stop staring inside. Somewhere in that room there were important things. Her mother rarely threw anything away and Ida knew that somewhere there'd be a draft of the play, or a notebook that Ida could turn into something for *The Guardian* culture bit at the very least. 'Ida – the true story', or 'The Elusive Bridie Adair'.

There might be other things too, personal stuff. Little bits of information she could piece together for herself, to make more sense of her strange, solitary ma.

And even though she tried not to care, maybe it would be

interesting to work out why her mother had written one strange, violent play, and nothing ever again.

"That was awful. The man was a total weirdo," said Alice as she stood in the doorway, watching Ida scrub the sides of the bath. It was so old the enamel had gone, leaving it rough with bare patches of metal in places, and Ida was having a hard time getting it clean.

"Well he would be, wouldn't he, he dresses corpses for a living."

Alice hesitated. "If you want any proper input let me know. It's going to be pretty simple. I thought I'd put her in her nice cotton nightdress with a rosary..." she waited for Ida to reply but she carried on scrubbing. "Anyway, thanks for doing the cleaning. Did you start on Mum's room?"

"No. Not yet. I'm not sure I'm the best person to do it. I'll do other stuff, tidying and whatever."

"Please help me. I can't do it on my own. And, I know you'll laugh at me for the pop psychology crap, but I think it would be good for you. You still haven't faced up to it all."

"I faced up to it a long time ago, actually, Alice. But fine, whatever, I'll help you. Can you take the bath mat with you when you go down? It needs to go in the wash."

By the time they started on the bedroom most of the cleaning had been done. Ida marched through her mother's door, staring at the opposite wall and concentrating on simply putting one foot in front of the other until she reached the clothes-covered bed. It didn't smell of Bridie which was one good thing; instead it smelled of antiseptic and air freshener. She sat down on its edge.

"I wouldn't sit there," said Alice.

Ida noticed the mattress was dotted with wet stains. "It's fine."

"Really? You don't want to know what that is. I'll get Tom, he's got some bungees in his car. He can take it to the tip. Fuck, he got more than he bargained for when he started seeing me."

Ida stood up and they both looked down at the bed, until a

laugh started to form somewhere in her throat. She could never stop herself when the worst things happened.

Alice sensed it.

"Did you speak to Peter?" she asked.

"Yes, thank goodness. He's coming down."

"I'm glad... for you. I know you're very fond of each other," Alice said. "He can help you through it all."

Ida had an almost overwhelming urge to push her sister, head first, onto the nasty bit of the mattress and it took a great deal of strength to turn and walk out of the room.

Chapter eight

~ 1976 ~

The first time the man shouted her name Ida thought she must have misheard. She knew it was a man, although Alice didn't, because of his height and the long, bendy legs in their stripy tights that came out from under his skirt.

"That lady wants you, that lady wants you," said Alice loudly in her little voice, standing up on her seat, making the people in the row in front turn round and laugh right in Ida's face.

Everyone was clapping. Ida knew they were waiting for something – something that involved her.

She closed her eyes and tried to breathe. Unlike Bridie, Da wouldn't have smelling salts, so Ida put her head in between her legs like she'd been taught to when she felt faint. Everything was scratchy – the red seat on her hands, her white woolly tights, her silky dress, her velvet headband. She tried to think about the scratchiness, to be annoyed about the scratchiness, and not to think about all the people who were waiting for her.

"Ida, Iddy Iddy Ida, I've been told you want to come up and see me," said the man from the stage in a kind of song. The clapping got slower, someone coughed and a baby started to cry.

"For goodness sake pull yourself together," her father whispered into her ear.

"She looks ill, Bryan, is she going to be sick?" It was the strange lady who'd come with them, a neat, smiling woman who smelled of tinned peaches.

"Ida, darling, my poppet, where are you hiding – watch out or you'll get a right good hiding," sang the man and then everyone in the whole theatre was laughing again.

"Right, that's it." Ida felt her father's hands round the waist of her taffeta party dress and she was lifted into the air, her eyes still closed tight, her arms by her sides and her head down. She had borrowed a book about sharks from the library and had been practicing playing dead for weeks.

As she was carried through the air people cheered. And then there were bigger hands on her waist, lifting her higher into the air and a new, kind voice whispering, "Stand up, sweetheart, it won't last long." She straightened her legs, took a deep breath and opened her eyes.

The light was so bright she couldn't see at first and felt all wobbly like she often did at Mass. The man took her hand and Ida put her other arm in front of her face to shield her eyes.

"Now, have you been a good little girl?" the man asked in his big loud lady voice.

"No. Not really."

Everyone laughed, and under her arm Ida could see children pointing up at her.

"What a serious girl. You're meant to say yes, sweetheart, or there won't be any chocs. Shall we try again? All together now – have you been a good little girl?"

Everyone said it together and Ida wondered if Alice and Da and the strange woman – *Terri* – would be saying it too.

"Yes."

"Well done deary. Everyone give her a round of applause." The man patted her on the bottom, handed her a Cadbury's selection box, and whispered, "Go along now dear," while the smiling blonde ice cream lady walked towards the stage and led her down some wooden stairs and back towards her seat.

"That was bloody embarrassing. Now you have to thank him for the chocolate and tell him how much you enjoyed it or that's it," said Ida's da.

They were walking through the stage door to Peter's dressing room. Peter was Da's friend.

There were people standing around in the corridor, some little girls still in the sequinned leotards they'd been dancing in earlier on stage. They had their hands on their hips, were chewing gum and even had make-up on, Ida could tell.

A door opened and there were some long skinny legs in suit trousers.

"Bry!" the man shouted and hugged Ida's da, while the strange woman held Ida's hand for the first time. Ida looked at her shoes. She wished she'd stayed at home with Ma, and watched her eat crystallised ginger, get drunk and mouth all the words along with *The Wizard of Oz*.

"Come in, come in, get yourselves comfortable. Sorry there's not much room, that stupid Jeanine tart has got the best dressing room obviously, despite being a terrible trollop and a bloody – excuse my French – awful actress to boot. Enough of that, here's the star of the show!"

Ida was jostled in until she was half under a rail stuffed with shiny dresses and feathery things. There was an electric heater in the corner, the fake-coal type that Bridie said was naff, and a table covered in make-up and brushes and vases of flowers. It was so cold Ida could see her breath and she jiggled from side to side.

Peter walked over and crouched down until he was face-to-face with Ida. She gasped, although she knew that was rude. Although he was wearing a suit and had short, grey hair, there was sparkly blue stuff all round his eyes and on his thin cheeks there were two red circles. Ida wondered if he realised.

"Thank you so much for the chocolate. I had a lovely time."

"See! She's a better actress than Jeanine, Bry, and she's, what, eight?"

"Seven and a half," said Ida.

"Only seven and a half! Goodness you're tall. Now you didn't seem like you were having a lovely time while you were on that stage, but I may well be wrong. And I have to say you look a little scared right now, of me in all my slap. But, your word is your honour, right?"

"Right."

"Good girl," he said and ruffled her hair.

From behind his back he brought out a big red flower. It had seemed real on stage when it had gone limp and straight again over-and-over – but now Ida could see it was papery and had wire inside.

She went to touch it and pulled back her hand. The man laughed.

"You can touch it, I'll show you how to make it work too. You know what? You're going to be famous one day, sweetheart. I've a nose for these things."

He sniffed the flower and pretended to sneeze.

The waiter had said the soup was homemade but Ida knew it was Heinz, which was fine as Heinz was her favourite. In the corner was a white piano, covered in red tinsel, with a man in a white suit playing it. Ida couldn't take her eyes off him – he had black hair and was moving his face around so much while he played that he looked like Jerry Lewis.

Alice sat next to her eating a runny boiled egg which was dribbling down her chin. "More soldiers, I want more soldiers," she said and everyone ignored her. Next to both girls were giant teddy bears with red sparkly bows round their necks and hard black plastic eyes. Ida and Alice were both scared of them but they'd said thank you politely.

"I've been gone for more than a year now," said her da.

"About eighteen months," said Terri. "It was just after you'd moved into the new house. And then you left... and we met." She turned to Peter, "I always say we met through the Yellow Pages. He called me to make some curtains for his new place... and that was it!"

Bryan ignored her and carried on. "I couldn't stay, she was being bloody unreasonable, and her drinking was getting out of hand. First she sacked the au pair, back in London, because she thought she was stealing. You know she takes these slimming pills? God they make her mad. Moving out of London was a last ditch attempt. She didn't want to move to Bournemouth but I thought it would help. We met here after all. We were happy here, once."

"And what about the girls?" asked Peter.

"If I could have taken them with me I would have done. But there isn't room in our flat. I mean, I think they're fine. They go to a good school, and it's better that we're separated than arguing all the damn time."

"Hmmm," said Peter, "you know I love Bridie. She's a good woman deep down – if she'd write, she'd be fine."

"Write?" said Bryan. "I don't know how she wrote that play in the bloody first place. She's never finished anything else. I don't think she ever will. She's not a finisher."

"I'll drop in on her tomorrow, we could go to Mass," Peter said.

"I'm not sure about Mass. I don't think she goes any more. I don't think she goes anywhere any more. We're going to Terri's sister's or we could have met you at the house."

Ida kept her eyes on the piano man. She would not look at Terri with her blue eyeshadow and helmet-hair. And if there was one person she loved in the whole entire world – more than any other – it had to be Jerry Lewis.

At six she and Alice watched *Batman* in the sitting room under the pink silky quilt they'd brought down from Ida's bed. Alice had her potty next to her as Ida had sworn she wasn't going to miss any of the action to take her to the loo. Alice had wet her pyjamas in the night, so was naked except for a red hat and mittens. Ida was wearing a blue towelling beach dress with a knitted green hat she'd found in the shed while playing hide and seek with Da before he left. The girls had wrapped the quilt around them so their bottoms weren't too cold, but their feet were sticking out which they didn't mind that much. They were both used to the freezing floorboards and quarry tiles in the downstairs of the house. It made it nicer, somehow, when Ida reached the red carpet in her bedroom – like she was taking her feet on holiday.

The television was black and white with a knob to tune it in. It was very small, which was why it felt too far away to sit on the sofa and watch it. Behind the girls was a low, glass-topped coffee table, and on it was their mother's wine glass and the half-eaten box of crystallised ginger. It was the adverts.

"Have a sweetie, Alice."

"Don't like them." She shut her mouth tight.

"They're different ones. These ones are like Fruit Salads."

Alice kept her mouth shut but opened her eyes wide. Ida knew she was thinking about it.

"But…"

Ida grabbed her sister and put her fingers in her mouth. With her other hand she took a piece of ginger, forced it between Alice's teeth, and held shut her lips.

"Chew it. Chew it, mmmm delicious sweets," she was cackling.

Tears rolled down Alice's face and her cheeks went red. She started to cough and Ida released her.

"Don't be a baby, Alice, for goodness sake. They're good for you. Like medicine. See?" She pretended to take one and eat it.

From nine until ten past twelve Ida sat on the back of the sofa eating cornflakes straight from the packet, waiting for him to arrive. Alice had cried for Ida to play with her until she'd sent herself to sleep and was lying by Ida's feet, rolled up in the quilt. From experience Ida knew that it was best to do something else, to make some tea or have a bath, while you were waiting. But this man was so interesting, so magical somehow, that she was scared to move from the spot.

From where she was sitting she could see the play poster, the one with the wavy-haired girl, which hung above the mantelpiece. Despite all the bad things that the the girl in the play did (grown-up things she wasn't supposed to know about) Ida wanted to be her more than anyone.

While Ida's face was rounded and monkey-like, the girl in the poster had a long thin face and a pointy nose. While Ida's hair was frizzy and full of knots, the girl in the poster had perfect wavy mermaid-ish hair. A couple of months ago she had used a whole bottle of conditioner while trying to make her hair as soft and lovely as the other, pretty Ida's. Bridie had been annoyed but then, as she got drunker throughout the day, had tried to help, cracking an egg on Ida's head and accidentally scrambling it when she tried to wash it off under the hot tap.

Next to the poster was the painting of her mother, the one where she was looking in the mirror with her bosoms out. This picture was one of the many reasons Ida couldn't bring friends home from school. Secretly she loved it though, the big splodgy brush strokes, the way her mother's skin was made of greens and reds, nothing like the 'skin coloured' crayon they told her to use at school. And her eyes were beautiful – black and mysterious as she gazed at herself. Other-Ida's face and hair, her own mother's bosoms and eyes – some of the things she prayed she'd develop when she finally grew up.

"Tea sweet pea, I'm dehydrating. Help!" shouted Bridie from upstairs at just past twelve and Ida did as she was told, stepping over her sleeping sister and walking into the kitchen over the cold tiles, lifting each foot high and treading lightly as if she were walking on hot coals.

"So is she thin? How thin?" asked Bridie. She was sitting up in bed drinking her tea while Ida lay by her feet like a cat, staring into the mirror opposite. The reflection showed Ida's frowning face, long legs and matted hair, but she wasn't interested in looking at herself. Instead she was looking at her wonderful mother, whose black hair was pouring onto her tatty blue kimono. Ida liked her best like this, make-up free and straight backed.

"Not as thin as you," she said.

"She's younger though. How young?"

"I don't know. Twenty?"

"Twenty!"

"I mean, a bit younger than you, but not much. Thirty?"

"She's either twenty or thirty. There's a ten year gap. You wouldn't like it if I said you and Ally were the same age, would you?"

"No, but you know we're not."

"Sometimes I don't know who's more grown up."

Ida frowned and bit her lip.

"Ally can't make tea."

Bridie laughed.

"Alright, you're a very grown up little lady who loves *Batman* and digging and her Sindy doll."

Ida tried to laugh but it came out as a squeak.

"Did you have a good time anyway?"

"It was okay. They made me get up on stage."

"'Okay' is not an 'okay' word for you to use. It might be worse than nice. Did you have a good time? Give me three words."

"It was... scary, and magical, and... scratchy."

"Ha! Now there's my daughter, you funny old thing. Happy Christmas – come here."

Ida crawled up the bed and into the crook of her mother's arm. She smelled of sweat and cigarettes, but Ida didn't mind.

"Did you like being on stage?"

"No. Well, by the end I didn't mind."

"You'll have to get used to it. Everyone has to get used to it."

Ida thought about that. She knew not everyone had to get used to it, not ice cream ladies or people in the bank, but Bridie always talked about 'everyone' as just being everyone she knew.

There was a knock at the front door.

"Who the bugger could that be? Tell them to piss off, Ida, tell them I'm working."

Peter stood on the doorstep in a cream suit with a dark blue coat that went all the way to the ground. With his thin, pale face clean of make-up, he was like a normal man and Ida was disappointed. He held a little bunch of flowers and a briefcase.

"Good morning, Princess Ida of Bournemouth. I come bearing gifts."

From his pocket he pulled two Milky Bars.

Ida took one and handed it to Alice who was standing behind her, shy and clinging onto her beach dress.

"Oh, thank you, Peter. Good morning – or afternoon. Mummy's working."

"Is she now? Well, I have to say that's a surprise. But a good one. I'll look in on her for a minute then, shall I? I'll take her up these freesias."

"Umm, she won't like it."

"I'll be quick. Open the door wide, there's a good girl."

He stepped through into the hallway and Ida felt a bit embarrassed, but mostly scared her mother would hit the roof. She knew it was dusty, and there were empty bottles on the telephone table, two of the reasons she was under strict instructions not to let anyone into the house.

"Christmas festivities I see! Have you had people to stay?" asked Peter, but Ida knew he realised that Bridie had drunk all the bottles herself.

"No," Ida said.

Peter frowned, sympathetically, and tapped her on the head.

"The queen is upstairs I take it?"

Ida didn't reply.

"Take my coat, there's a good girl."

It was very heavy and Ida struggled to hold it while Peter bounded up the creaky stairs three at a time, clutching the little bunch of flowers. Ida closed her eyes. She hadn't got a clue what was going to happen. She dragged the coat into the sitting room and sat, listening hard for raised voices, as Alice sucked her chocolate through the foil.

It was almost four before they came down the stairs for good. A few hours before, Ida had heard the bath running, and when Bridie walked into the sitting room Ida could tell she'd had a wash. She was wearing her best beaded black dress, and on top of her clean hair was her wavy hairpiece that slid in with a comb. Her make-up was different to normal, prettier and sparklier, and she was smiling, although her eyes were puffy as if she'd been crying.

Ida ran over and hugged her legs.

"Isn't she divine?" asked Peter.

He was next to Bridie, wearing her best mink coat, with soft pink blusher on his cheeks. He didn't look scary now, he looked fantastic. Even Alice seemed to think so, and toddled up and touched the fur. Peter leant down to kiss her forehead and she didn't cry, which was almost unheard of with strangers.

"My dear princesses. What pretty little things you are. Sorry we took such a long time, we had important business as you can see. And now, as it's four –" he pointed at Bridie, "we can have a drink. Because four is an alright time to have a drink on Christmas Day. But never, ever before."

Ida knew that he thought Bridie hadn't drunk that day, which made her realise that he wasn't as clever and magical as she had first imagined. There was a bottle of whisky in the back of the loo and Bridie would have drunk that when she'd been having a bath. Ida couldn't tell Peter the truth. Everything was far too lovely to ruin.

He lay his briefcase on the sofa and opened it with a click. Inside were two parcels wrapped in sparkling gold paper with a purple feather stuck to each one.

"Here you go, darlings."

Ida held Alice back with her arm as she opened both parcels. Alice would rip them and Ida needed to keep the paper – it was beautiful.

Inside each package was a scarf, one purple and one silvery, and a pile of enormous jewels, including the nicest clip-on earrings Ida had ever seen.

"Treasure," said Peter winking. He whispered to Ida, "You can have the pick darling. Not sure your sister is that bothered. And I'll show you how to make yourself a sari with the scarf, like a real Indian princess."

Bridie asked Peter about what London was like now, about Soho and the theatres. Ida didn't know why she asked, she always cried if people talked about London.

Peter tried to change the subject and her ma finished another bottle of wine, and then Ida knew she was really drunk because she started singing Irish songs and talking in an Irish accent, even though she'd been born in King's Cross.

'You're never a real person,' Ida's da used to say to Bridie, 'you're always pretending to be someone else, even when you're rat-arsed.' And he was right, Ida supposed.

Then Bridie started sobbing while Peter hugged her. "No one understands why I didn't want to move down here. How much I hate it here. No one except you."

But Peter changed the subject and poured more wine and soon they had drunk two bottles each, the amount Ida found made adults the most fun. It was getting late but there'd been no mention of bed and Ida had the feeling she wouldn't have to stay still and be quiet to be allowed to stay up. They were having a party, a real grown-up party with candles and music, and Ida was part of it, not at the side of it or in another room like at most grown-up parties.

Bridie got her records out for the first time in ages and they all sang along, Peter giving the girls turns at dancing on his feet, him holding their hands. And then it was Cher and they all sat on the sofa and watched Bridie dance, and sing in a deep voice while throwing freesias onto their laps, and they all believed that she was a gypsy, and that she'd been born in a travelling show and Ida was in love with her mother and in love with Peter and everything was wonderful.

Then she bowed and sat down and Peter sang a funny song called 'Jellied Eels', but in a really serious voice which made it funnier and Ida thought she might pee herself laughing.

"Your turn, Princess Ida," he said and reached for her hand. She tried to pretend she was drunk like the grown-ups and that she didn't care about anything.

"Now for one of my old favourites," she said in a pretend cockney accent and everyone clapped. She sang 'Oom Pa Pa', and danced round the sitting room, taking each of them in turn and making them spin round the room with her while she flapped her skirt around like she was Nancy. They were all breathless by the end but they stood and shouted 'encore' and she sung a few verses of 'I'd Do Anything', then curtsied and caught some imaginary bouquets.

"God, you're your mother's daughter," said Peter as she joined him on the sofa. Ida grinned.

Bridie was singing again now, another of her favourites, 'One For My Baby', originally sung – as Ida was always being told – by her namesake, the olden-days actress Ida Lupino. Normally Ida would have been delighted, Bridie had sung it to her when she was really small, but she was slurring the words and looked like she might fall over.

Ida stared at the poster she loved, the one for her ma's play, and tried to copy the pose of the girl in the drawing, flicking out her hair and parting her lips.

"A bit of practice and you'll be there," Peter whispered into her ear and Ida could feel her face go red.

"Nothing to be ashamed of, dear, I spent my childhood wanting to be Bette Davis. And look – it worked!"

He leant down over Ida, making a manic, smiling face, as he pretended to strangle her. The sleeves of his mink coat tickled her cheeks and she laughed and laughed and begged him to stop, though really she hoped that he would go on forever.

Chapter nine

~ 1999 ~

The plan was to be ruthless, but by the time Tom got back from the tip Alice and Ida were sitting in the half dark on Bridie's threadbare bedroom carpet, surrounded by piles of paper, jewellery and faded photos. They'd found a couple of cine-films too, but neither of them were sure how to work the projector.

Ida had begun the sorting-out by moving things meaninglessly from pile to pile, convinced that Alice would take the lead, but so far Alice was doing much the same thing. In fact, Ida soon realised it was she, and not Alice, who was becoming frustrated with their lack of progress. She was beginning to wonder, as she frequently had when they were children, whether Alice was slightly slow or something.

"Shall I put the kettle on?" Tom asked. "And a light?"

"There's no bulb in the centre one. She hated centre lights. Thought they were naff. But tea would be good," said Alice.

"She was a mad old cow," said Ida, "look at all this stuff. You know, I think we need to be clearer about what we're keeping and what we're chucking. We can't keep all of this. Where would we put it?"

"There are so many photos. I didn't think she kept them all. Who knew she was so sentimental." Alice was smoothing down the edges of an ancient picture of Ida's old room.

"That can go for a start," said Ida, snatching it from Alice. She wanted to say that her mother had been too lazy to throw anything away, but managed to stop herself.

"People can be funny creatures," Tom said, walking into the room, sitting on the floor and touching Alice's bony knee. "When my granddad was about to die he told me he'd always loved me and gave me some poems he'd written. They were terrible, of course. But this is from a man who didn't cry at his own wife's funeral."

Ida didn't say anything but shuffled some bills. She had managed to resist looking at the photographs her sister kept trying to show her. Now Alice was passing some to Tom.

"Look at Ida here. She'd cut all her hair off. You must have been what, fourteen?"

"Thanks Al."

"What? It doesn't look that different to how it does now."

"But I was so spotty."

"God, weren't we all. What about this one then," Alice said, flicking through a blue album with red wine stains on the front. She held it out to Tom.

"Ida at her First Communion in her white dress. And look at Mum in the background – she looks so bloody glamorous in her patent sling backs. She always did. Oh Ida, look, you're holding a Bible, how sweet."

"Fuck off Alice."

Tom laughed, examining the photos closely. "You do look sweet. You're still like kids you two, arguing."

Ida clambered to her feet and stretched her arms towards the ceiling, her fingertips brushing the plaster.

"Well, I'm going to put the kettle on. I can cook too if you like. Tom, why don't you help Alice? Not that we're getting anywhere. What the fuck are we meant to do with all of it?"

"I'll stop in a bit too, to be honest," said Alice, "we've got to see the funeral director tomorrow and need to plan for that. You need to choose your reading. I've done a shortlist..."

"Old Testament please."

"Okay, fine. Well, I've done the basics. I'll leave as much as possible to them, put it on my credit card and pay it off when the house is sold. I can't bear it, any of it, and goodness knows what she actually would have wanted. I only know what she didn't want."

"She was good at what she didn't want," Ida said.

"She certainly was," said Alice.

Ida hadn't attempted to cook a proper meal for years and was almost enjoying rooting through the cupboards and examining the cans. There were all kinds of vegetables in the fridge and above the sink was a spice rack filled with things Ida had never heard of. When they were children they'd lived off spaghetti hoops on toast and fish finger sandwiches and she wondered how on earth Alice had learned to cook.

There were chicken drumsticks in the freezer and Ida guessed she couldn't go too wrong with some meat and some veg and lots and lots of wine.

Tom came through the kitchen door with a shopping bag full of rubbish. "Shit, there's some amazing stuff up there, the original script for the film, signed by Anna DeCosta. Your mum's written 'bullshit' on the front in felt tip but I think that kind of adds to its charm."

Ida felt suddenly cold. "That's mine. She sent it to me after the premiere."

"Really? Cool. God, it's got to be worth something."

"I'm not going to sell it. I do have some nice things you know."

"Of course not, no, of course you wouldn't sell it."

"Do you think Alice will let us have some wine tonight? A glass or two? It's normal to have wine with dinner, that's not me being an alchie."

"I think she actually might, you know. She's feeling worn out. I'll talk to her. I worry about her. She's so controlled about everything. And she's funny about food. Don't tell her I said anything," he started to whisper, "but a glass of wine might do her good. Is that chicken? She bought that for Bridie. You do know Alice is vegan?"

"Of course she is," said Ida. "Of course she's a bloody vegan."

They sat and ate in front of the TV, drinking red wine that Tom had gone out to buy. Ida was trying to drink hers slowly, aware that her access to alcohol for the rest of the week depended on her conduct this evening. Although things could have been awkward, Ida found it hard to feel uncomfortable when everything was so clean and warm and there was food in the cupboard. Alice was picking at her vegetables while Tom looked at Teletext to see what was on. "I normally watch Barry Norman. But, I don't know, there might be something on it about your mum," he said.

"I don't mind, do you mind Al?"

"I don't mind about much, this wine's gone straight to my head."

He turned over. It was some balding director Ida didn't recognise talking about an action film. Ida went to her room and added some whisky to her wine.

She came back to see a face she knew on screen and stood still in the doorway.

"Look at her Ida. Fuck, look at her face, she's not even old!" said Alice, turning round. "At least Ma never got round to plastic surgery. That's one horror we managed to avoid."

"Anna DeCosta. You know her real name is Anna Furkin, right? No wonder she changed it," Tom said.

It took a few seconds to work it out, but yes, it was her, Anna DeCosta, puffed up and shiny like a deranged Barbie.

"Apparently she's touring in some show at the moment. I'm amazed she can stand up," said Alice.

"Yeah, that's not just surgery, she's been in rehab like, ten times or something. My mate David says she offered to suck him off for two hundred quid on the set of *Night Terrors*."

"Tom! Ida, you used to love her, didn't you? You had posters of her on your wall."

Ida tipped back her glass and finished her whisky-and-wine in one big gulp. She wiped her mouth with her hand. "Actually, on the night of the premiere, I shagged her, so there."

Alice rolled her eyes.

"Right Ida, you shagged her. You're always so dramatic, and

you talk such shit. You're exactly like Ma that way."

Tom was looking up at her, wide eyed and serious. "Really?" he asked.

"Pretty much," she smiled.

"Shhhh, I can't hear," said Alice.

Ida sat down.

"She was a real class act, everyone said so. So beautiful and glamorous. And of course I was a fan of her work before I was asked to play the part. She told me I'd done the role justice, well, that was all I cared about."

"What a load of crap, turn it off." Alice started to cry.

Chapter ten

~1983 ~

When the man came round with his trolley Bridie ordered two glasses of Chablis, paying with the torn ten-pound note Ida had frantically helped her search for earlier.

"Keep the change," she said, and Ida had to clasp her hands together to stop herself reaching out for it. She tried not to think about how they would pay for a cab to the hotel when they got off the train – it would all be alright, it was normally all alright.

The women sitting next to them shared a brief wide-eyed look; shocked either at her mother's large tip, at Ida's age, or perhaps because it wasn't yet lunchtime. Next to these neat-haired women Bridie looked mad, her long hair piled up with two black chopsticks sticking out of it, her shakily draw-in eyebrows over her gaunt cheeks, and long thin fingers moving manically as she spoke.

"I mean what can you learn anyway at that crappy prim school, buried up to your ears in bloody geography books? I can teach you the important stuff."

"Yes," said Ida quietly. The film company had sent first-class tickets and she was trying hard to fit in, stretching her legs out slowly, attempting elegance and reserve, staring out of the window with a serious expression.

"Why are you speaking like that? Like you've got something up your bottom?" asked Bridie.

Ida didn't reply but took a swig of her warm wine and tried hard not to retch. Her mother was still talking but she blocked out her words, noticing instead the regular sounds of the train and the colours of the blurred and drizzly world outside. She thought about the high shoes she had for later, and the red, strappy dress that showed off her boobs. She was secretly hopeful that she'd be spotted by someone important, someone who'd notice her 'je ne sais quoi.'

For years she'd been practicing this night, the conversations she'd have with people, and how she'd pose for the pictures. And Anna DeCosta! Before Ida had left Greenlands she'd told nearly everyone in the class she would get them her autograph. Ida couldn't understand why Bridie wasn't more excited about it all, surely this was what she'd been waiting for – recognition, money, glamour, even fame. Instead she seemed bored, as if she'd been going to film premieres on first-class trains every week for the last ten years. She had in her mind, Ida supposed, all those days spent in bed in their dirty, cold house, pretending desperately she was lying in some glamorous hotel.

The windows went black as they entered a tunnel, the noise of the train becoming louder and more highly pitched as Ida's reflection appeared in the window. She vowed silently to the image of her own lips that she would always be excited and grateful about good things, noticing with alarm her crowded bottom teeth, slight moustache and acne-covered chin.

When they got to Waterloo Bridie marched so quickly through the station that Ida had to run to keep up. She knew her mother, and the marching was a sure sign she didn't want to be questioned or hassled about the next stage of their journey. Just before the exit a short elderly man wearing a pink turban appeared. He was holding a sign saying 'Bridie Adair and daughter'.

"I've been told to look out for you. Are you Ms Adair?" he asked.

"I am indeed, and this gangly thing is my daughter, believe it or not."

The man smiled nervously while Bridie guffawed.

The car had tinted windows and Ida couldn't believe it. She was being driven by an actual driver, in a car with blacked-out windows, like she was a film star. She tried to look straight ahead and ignore her mother, to pretend she was Anna DeCosta and that she travelled like this every day. As they drove over Waterloo Bridge she noticed some people stop and stare and it took all the strength she could muster not to wind down the window and wave. *New starlet, Ida Irons, arrives for the premiere of her latest film.*

Bridie sighed and turned away from the window. "The thing is, it's the English I hate, any other race I absolutely adore. Where are you from originally?" Bridie asked the driver.

Ida closed her eyes.

"Ummm, well, Ealing," the man laughed, even more nervously than before and Bridie appeared not to hear his answer.

"Oh God yes, the English with their tracksuits and their fat arses and their bloody vol-au-vents."

Surely they're French, Ida thought, but she knew better than to speak.

"Where are you from? Originally?" the man asked.

"Ireland," she said, as if he was stupid for asking. "Well, I'd Irish parents. People know how to live there. It's not all pot-pourri, en-suites, Bruce Forsyth... and bloody dogs in prams."

The man didn't make a sound and kept his eyes fixed straight ahead. Ida didn't know whether to laugh or cry.

They pulled up at the Hilton and the driver walked round to Bridie's door.

"When we were younger we'd avoid the Hilton like the plague," she said. "I suppose beggars can't be choosers, eh."

Bridie let him help her out, extending one leg slowly and straightening her back. She was getting into character, Ida knew the signs, and despite her protestations Ida could see that her mother was at least pleased to be away from Bournemouth, to be the old Bridie once again. She prayed that it would all be okay, that her mother would be normal and that people wouldn't laugh.

The staff had emptied the minibar and Bridie was irate.

"I'm not a fucking baby, am I? Do I sound like a baby? A

child?" she was shouting down the phone to reception.

Ida lay on her bed. It was so soft she felt like a bird in a nest.

Outside she could hear the hum of traffic and, if she sat up slightly, could see over the road to Hyde Park, where people were walking dogs and jogging and playing with balls. If Terri were there she'd make Ida walk round the park now. First she'd lay her things out, all neat and in rows, then she'd feel the towels, inspect the bathroom for dust and then, when she was happy with that, she'd make Ida go for a long walk, followed by hot chocolate. Always hot chocolate.

There was a knock at the door and Bridie opened it.

"Two bloody marys madam," said a man with a wide, false smile under his silly blue hat.

"Charge it, please," said Bridie briskly, tipping him their last full five pounds. He bowed and left the room.

"Don't let anyone treat you like a child, you hear me?" she said, placing one of the drinks next to Ida. "I've never treated you like one, have I? Women should be able to do whatever the hell they want, and you have to fight for that. These bloody film execs will have your guts for garters." She took a large sip.

Ida sat up, took the drink from next to her and sniffed it. She hated walking, anyway.

The driver was coming back at six thirty and it was ten to six. Ida felt sick. She wasn't sure if it was the booze or the nerves or a combination but she felt so nauseous she could hardly speak. She had taken a long bath which had been lovely – the water at home was tepid at best. Then she had laid out her clothes and jewellery and carefully got dressed.

"Don't forget deodorant, we don't want you smelling like a horse," Bridie said. "And brush your hair."

The thing was, the more she brushed the frizzier it got, until her long, mousey hair resembled something close to the roof of derelict barn. Her skin was so bad that the more cover-up she layered on, the worse it looked.

As she did her make-up in the mirror she watched her mother getting dressed behind her, pulling velvet trousers over her spindly legs and slipping a man's white shirt over her ribs. Bridie had always been thin as anything but now a fine layer of downy hair covered her arms and she rarely let Ida see her get dressed.

"You need to eat more, Mummy, you look so ill," she mouthed the words to herself in the mirror before realising, to her horror, that she'd said them out loud. There was a long pause while Bridie carried on buttoning her shirt. After a minute or so she spoke.

"Why don't you mind your own business, eh? I don't go poking my nose into everything you do, do I? Like you having it off with that oik from St Luke's?"

Ida went bright red.

"We didn't..."

"I don't want to know the details, dear – snogging, or fumbling, or actual in-and-out. Now are you going to help me with my hair? Your spots won't show anyway, well, probably not. The lights won't be bright, thank God, we're not in the suburbs now."

Bridie sat on the bed and Ida turned and sat behind her, pulling the chopsticks out of her mother's hair and beginning to brush.

They were expecting more drinks but the man was empty-handed. He wasn't wearing a uniform, but instead a black suit, and behind him a young blonde waitress carried two coffees on a tray.

"Ms Adair. We have brought you some coffee."

"Where are my drinks?"

"Ah well, there was a little problem with that. The studio would prefer you had some coffee."

The man was smiling like this was a gift. He was good, Ida could see that, but he could never be good enough to defeat her mother. She sat on the bed and looked outside. That was that then, they'd be here all God damn night.

"I need the drinks I ordered, now. If that bloody studio think I am going stone cold sober to some terrible thing where people will insult me, and my work will be ripped to shreds by morons, then they've got another think coming."

"It's also come to our attention that your daughter is underage."

"Both the drinks are for me."

"I'm sorry we can't help more, Ms Adair, maybe you could take it up with the studio?"

"You know I know every reviewer in this town? Just you wait, you stupid, foolish man."

He bowed and started to leave.

"My apologies, Ms Adair, if there was anything I could do –"

"You could do plenty, couldn't you? It's that you won't."

He closed the door but Bridie didn't move. "I bet this has to do with your father, you know. Bad mouthing me to all and sundry, spreading lies in that bloody trashy mag he writes for..."

The Radio Times, thought Ida, he writes for *The Radio Times*.

"Get your shoes on then, count up the money from the bottom of my bag. There must be a shop near here you can get to."

"But the time, Ma."

"I'm not going anywhere 'til I'm at least three-quarters pissed. Not tonight. Not tonight of all nights."

By the time Ida got back the driver had been sent away twice and it was nearly seven o'clock. She had a dusty bottle of brandy she'd bought in a tobacconist; the old lady behind the counter was long-sighted enough to have taken Ida's height as proof she was over eighteen. Bridie's hands were shaking as she took it, and she downed almost a quarter of it in four gulps. She exhaled.

"He'll be back in ten minutes, that's what he said. Wash your face, darling, you're sweating."

Ida couldn't stop shaking in the car, and for the first time she wished Alice was there. She realised that it was, perhaps, the first time she'd been away from her sister overnight. If Alice was there she would have been kept busy answering her maddening questions and making sure she ate. Without her there Ida wasn't sure what to do. But it was a grown-up film, not one for irritating girls like Alice who wet the bed and cried at *Lassie*.

It was dark outside but there were people everywhere and more lights and sounds than she could possibly take in. She wound down the window and took a deep breath, tasting petrol and fast food and things she couldn't name. On a street corner two men were dancing while other people watched, and as they turned she saw a group of girls with red Mohicans and leather jackets. She was filled with a joy she'd not known before, the kind she'd been told she would feel when she'd been confirmed. She wasn't sure whether God would possibly choose to reach her through some scary looking girls, and some smells, and some dancing young men, but it certainly felt like it.

Bridie was jiggling her leg and looking out of the other window and Ida could tell she was nervous, drumming one finger on her collarbone. Her hair was up in a twist, Ida had pinned it, and she had dark red lipstick on her full lips. Over her white shirt she wore a black tuxedo jacket, which Ida was surprised to recognise as an old one of her da's.

Ida looked down at her own legs. She was wearing thin black tights under her dress, the kind that always ripped, and had a spare pair in the red clutch bag Terri had given her to bring. Over her dress she wore her mother's pale mink coat, and although it made her feel bad for all the little minks, she did feel lovely and warm. Her hair was loosely up now, pinned with bits round her face, and in the end Bridie had helped her powder her chin so it didn't look too bad. She had only been back to London a few times since they'd moved to Bournemouth, and had always felt scared and out of place, standing on the wrong side of the escalators and being tutted at in the street. But now she felt she was in a different city entirely, a city that she owned, where she was driven in fancy cars and wore fur coats and heels. She took more deep breaths. It was all going to be okay – she knew it would be okay. She could feel it in her bones.

Ida had thought they'd pull up at the theatre but instead they stopped nearby. They were too late to drive up outside apparently, the stars were arriving now.

"Fine, fine," said Bridie, like it wasn't fine at all, "thank you for all your help today, you've been marvellous. Come on sweetheart, let's leave this man in peace."

They climbed out of the car and onto the busy pavement.

"Come on, this way, I know London like the back of my hand," Bridie said, grabbing Ida's arm painfully and pulling her along while she tottered on her new high heels, apologising as she bumped into people. As they turned the corner into Leicester Square Ida felt an embarrassing grin creep across her face. To the left of them was a cinema and a sign with tall black letters read 'Ida, starring Anna DeCosta, premiere tonight'.

From the door lay an actual red carpet, and on each side were barriers with gold posts and black ropes. Behind them were fans, two or three deep, waving autograph books and squealing as car doors opened and people got out. Ida watched as they emerged from their cars – shiny shoes followed by thin legs, then sparkling dresses, white smiles and smooth, immobile hair. She touched her own frizzy scalp.

"Darling, you're shaking, pull yourself together. No one's here for us, are they? Just keep quiet and try not to fall."

They walked towards the corner of the barrier where a woman stood with a clipboard.

"Bridie Adair, I wrote the damn thing."

The woman grinned broadly, and slightly meanly, Ida thought, as she skimmed the clipboard with her eyes.

"Of course. Fantastic, please go through in a second. You're a little late. Miss DeCosta is arriving now." She held her arm out in front of Bridie and Ida as if they were liable to jump over the rope.

People began to scream and from behind someone pushed Ida hard in the small of the back. She fell forwards slightly, her ankle twisting to the side.

Less than three feet away from them stood Anna DeCosta, far thinner and more beautiful than Ida could have imagined. Her dark blonde hair waved softly at the ends, and she smiled at the crowd as if, Ida thought, she'd just heard a wonderful private joke. Her dress was pale pink and she wore brown cowboy boots beneath it. She wasn't that much older than Ida, nineteen or twenty, but she looked like she knew things Ida couldn't even dream of. Ida immediately wished that she'd worn flats instead of her painful high heels.

"I don't know what all of the fuss is about. She looks like a girl who'd work in Safeway," Bridie said loudly, and the woman with the clipboard frowned.

"She'll be a minute with the press and then you can go through Ms Adair, and...?"

"Ida," Ida said, trying to ignore her throbbing ankle.

The woman looked confused but smiled blankly, then unhooked the rope and ushered them through.

Ida's legs were shaking so much she was grateful for Bridie's iron grip on her arm, and even for the stage-whispered instructions she was being given as cameras flashed and people shouted things she couldn't understand.

"Side on, remember your hips are wide, that's it, smile, pose, smile, turn, pose. That's enough." Bridie put one hand on Ida's back and pushed her along the rest of the carpet and through the door.

"I'll probably get Bryan Irons' wife in the captions, I wouldn't be surprised. This whole thing's a farce."

Two women took their coats and they were handed flutes of Champagne by waiters who stood either side of the entrance in short rows. The lights were bright in the foyer, not dim like Bridie had said they'd be. A woman in a dark suit walked towards them. "Hi! You're a bit late, if you wouldn't mind coming straight through, Ms Adair, I'll take you to your seat. The one next to you has been taken I'm afraid, we had to shift things around, but don't worry, we'll fit you in," she said, looking at Ida.

For one moment Ida wondered about popcorn before realising how hopelessly unsophisticated she was and feeling ashamed. They followed the woman through the doors into the dark cinema. There was a low mumble, broken by nervous laughs and at the front a band played some unfamiliar, sad music. It wasn't like the Odeon in town, all concrete and neon signs. Instead it looked like a theatre, with cherubs and fancy carvings all over the walls. Ida struggled to walk in her shoes, hold her glass, and look for famous faces at the same time.

"Ms Adair, you're in row G with Mike Saunders, and your daughter, well..." she scanned the crowd and Ida followed her eyes. There, in the row in front was the honey-coloured head she was looking for. Someone was whispering into her ear and she was laughing hard.

"If you don't mind I think you may need to sit over there, you lucky girl." She pointed to an empty seat, where a pale pink handbag was lying.

"But..."

"Don't be shy, excuse me," the woman stepped forward and spoke to the people at the end of the row and they began to stand up, giving Ida no choice but squeeze past them to her seat.

"I'm so sorry," said Anna DeCosta, standing up and lifting her pink handbag off the seat as Ida brushed past her, pulling in her stomach as far as she could. "I didn't think anyone was sitting there, here, sit down," she patted the back of the chair. "What's your name? I'm Anna, Annie to my friends. Nice shoes," she whispered as Ida sat down, feeling very aware of her big hips, spotty chin and possible bad breath.

"Thanks. Yours are nice too."

"Ha. Thanks. I wasn't sure. At home they would hate it, boots at a premiere, but in Britain you can get away with more. A refill?" She lifted a bottle from between her feet and without asking filled up Ida's glass.

As soon as the opening credits began Ida could tell it was going to be different to the play. She had imagined a slow and serious film, quiet with lots of silences, but instead it opened in a loud, nasty disco, with shots of different almost naked people sweating and dancing and kissing. And then there she was, Anna – Other-Ida – sitting crying in the loo, wearing a waitress outfit with her hands over her ears, scared of the noise and the people and her sleazy boss.

Ida could hardly breathe or blink and from the corner of her eye could see Anna's perfect long fingernails, her little fingers resting on her leg. She hoped she was happy with the way it was going and with how she looked on screen.

The scene changed. Other-Ida was going home from the club on the subway and there was no music now. Instead the only noise was the horrible screech of the train as the camera panned round slowly to show the miserable, scary faces of the people in the carriage: a homeless man with broken shoes, two ill-looking girls with matted blonde hair, a dirty woman holding a snapping dog. When Other-Ida got back home she tried to sneak in but the lights came on and there was her sister.

For the next twenty minutes she hadn't a clue what was happening. She noticed colours and faces, but couldn't join them up. Instead she imagined herself in the film – living with her sister in a house in New York.

She imagined she was thin, with sleek straight hair – that she was mysterious and tragic.

Occasionally she turned round and tried to catch Bridie's eye and felt anxious when, after half an hour or so, her mother disappeared. The thought of asking all those people to stand up and then showing her awful hips to the whole cinema was too much to contemplate so she stayed where she was, biting her nails, and gazing at the wonderful Anna on screen while trying hard not to look at the wonderful Anna right next to her. Then there were Anna's small round boobs, made massive on screen, and Ida couldn't resist subtlety touching her own for comparison while trying hard not to sneak a glance at the now famous breasts which were inches away from her.

She drank her champagne quickly and Anna noticed each time her glass was empty and filled it straight back up. "A girl after my own heart," she whispered approvingly.

They were on the beach. It was nearly the scene Ida was waiting for and her palms were sweating. The two girls were naked – there were lots of shots of their boobs – and they laughed as they swam further and further out. And then it happened. On-screen Ida turned, and held her sister under the water, not flinching or pausing, a fierce, determined look on her beautiful face.

People around them gasped.

"Do you think my teeth are too yellow?" Anna asked as, on screen, she opened her mouth wide and screamed. As she moved away Ida could still feel the heat of Anna's breath on her ear and wondered whether any particles of spit or something would be left on her skin. Alice would know, Alice was good at science, but it wasn't a question she could ask, really. Just in case she decided she better not wash her face for a while.

Most bits were totally different to the play. She went to a clapped-out fairground by the sea where the sounds of the games were very loud, and the camera moved so jerkily that it made Ida dizzy.

Exhausted, she walked back down to the beach, strode into the sea, spread her arms wide and confessed what she'd done to the grey sky and suddenly Ida imagined she was there, at that beach, with the warm American sea on her legs and the tinkling sounds of a fair behind her.

The champagne had made Ida feel strange and, closing her eyes, she found she could actually feel the sea on her ankles, the painful crunch of shells beneath her feet, and a wind so strong her hair wrapped right round her face.

But instead of fairground rides there were peeling beach huts, a small girl, shivering in her nightdress, and hundreds and hundreds of furious gulls. "My breath is the slow creep of the tide," she whispered to herself, and opening her eyes, noticed Anna had turned to look at her. She felt herself blush.

'The End' appeared before Ida expected it to, and the audience broke into loud applause. There were cheers from the balcony and all around her people stood and clapped, so she got unsteadily to her feet.

"What did you think, kiddo?" Anna whispered, turning around and waving at people behind her.

"I loved it."

"Aren't you sweet? What's your name? I didn't catch it."

"Ida," she said.

"I'd heard you existed! They said you did. I wanted to meet you, you know, for research. And here you are! It was meant to be."

People cheered, hoping Anna would wave again or something, but instead she held onto Ida's arms with both her hands and stared right into her eyes. Her face was so small and she looked so excited, that Ida almost hugged her.

"You've got to come out with us, to the afterparty. Wow. The real Ida. Right here. That's neat, you know?"

"Yes," said Ida, "I suppose so."

Because she was sure it was meant to be, and because she was drunk and hungry and very tired, Ida didn't protest. She was led happily outside and into a waiting car, and felt she had about as much control over the situation as she'd had over the action in the film they'd watched. Somehow these events had begun and she was powerless to stop them.

"Hey Shirley, look at her coat! It's kind of fifties. It's cool."

Anna was pointing at Ida's mink jacket.

The girl, Shirley, nodded in agreement from under her heavy fringe. She offered Ida a cigarette, which she gladly took.

"So where's good to hang out in London, Ida, where's good to just hang?" Anna sprawled across the seat with her legs open and she and Shirley started laughing.

"Um, I don't live in London. I'm not sure." Her own voice sounded stupidly posh. She felt dizzy again.

"I don't live in London," Anna said in a fake English accent and she and Shirley laughed. Ida tried to as well. The way Anna was saying things was the way mean girls at school said them, but oddly this was a kind of nice mean – she wanted Anna to tease her.

"I'm kidding Ida, you know that, right? Jimmy's taking us to the afterparty now anyway, aren't you Jim?" A small dark-haired man in the passenger seat turned around.

"That's right, Annie, as long as you keep your legs closed and your boobs in. We've all seen enough of them for one night."

"Yeah right, Jim, you love my tits," she leapt into Ida's lap, pulled down the top of her dress and there was one small breast, just inches from Ida's face. She was so light that Ida had the inexplicable urge to jump out of the car, pick her up and run away with her. For what felt like the millionth time that day she thought she was hopelessly weird.

"She looks petrified! Doesn't she look petrified!" shouted Shirley.

"Shut up Shirl. I don't blame her." She pulled her dress back up. "We'll be better behaved from now on in. Scouts' honour, namesake."

She smiled, as if she and Ida shared a secret, and Ida felt, on some deep level, they really, actually, probably did. She was about to say just that when the car came to a halt.

"Alright girls, we're here. Mike and the others are in there I think, walk straight through the lobby to the Grill Room."

Nothing about the Café Royale Hotel's concrete façade had prepared her for the Grill Room. It was Annie's first time there as well.

"Fuck me. Fuck me!" she said as they walked inside.

"Fuck me," repeated Ida, and immediately felt like an idiot.

The walls and ceiling were gold and completely covered in mirrors, and around the edge of the room there were mirrored tables surrounded by red velvet seats. There were candles and oil lamps but no other lights and the band from the cinema was playing music from the film in the corner.

Applause erupted as they stepped into the room and a handsome, fair-haired man stood up and bowed. He signalled to the band to stop.

"Our glorious Annie," he said and everyone clapped again. A girl took their coats and Annie took Ida's elbow and led her towards the man. As she walked Ida could feel people's eyes on her dress and her shoes and her hair but it wasn't like at school. Instead of judging her they wanted to be like her, or at least they were wondering who she was. A warm feeling of pure wonder rose from her stomach to her cheeks, and she felt like Lucy must have done when she first went through the dark wardrobe and found herself in the snowy woods of Narnia.

Everyone loved Ida. They asked her questions about her life and her mother and her house and repeated all the British expressions that she used. They were Americans, most of them, and were sniffing drugs from the table through a rolled-up ten-pound note.

First they'd cut it up using Mike's American Express card, slicing it then pulling it out to make lines. It looked difficult, and Ida was both shocked and fascinated but tried hard not to stare. From the corner of her eye she carefully watched how they did it, in case they offered some to her.

"Is your Mom okay do you think? I hope she wasn't too upset. I figured she might not like the mad Catholic angle, I know she's kind of into religion," said the blond man.

"I'm sure she's fine. She, well, she sometimes does things like that."

"She's a wino, isn't she?" asked Shirley, giggling, her angular head lolling under her dead-straight hair.

"That's enough," said Annie, then, "don't listen to her. Here..." She passed Ida the rolled-up note and Ida took a quiet breath for nerves, then leant over Annie's thin legs and snorted the thick line of white powder. She felt like someone had poked her right in her brain, and she couldn't help but jerk up her head and open her eyes, wide. Everyone laughed. With a 'pow' the wonder she'd been feeling spread, from her head to her arms to the ends of her hair. This is what heaven feels like, she thought, catching her glowing reflection in the gilt mirror to her right and grinning.

"Wow. No you're right, Shirley, she's a wino, my ma," said Ida, blinking. "She's a wino. And a fucking bitch."

Everyone roared with laughter.

"So I guess she didn't like the film," said Annie shrugging, scraping together another line with the card, "but did you like it? Really? That's what I want to know."

"Yes – I loved it. It was intense and dramatic."

"Exactly. It's all about the mood, it's sinister and strange. You have to be more mature to get it completely," Mike continued.

Ida nodded.

"I wonder how many people have snorted coke from this very table," said Shirley, almost inaudibly, her chin on her chest.

"Lots and lots," said Mike. "Maybe even Oscar Wilde. You know he used to bring his boyfriend here – to this exact club. They would have been sitting where you two are, Ida and Annie, holding hands, looking lovely, making out." He raised his eyebrow at Annie, a private joke Ida didn't understand.

"Come and dance," said Annie, rubbing her nose and squeezing Ida's hand.

The band was playing a jazz tune and the two girls waved their arms about stupidly and pulled faces. Ida was glad that Annie was being so silly, she'd never danced outside her bedroom and wasn't sure she could. Round the edge of the room good-looking people stood and watched them. Annie took her hands and they both leant backwards and span round and round 'til the gilt and the mirrors became one gold blur.

Panting, they stopped and leant towards each other. Annie touched Ida's elbow.

"You want to know a secret, Ida? I thought the film was kind of shitty and confusing," she breathed hotly onto Ida's cheek. "It might just be me. I mean, I read your Mom's play but I couldn't make it out. It's just that bit on the beach, man, that has some honesty. There've been loads of times I wanted to walk right into the ocean and let it all out, you know?"

"I know," said Ida.

"Fancy some air?" asked Annie.

Ida collected their coats while Annie hid in the loo and they ran together, the sweat cooling on Ida's skin as they hurtled past the doormen and round the corner into an alley. Annie took her arm. She was so small Ida felt like more of a giant than ever.

"They'll kill me when they find out I've gone. We can't be long. Where can we walk to, kid? I'm drunk. Or pissed, don't you say pissed?"

"Yeah. I'm pissed." Ida tried to smile. She wasn't sure what was funny, her feet were hurting and she felt a bit out of her depth.

"Take off your shoes. I dare you," Annie said.

Ida did as she was told. The ground was cold through her tights, but not unbearably so. Everything felt sort of warm and exciting.

"Hey mister," Annie called out to a man walking past, "where's good to walk to from here? Somewhere totally pretty and kind of magic."

"Let's head to the river," said Ida. "It's magic there."

They walked through Piccadilly Circus and Annie asked her questions about the streets and the buildings while Ida made up answers as best she could. Although Ida noticed people recognise Anna, pointing her out to their friends, she seemed to be oblivious, gripping Ida's elbow and gossiping about the crew on the film. At any moment, Ida was sure, she would realise she had made a terrible mistake, notice the acne on Ida's chin, and make her way back to the party.

As they walked past the entrance to the National Portrait Gallery, with the steps of St Martin's over to their left, Ida began to walk more quickly, pulling Annie gently along.

"There's something at the end, here," Ida said. "You're going to love it, you'll see."

They stepped into Trafalgar Square and both stood still, barely breathing, as Ida tried to work out the way she felt. It was joy, she decided, a strange, scary joy at being dwarfed by magical buildings with a magical girl on her arm. Even her blood felt magical, pumping quickly round her head. There were drunks on the steps, and people kissing, but Ida had never seen it so quiet.

"It's like a huge dancefloor, just for us. Man, if it was summer I'd be in those fountains like a shot," said Annie.

"Not summer in England you wouldn't. It's eerie here, isn't it? With Nelson standing over us – all the way up there. He seems alive today, I swear. Everything feels funny today, like things are changing."

"Yes! The whole world's changing."

"I mean, for me, tonight. I feel kind of, I don't know, electric."

"I can feel it. Man, I can really feel it." She touched Ida's fingertips with hers.

Ida closed her eyes, felt Annie lean towards her and then, a soft mouth on her bottom lip. Ida shuddered slightly, opened her eyes, leant down, and before she could stop herself, kissed her full on the mouth. A charge ran from her head to her shoeless feet and she pulled Annie as close to her as she could, amazed at what was happening, noticing everything around her – the low rumble of the cars driving past, the cold air on the tops of her ears, each small place where their bodies touched. A group of men walked past and whooped and Annie pulled away.

"Thanks guys," she shouted, looking up at Ida and smiling. "Let's get moving, down to the river," she stood on her tiptoes, kissed Ida's nose and stroked the fur of her coat.

They found their way to Embankment, then up onto a bridge and stood looking out over the black Thames. Ida had never been there before. It was far less glamorous than the other bridges she'd been to – Tower Bridge, Westminster Bridge – just a manky railway bridge with a narrow walkway. But the view of the Houses of Parliament was pretty spectacular.

She awkwardly put her arm round Annie's waist and wondered if she could get used to this. Annie was so sweet, so beautiful, so delicate, she felt almost scared. She wanted more drugs.

"Look at all the lights. Think of all those guys in their houses, watching TV with their ugly husbands or wives," Annie said. "When we're here being all cute and happy and magic. What would you like to do with your life, Ida? If you could do anything?"

"I don't know..."

"You want to be an actress. Any girl who kisses another girl in front of loads of guys, in Trafalgar Square, well, she wants to be an actress for sure."

"It wasn't like that. You kissed me. And I didn't know they were there."

"I just got caught up in things. You started it. 'Ohh Annie, I feel electric.'"

Ida could easily have cried.

"I'm kidding, I'm kidding. I do feel electric. You are electric. You could be an actress, why not? There are parts for big girls. I think you'd be great."

Ida didn't know what to say so didn't reply and looked out towards the pointed silhouette of Westminster Palace, the dark houses to the left of the river and the hundreds of thousands of flickering lights. There was a rumble as a train drove onto the bridge, an almighty roar as it sped its way behind them. Ida hugged Annie as tight as she could, worried – ridiculously – that they'd get knocked over the edge and into the freezing water.

"I used to make up plays with my sister, you know, we used to film them on the beach. Ages ago," Ida said, appalled at the memory that their last film – the most embarrassing one of all – had only been made the year before.

"I bet they were cute."

"They were weird and terrible. We did stuff from *Ida* too, I even did the scene on the beach, you know. Well, my own version."

"I bet you were good at it. I bet you could do anything you wanted to."

"Nothing that involves learning anything, I've just had to leave school. My mum called the headmistress a stupid cow and took me out."

Annie laughed. "School sucks. How old are you anyway? Seventeen?"

"Yes," Ida lied.

"I'm twenty-three and I haven't been to school since I was nine, not properly. I was meant to have a tutor, you know, on set, but he was just some pervert and I never listened to a word he said. You'll be fine."

"Promise?" asked Ida.

"I promise."

Annie gripped the railing with both hands and leant over the edge. "Imagine jumping off. It would be cold, wouldn't it? I've been nuts enough to do it, not tonight, but I have been. Maybe you'll push me."

Ida kissed the back of Annie's head and she turned round, reached up, held Ida's face and kissed her again. Her shoeless feet were numb now and for one glorious moment Ida felt she was floating somewhere above the river, held up by Annie's arms.

The coke was starting to wear off and Annie got worried that she'd be in terrible trouble for leaving the party. Getting back was tricky, and as they neared the Café Royale Ida felt faint and hungry but didn't say anything to Annie. She was worried about her ma. The streets were quieter now, it was very late, and there was always the fear, which she could barely acknowledge, that Bridie would choke on her own sick, fall and break her back, or end it on purpose, properly this time.

Annie was talking about the suite she was in at Claridges and how much Ida would love it. But Ida felt scared. She had no idea what she'd do with Annie if she got to the hotel and the thought of this perfect woman seeing her naked, or whatever she was planning, was too much to cope with.

"I need to go home, I think, well, to the hotel. Shirley was right. My mum can be, well, dangerous."

"Boo. That's a shame. It would have been fun. All the guys would have been there, partying. No problem though – some other time."

"The thing is, I don't have any money for a cab, I don't think."

"You serious? A girl like you doesn't need cash. I never pay for anything. Watch this."

She hitched up her dress, stepped into the road and stuck out her thumb. A black cab from the other side of the street did a U-turn and pulled up next to them.

"Where to?" he asked.

"Hyde Park – the Hilton. The thing is – I don't have any money."

Annie slapped her gently on the back, got into the front seat and, without hesitating, kissed the middle-aged driver passionately, her hands on his chest. Ida was jealous and proud at the same time. Annie pulled away. Ida leant in to hear what they were saying.

"It's okay, isn't it, you'll take my friend home, yeah?"

"Ummm," the man looked confused.

Annie sighed. "Here, give this to your wife for her birthday, it's worth a thousand cab rides, I promise."

She took off a narrow bracelet, set with something that looked like diamonds, handed it to the man, then climbed back out of the cab and stood in front of Ida. "Don't worry, all that crap is insured," she said.

Then she kissed Ida in the hollow at the base of her neck while the cabbie looked at them and shook his head. "Get in then, kiddo. Sleep tight – great to meet you. Remember, you can do whatever you want to. You've got the power! You're electric!"

Ida threw her shoes onto the back seat of the taxi, climbed in after them and sprawled across the seat. The car pulled away and she sat up and turned to see the tiny figure of Anna DeCosta waving at her through the rear window, smiling her lovely, secretive smile. Ida turned away and without any warning burst into tears.

"Fucking hell," murmured the cabbie.

"I'm sorry, I'm tired," Ida said.

She held her breath as she let herself into the room, unsure what she would find. To her surprise the lights were on and Bridie was sitting on the bed, straight-backed in her white cotton nightdress, her hair down and brushed out, watching *The Munsters*.

Bridie turned round, slowly. Her face was completely free of make-up and she looked very old indeed.

"So there you are. Did you have a good time?"

"Yes."

"Well, I see you've been crying. That's a shame. It would at least have been nice for you to have a good time. There's not much for you in bloody Bournemouth is there?"

"I did have a nice time."

"But why are you crying?"

"I don't know."

"As long as you don't think those people liked you, Ida, any more than they liked me. They're a fickle lot, I've told you that. You've got the name for it, but not the looks, and probably not the talent. Don't let them fool you for one God damn second."

"Okay." Ida lay on the bed and turned away.

"At least wash your face before you get into bed. Your skin needs some air."

Ida stood up and walked towards the brightly lit bathroom. Her hair was a mess and she had make-up smudged round her eyes but, from where she stood, she couldn't see her spots in the mirror. Instead what she noticed was a faint, peach lipstick mark, just below her neck. She turned round.

"I'm not having it anymore, Ma. Some people do like me – they think I'm clever and funny and interesting – even pretty. And if you think I'm not, well, that's the way you and Da fucking made me and that's your problem. I won't listen to you being horrible to me anymore. You're a wino, and a fucking... a fucking, bloody, horrible bitch. And everyone, absolutely everyone thinks so. Okay?"

Bridie sniffed and turned back towards the TV. Herman Munster was dancing. "Someone's grown up," was all she said.

Chapter eleven

~ 1999 ~

They had given up on TV. Tom had been out for more wine before the shop shut and they sat around the kitchen table with a glass each. Radio Four was on, quietly, and Ida could see her hunched reflection against the night sky in the glass of the back door. Behind her she could see Tom rubbing Alice's back. She had a sudden, sharp wish for Elliot to come. Not that he'd dream of rubbing her back.

Alice was writing things down and explaining them as she wrote. She was slightly slurring her words. "So, I've ordered the willow coffin and the Mass cards, Hendon's are dealing with them, and Father Patrick is doing the service, she always liked him."

"I can't believe he's still alive," Ida said, picking the wax off the candlestick that stood on the table.

Alice didn't answer.

"What about the eulogy?" Tom asked.

Ida and Alice looked at each other.

"I think she'd hate it," said Alice. "I've asked the priest to say a few words about her, and us and her work."

"No, that's one of those things she would say she'd hate. People going on about how great she was? She'd love it!" Ida said.

"I don't think so. Anyway, it's arranged."

Ida kept quiet. She had no idea why Alice was asking her questions when she didn't want them to be answered. At least there was more wine. But nowhere near enough.

"You know what," Alice said, "I could actually do with a fag."

Tom and Alice were lying on Bridie's bedroom floor laughing hysterically and smoking. Alice had lit candles and put them round the room and Ida felt inexplicably angry and miserable while she watched them rolling about. She supposed it was the drinking; she often got bored drinking with normal people as they always got drunk so quickly, leaving her in the unusual position of being the sober, sensible one. Tom had suggested coming up here to smoke, the room still smelled of cigarettes anyway, but it was Alice who had suggested reading the film script out loud. There it was, the curled bundle of A4 sheets, signed by Anna DeCosta, with 'bullshit' written in huge letters on the front.

"Read us another bit, please. Dear God, oh God I'm going to wet myself," Alice said.

"All my cells are broken, crushed, you don't know what it feels like," Ida read, frowning. She was being the sister – Kate – the pathetic one; the one they'd discovered had the best cheesy lines.

"All my cells are broken, Tom, you don't know what it feels like," Alice said to Tom and he tickled her.

The wine was nearly finished.

"I think I might go to bed, it's after three," Ida said.

Tom stopped tickling Alice; sat up and turned towards her. "Don't do that, read some more," he said.

"Alright, but not this shit, I'm reading from Ma's actual play. You are as well. Come on, sit up you two."

Ida crawled towards the wardrobe and opened the door. She closed her eyes. She wasn't ready to see her mother's clothes and the smell of damp and Chanel No.5 was almost too much. She reached in and pulled out a box. It was still there, it had been there for years.

"Here it is," she said, opening it to reveal a pile of black and red books. "Take one and pass it on."

Alice had forgotten about her no spirits rule and was drinking a glass of whisky, kneeling on the carpet and gesticulating with her free hand, her hair coming loose from its band and falling over her face.

"This is what I trained for actually."

"You did English and Drama at some knobby university, now you work in what? Some bank?" Ida said.

"Falmouth is pretty good for drama," said Alice.

"And you were always too scared to even read in church," Ida said.

Alice ignored her and looked at Tom. "It's meant to be based on some Greek tragedy. There's a bloody chorus. I want a chorus following me around."

"Alice went for a joggg," Ida sang, operatically, "now she's eating some pulses or maybe some veg-e-tables!"

"Ida had ten billion drinks," Alice sang, "now she is taking some drugs and having sex with strangers and going to hos-pi-tal."

"Brilliant Alice," Ida said. "Your student grant was money well spent. Let's get on with it."

"Ready? Let's pick a page," she closed her eyes and flicked through. "Here, page 30. Okay. We can't escape it –" Alice read.

"Pah! We can escape anything – we're so much stronger than you think," read Tom, putting on a comedy cockney accent.

"You sound like Dick Van Dyke," Alice laughed. "They're meant to be Irish."

She noticed Ida was looking pissed off. "Alright, don't get your knickers in a twist, I'm reading it. Anyway, you should be playing you, not Tom."

"Fine. We can escape anything – we're so much stronger than you think. We could build a boat –" said Ida.

"With what?"

"Branches, leaves – a hollowed tree –"

"You're mad."

"If I am, you are too. We are the same, Kate, the whole way through. Your blood is my blood – dangerous blood."

Tom started laughing. "Dangerous blood. Have they got hepatitis?"

"I thought this was meant to be good. It's so over the top," Alice said. "I feel bad for saying it. I mean, I like the film in a trashy way but the play has dated."

Ida stood up, flustered. "Of course it has. Mum wrote it ages ago for fuck's sake. I'm going to bed."

She walked downstairs clutching a copy of the play and lay on her low bed. She knew this rage, the anger born of some kind of loyalty; she felt it often for Elliot. But why now? Why tonight? She hated her mother and she hated the stupid play.

She turned to the first page. She had forgotten it started with a lullaby. Bridie had often sung it to her when she was a child; Seoithín, Seohó. Ida didn't know what the words meant, but she knew the gist. A child had to get to sleep or the bad fairies would come to take her away. A threatening lullaby; no wonder her mother had liked it.

Above her a spider had made a cobweb, and again she noticed the curling paper, the rose pattern underneath. Without meaning to she remembered the study as it had been when they first moved in. She sat up. Yes, it was rose papered, big, old-fashioned roses, and the carpet had been... She looked at the beige carpet by her feet and squeezed her eyes shut. She remembered people coming to change it, squishy underlay and the cat, Boots, playing with the off-cuts. She must have been seven or eight at most.

Above her she could hear her sister laughing, rolling around with her stupid boyfriend. She reached for some tablets and prayed silently to Our Lady, as she had done, secretly, for most of her life.

She was almost asleep, with the book open on her chest, when she realised what was wrong. It was so simple she could hardly believe it. She was the play, wasn't she? It wasn't just her stupid name. And if it was so terrible, so irrelevant, then what on earth was she?

Chapter twelve

PRODUCTION NOTES

The stage comes forward to meet the audience and the exact place where the stage ends and the auditorium begins is not clearly defined.

IDA and KATE sit downstage and the audience enter. IDA is kneeling and plaiting KATE'S hair and KATE is sitting cross-legged and smoking while idly playing with a pile of pebbles next to her.

It is not clear to the audience whether a fourth wall is present; the girls occasionally seem to acknowledge the audience with a glance or nod, but it is hard to be sure.

The verses or poems should be chanted/sung by the girls and/or the chorus (where indicated), according to the needs of the situation.

IDA: Dark, Irish, tall, aged about eighteen. Bold, funny, crude, with an explosive laugh, but moves gracefully and her singing voice is strong. Not pretty, but striking and knows it. Has made herself up to her full advantage.

KATE: Dark, Irish, smaller, aged about fifteen. Potentially more beautiful than her sister but shy and unsure of herself; occasionally mumbles for this reason.

******

KATE *and* IDA *are already sitting downstage. There is no change to the lighting and the only indication that the play has started is that* KATE *begins quietly singing a lullaby. The audience should be allowed to realise this in their own time and not hurried to settle/be quiet by means of* KATE *singing more loudly. As is traditional in Irish songs both girls hum in between the verses.*

KATE: (*Quietly, in a pretty but ordinary voice*)
    Seoithín, seohó, mostór é, moleanbh
    Mo sheoidgancealg, mochuidgantsaoilmhór
    Seothínseoho, nachmór é an taitneamh
    Mo stóirínnaleaba, nachodladhganbrón.
    A leanbhmochléibh go n-eirí do chodhladhleat
    Séan is sonasgachoíche do chóir
    Támise le do thaobh ag guídhe ort nambeannacht
    Seothín a leanbh is codail go foill.
    (IDA *begins singing with her sister in a much better and more confident voice*)
IDA/ KATE: Armhullachantításíodhageala
    Faolchaoin re an Earra ag imirt is spoirt
    Seoiadaniariad le glaocharmoleanbh
    Le mian é tharraingtisteach san liosmór.

Chapter thirteen

~ 1999 ~

Although Ida slept until late there was no note under the door. She was too annoyed to cope with a note today, something Alice must have sensed. At least the house was empty, and she could pad around, braless, smoking and looking for medicines. She was shaking and there was no booze left in the house – she needed something to keep her going.

She walked up the stairs to her mother's room. She wanted to find it messy, full of fag butts and bottles, but irritatingly Alice had tidied up. Things were just as they had been before they'd started drinking and Ida briefly wondered whether she'd dreamt the whole thing. Realising that she hadn't, she hoped that the shame of drinking and smoking wouldn't make Alice behave like even more of a cock. She would try not to mention it although it would be hard.

To her left was the chipped cream door of her old bedroom, the room Alice now said was hers, and Ida stood outside it. Above the handle there was a ripped-off sticker and Ida traced the tip of a lightning bolt. She touched it and remembered it had been a T-Rex sticker that Terri's unfortunate nephew had given her. Given? Or was that the story she'd told? She'd a funny feeling she'd nicked it from his bag.

She grasped the Bakelite handle and turned. It opened a crack and she said 'hello' stupidly, before remembering there was no one there. She pushed it open and peered inside. Her bunk beds were gone. Instead, there was a double bed, and rather than hundreds of posters and records there were framed prints, potted plants and two neat racks of CDs.

By the window was a desk with a computer on it, a newish looking computer and a pink plastic pot filled with pens. Next to the desk were a suitcase and a rucksack, and on the bed were neatly folded clothes. For the first time in a long time Ida wanted to smash everything up. She wanted more than anything to throw around the clothes, piss on the bedclothes, stamp on the computer and kick apart the drawers. Where the fuck were her bunk beds? She'd bought them with her own fucking cash.

"I'm glad you're dead!" she shouted at the top of her voice. She hoped the flash new neighbours could hear.

She took a deep breath and walked further into the room, pulling the pine chair away from the desk. Standing on it she peeled the loose paper away from the light fitting and found, as she'd known she would, yellowed Sellotape holding a piece of card over a large, shallow hole in the plaster. She pulled at the edge and there was the brittle plastic bag saying 'Safeway' in an ancient font, stretched out over the book it contained. It had been hammered into the ceiling – God knew where she'd got that idea – and she ripped it away from the nails, replaced the card and the ceiling paper, stepped down from the chair and wiped the plaster dust off her hair and clothes. Her hands were shaking. As she walked from the room she resisted the urge to slam the door and went back down to the study.

Sitting on the chair bed she took the book out. 'Magical Days Book' it read in Tippex across the ripped black front cover and tied around it, to hold in the letters and loose papers, was the wooden rosary Bridie had given her for her First Communion.

10th December 1983

So I'm going to write to her. I'm getting together the strength of mind and will and I prayed about it, which is embarrassing, but I thought I might as well. Not that the Bible says anything about being a lez. I checked. The other day Ma had Hello! and she was in it and I nearly puked right over it. Not because she was ugly (anything but!) but because I love her SO MUCH. Here it goes. (YOU CAN DO IT

IDA, YOU'RE ELECTRIC!)

Dear Annie
Thanks for the script. I feel like such a dork telling you this but I showed some of the girls I used to go to school with and they were pretty impressed. Also showed this boy I used to snog (make out you would say!) which is embarrassing because he is sort of ugly and used to drink his yogurt at Sunday school. I didn't tell him about the kissing, kissing you I mean. I wouldn't tell him that. I don't know why I'm telling you any of this.

IDA YOU ARE A FUCKING IDIOT STOP WRITING SUCH CRAP LOVE IDA.

Dear Annie
I love you. I love the idea of you and the actual you. I mean, I love seeing you on screen, your wonderful little face and then the actual you – the way you smell, and the way you dance and the way you kiss. I didn't know such a small mouth could make me feel so churned up. I feel broken, Annie, I'm in bits. Because of you!

IDA YOU ARE AN OVER ROMANTIC DICK HEAD IDIOT WHO SHOULD BE SHOT.

1st Jan 1984

So I wrote to her (a better letter than the ones I practiced, promise!) and she DID NOT REPLY. I didn't hear from her over Christmas or even New Year although the phone did ring and someone put it down when I answered, but that couldn't be her unless she got our number from Ma's agent or someone. I am HEARTBROKEN. How will anyone ever compare to her? I told Martin (the boy from St Luke's who I kind of had sex with) and he did not believe me, obviously, which is ridiculous as I am not a liar. However, he told everyone what I said and so I said HE was making it up so the joke was on him. HA!

I am now taking a vow of chastity and this book will not be about romance but will solely be about secret, amazing things that happen to ME. And not just any old thing. I'm talking about magical things. These could include:

Ghosts
Unexplained powers
Poetry/plays/literature
UFOS
Telepathy
Strange feelings
Furious anger
Artistic excellence
Beauty in all its forms
Fortune telling
Musings on death and the afterlife
My glorious, inevitable fame and success

This new theme has been inspired by (this is the last time I will mention her, promise!) my kiss with Anna (or Annie to me) DeCosta which has made me feel different, powerful and above all MAGICAL. We kind of swapped I think, like in Freaky Friday, and I got her powers and bits of her personality. And maybe even some of Ida in the film which is scary because she is a murderer. IF YOU ARE READING THIS FIRSTLY: FUCK OFF, SECONDLY: THERE ARE SOME THINGS YOU CAN'T EXPLAIN (EVEN YOU, SMART ARSE, IF THE SNOOP IS ALICE) SO

THERE IS NO NEED TO LOCK ME UP. WHAT I AM
SAYING IS TRUE. I AM A CHANGED WOMAN. IT
IS A MIRACLE OR A CURSE. I am not sure which. It's
a mystery. That's all I can say for sure. Only time will tell...

(To be continued. Ha!)

Ida put the book on the bed next to her and laughed out loud, realising that for some unknown reason she'd been reading it with one eye shut, as if watching a horror film.

Then, after the laughter, she felt another emotion, a strange mix of sickness, confusion and annoyance. She only remembered rage from her youth, but here she was, sweet and stupid like any other teenage girl. She felt a surge of depression in her stomach as she realised that for a long time she'd been clinging onto the hope that somewhere inside was the strange, creative girl she once was. But maybe that girl never existed. The thought was almost too much to bear.

For a second or two she contemplated burning the book, or throwing it into the sea. But even those were the actions of a stupid fourteen year old. And she was very nearly bloody thirty. She wanted Elliot. If he'd come they could get drunk, have sex, and take those pills he'd got in Tijuana. And being around him, well, it gave her something to think about that wasn't her stupid self. But contacting him was always hard, and ever since the Christmas party (which she tried not to think about) even his gallery put the phone down whenever she called. She closed her eyes as hard as she could – an old trick from when she was bored in Mass – until she saw colours and shapes and felt dizzy.

"Please, Jesus, Mary, Joseph, Allah, the Universe, let him come to see me," she said out loud, realising to her horror that they were almost the exact words of the stupid teenage girl from her stupid, secret book.

Ida was in the bath when she heard Alice and Tom come back. She'd been in there for hours, spaced out on some double-strength codeine she'd found under her mother's bed. Every half an hour or so she'd top up the bath – the water was still tepid as it had always been when she was younger and her knees and ears were chilly, but the codeine took the edge off and she was enjoying listening to the radio and singing along in her loud, flat voice. The bathtub still felt the same and the cracked surface scratched her skin. She remembered the feeling from being a child, sharing with Alice, or, later, escaping from her ma. Maybe she should write about it, the scratchy, dirty bath. A poem. She could write one, if she wanted to.

Ida came to, shivering in the freezing bath. Her limbs were stiff and she slowly stood up, stepped out of the bath and wrapped herself in someone else's damp towel. She was about to leave the room when she heard, faintly from downstairs, the sporadic, electric crackle of a police radio. She put her ear to the door. There was an engine running outside the front of the house.

"I have no idea who he is or why he's here," said Alice. "But I wish he'd fuck right off."

She took a deep breath and tried to walk as tall as possible as she began down the stairs. Her vague plan was to behave as if she wasn't only wearing a towel and as though Alice was ridiculous, hysterical and borderline insane.

Her sister was sitting at the bottom of the stairs, hugging herself, while Tom sat next to her, rubbing her bare foot. The front door was open and just inside the hallway stood a policeman – spotty, greasy haired and very young, grasping his radio like a comfort blanket.

"Where is he?" asked Ida.

"Who?" asked Alice, turning round. She looked tired and pissed off.

Ida looked at the policeman. "I'm sorry you've been bothered. If my sister had got me out of the bath this whole thing would have been cleared up. You have a man here? Is he outside?"

"We tried, you just grunted for fuck's sake! And he wouldn't say who he was. Well, he couldn't say who he was." She let out a short, annoyed laugh and Ida nudged her, hard in the side with her foot as she walked past. Alice let out an angry yelp.

"There is a gentleman in the front garden, yes," said the policeman.

Ida stood facing him and tucked the towel securely around her chest.

"Right and you left him there? Lovely."

"There is another officer outside with him, we're expecting an ambulance. He's been abusive to these people –"

She walked out into the front garden, sighed and bit her bottom lip. It was evening now, and cold, but she refused to shiver, despite her wet hair and bare feet. Below her, on the garden path, lay the bony, pale figure of her stupid, lovely boyfriend, staring up at the sky, a bottle of red wine still clutched in his right hand.

"For God's sake," she said, forcing a smile as she jogged down the steps, shouting back up at the house. "You fucking people. Is it so strange I might have been expecting someone? I do have friends. And you both go and call the bloody police."

"Sweet pea," Elliot shouted up at her, showing off. "They're trying to arrest me or some shit. Look, there's our star." With his empty hand he pointed at the North Star, their star – the commonest star of all. Ida laughed, leant down towards him and kissed his clammy forehead.

"Oh you stupid wanker – let's get you up, are you going to help me, or what?" she said to the policeman.

They took an arm each and, with the effort, Ida's right breast popped out of her towel. Opposite a man who had been pretending to wash his car shook his head with disgust.

"What the fuck are you looking at you old perv?" she shouted over the road, and Elliot kissed her on the nose.

"Wind your neck in, Irons," said Elliot, leaning on Ida as she turned him towards the house.

"Should we wait for the ambulance, miss? I would advise we wait for the ambulance," said the policeman to their backs.

Tom jogged down the stairs. "Let me help you, you can't do this alone. I'm sorry, we didn't know who he was and Alice insisted we call the police. I feel like a right twat now."

"I'm sorry if we got off on the wrong foot," said Elliot.

"That's okay, it's fine. But you have to leave the wine out here I'm afraid. There's no booze allowed in the house."

"Apart from when Princess Di over there says it's okay," said Ida and Tom raised his eyebrows in what looked like it might be agreement.

Alice was still standing by the front door, her arms crossed, like a tiny bouncer.

"He's not coming in. No way. He can sleep in the garden."

"Alice," said Tom, managing to sound both placatory and exasperated.

"Firstly it's not your fucking house, secondly he's my boyfriend and it's my birthday tomorrow – yes, you forgot that, didn't you? – and thirdly, fuck off," said Ida.

Alice scowled but stood to the side as Ida and Tom dragged Elliot up the path while he apologised and thanked them and offered them his wine.

"We'll talk about this later," Alice whispered loudly to Tom, and Ida smiled as they stepped inside.

Chapter fourteen

~ 1995 ~

Ida sipped her wine and looked around. The room was immaculate, vast, and filled with skinny blonde women, standing about or perching on chairs while they talked to balding men. In the middle of the room was a glass coffee table, where – perfectly centred – lay a copy of *Captain Correlli's Mandolin,* like some sacred object. Ida laughed under her breath.

Claire was a corporate lawyer and distant family friend and Ida had only come for the free booze. She lit a fag.

"I'm so sorry, but could you do that on the balcony," Claire said. Ida didn't put it out and didn't reply but smiled and walked out of the room and along the corridor. The balcony was through Claire's bedroom and as Ida entered she noticed a man was already standing out there, hunched over the railings. He was wearing a tight, grey suit and silver shoes, his short light brown hair slicked to the side and he turned as he heard her. He was terribly thin.

"Nice look," she said as she stepped through the double doors.

"Do you think I'm pretentious?" he asked. "See I wasn't sure."

Ida laughed but was surprised by his grumpiness. She wasn't used to being called up on what she said.

"Well, yeah," she said. "Of course."

"And you're not pretentious. I see. Well, nice look," he said, wafting his hand towards her. She felt annoyed.

"They're from a charity shop," she said. She was wearing her red boots and a stained tea dress. They were both from Oxfam but she kind of knew what he meant.

He took another look at her. "Jesus, I thought grunge was dead."

"Fuck off," she said, half appalled, half delighted.

"My suit cost me £20 from Camden Lock," he said. "If it's about money then those tarts in there are the most pretentious of the lot." He smiled and leant back to get a better look at her as he sucked hard on his roll-up. His movements were jerky and he was wiry and small – inches shorter than her. His voice was cockney, but knowing Claire's friends, Ida wasn't fooled. She was certain he was a public school boy who was putting on an act.

Ida didn't reply and sucked on her own fag as he began to roll another. The view across Primrose Hill was amazing, the sky, lit by a million bulbs below, an eerie electric blue. She tried to think of something to say.

Claire came out of the French doors with a plate of asparagus and parma ham. "I didn't want you two to miss out," she said.

The man took a piece of ham and ate it in one go, staring at sky as he did.

"Have you been introduced?" asked Claire with a hint of panic in her voice. Ida knew what was coming next. Claire had an irritating habit of introducing people with interesting facts – she liked showing off her collection of friends.

"Elliot, this is Ida – THE Ida Irons – inspiration for her mother's play, and the film," she said. Then, looking concerned, "You do know it?"

"I wasn't exactly –" Ida started to protest. The play had been written before she was born, how the fuck could she have inspired it?

Claire was oblivious. "And Ida, this is Elliot Hill, he's an artist, he's exhibited in loads of fancy galleries and his father is this massive art collector, isn't he Elliot?" Claire said, turning to go back inside.

"Massive," Elliot mouthed, indicating someone fat with his arms.

"Claire, I think you've got it wrong about Ida," he said, and Claire turned back towards him. "The play was written before she was born. She wasn't its inspiration."

"No need for introductions," Claire said happily and went inside.

"You're right," Ida said and shook the hand he'd stuck out

towards her. "How the fuck do you know that?"

"I'm a fan," he said. "So, what's it like having a murderer's name?"

They drunk almost all the wine and, as it had started to rain, smoked in Claire's pristine bathroom, giggling as the blondes coughed politely outside, shouting, "in a minute," and roaring with laughter when someone politely said, "sorry but I'm pretty desperate for a wee." By eleven Claire took Elliot to one side and spoke to him. Ida was busy with the stereo, sorting through the CDs and shrieking about how awful they were. "Wet Wet Wet. Fucking hell."

By eleven thirty they were outside.

"You'll get her home safely, won't you?" Claire asked from behind the front door, flicking her eyes back and forth between Elliot and Ida, who was busy throwing gravel at passing cars.

"I don't think she needs my help," he said.

As Ida sat in the cab she realised she was horrifically drunk but had moments of lucidity as they talked about the shapes of the buildings outside, about the light and the posters and the people. For a few seconds she would remember that this was a man she barely knew, write him off as unsuitable, before being drawn into a conversation about a crane or a bag lady's coat and forgetting herself all over again. She lost track of where they were and he laughed as she tried to place herself and got it wrong. They weren't in Camden, or Islington, or the West End either apparently.

The cab fare was sixteen pounds. Ida had three in her purse.

"I'm not doing this to show off," he said. "You owe me, you spoilt cow, come on." He clicked his fingers and put his arm out for her to take as they walked past empty factories and shops. It was an old theatre or something they were going to and everyone in the queue was dressed up, the girls in sixties dresses with bouffant hair, the men in suits and ties, women holding handbags on their heads as they smoked in the rain. As they walked, people said Elliot's name, a bit like he was famous.

"Do you owe them money or something?" Ida asked.

"I see you're back from the dead," he said.

It was hot and packed inside and a band was playing on the stage, all wearing suits and trainers, their hair hanging over their eyes. Then there was a DJ playing music Ida didn't know – 'northern soul' Elliot said – and Ida danced and danced as he talked to his friends. She didn't mind, she could see him watching her, occasionally catching her eye.

She was sweaty and out of breath by the time he led her through the crowd. A skinny red-haired girl was sitting on a stool next to the stage and she turned a key to let them through the door behind her.

"Hi Elliot, great night tonight," she said, and smiled at Ida while looking her up and down.

The room through the door was long and dark with a skittle alley at the end. People were sitting on white leather sofas and purple beanbags.

"This is Ida," he said to everyone as they passed. She was pretty sure she recognised some of them, maybe from the TV though she couldn't be sure. There was a bar in the corner with no one serving and Elliot went behind and made them drinks. She sat on a high red stool and watched him.

"Rum and ginger ale, Ida Irons? With some angostura bitters. Now that's a drink," he said, leaning down to the fridge. "I suppose you think I'm a total dick," he said, "showing off like a wanker. I'm sure you know loads of famous people. You're not going to be impressed by some sixties club night in the East End," he said.

She didn't protest, but she was – very.

"I'd like to say I brought you back here because of the free booze, not because I was trying to get in your pants," he said, stirring her drink with his finger and taking out his tobacco tin. "But the truth is –"

Ida cut him off. "Let's go and play skittles," she said, hopping off the bar stool.

He nodded, opening the till with a key and slipping a handful of notes into his pocket, holding his finger to his lips and winking.

Ida laughed.

Elliot was amazed to discover that Ida had never played skittles, or been bowling, in her life.

"What have you been doing with yourself?" he asked.

"Sitting in the pub," she said. "I hate sport."

"Skittles isn't a sport, Ida," Elliot said. "Skittles is for children and drunks. You should be good at it."

Ida tried to hide her smile. She was delighted by his familiarity. She didn't mind about the insult, she rarely minded insults, and coming from him it sounded like a compliment anyway.

Walking up to the line she chucked the ball at the pins as if she was throwing something on the ground in anger. Two fell.

"I have never seen anything like that in my life. You're meant to do a run up," Elliot said.

He set them back up and ran towards the line, ducking down and swinging his arm right back before bringing it forward and letting go. Nine fell.

Ida thought he looked like a twat.

She set them up again and walked forwards. Staring at the centre pin she tried to imagine that someone's life depended on getting a strike. She tried to think of someone she cared about, to imagine their life hanging in the balance but she couldn't think of anyone at all. Raising the ball to her chest, she threw it down the alley like a netball.

"Strike!" someone shouted from the sofas behind them.

Ida failed to hide the delight on her face as she turned towards him.

By three thirty she was tired. "Let's go home," she said. She had kind of meant to go to her home, and for him to go to his, but when he asked the taxi driver for an address she didn't know, his address, she didn't argue. Normally she hated people making decisions for her but tonight, for some reason, she was quite enjoying it.

They drove through streets she didn't recognise, past shops selling watermelon, still open despite the time, past two girls pulling each other's hair, past a dead dog and a mosque.

He told her about Hackney, about its geography and bus routes and size. It was the next place to be, he was sure of it. A couple of years at most and the artists would be packing it out.

For once she did nothing but listen.

They fell in the front door and crashed through his house, tripping up the stairs and over rugs, shhssing each other and laughing. His room was on the top floor and apart from a double bed and an art deco wardrobe he had no furniture. On the walls were giant sheets of white paper, blu-tacked up, and covered in detailed sketches and lists, and in the far corner was a tower of books and CDs.

Ida threw herself straight onto the bed and with a crash realised that it had cracked, that her arse was now nearer the floor than her feet. She struggled to get up.

"Fucking hell, you big ball of chaos," he said, walking over, kneeling next to her and lighting a candle. "I've never met anyone like you."

She looked at him the low light. He was so angular and perfect. He was beautiful.

"Elliot," she whispered. "You're not really a fan, are you?"

"Of course not. My ex was though," he said, as he started kissing her legs.

"Should I be embarrassed about the bed?"

"Oh God no. Be proud. I'll remember you, won't I? And who needs beds anyway," he said as he gripped her legs and pulled her, screaming, onto the floor.

Chapter fifteen

~ 1999 ~

They were so squished up on the low single chair bed that by the morning almost every part of their bodies was touching and Ida was, for the first time, pleased that her sister had stolen her room. She couldn't remember them being this close and she felt grateful. Her eyes were still shut and she kissed the greasy back of Elliot's dirty blonde hair, smelling fags, and the tube, and days old cheap shampoo. She laughed out loud to herself.

"What's so funny?" he asked, still more asleep than awake.

"Oh God, everything. Alice is going to be so fucked off you're here but she can't say anything because it's my birthday and –"

Elliot turned over and kissed her hard on the mouth without opening his eyes. She was still wearing a towel and within seconds they were fucking, their bodies barely moving apart, her arms pulling him painfully close.

Just outside Ida could hear her sister on the telephone, talking politely to someone, and Ida groaned, far louder than she ever did back at home. Elliot opened one eye and smiled at her. He knew her very well and began thrusting hard and fast. She panted into his ear. She hoped Tom was outside the door.

"Can I come inside you?" he whispered.

"Please, yes," she whispered back. Although she knew it was wrong she enjoyed the danger, and loved the feeling of keeping him inside her for as long as possible.

He came, opened his eyes and kissed her on the nose. "Happy birthday you big mad cow."

"Thanks, piss head." She pushed him over and sat on top of him, her legs round his hips. "It's my fucking birthday," she shouted as loudly as she possibly could.

"There's some vodka in my bag, your birthday present dearest. Crack it open will you? Brought you some more Valium too. "

They showered together and Ida made sure the others knew it, dropping things and giggling loudly. When they finally made it to the kitchen Alice and Tom were at the table with *The Guardian* and a pile of pancakes.

"They're cold now but we can make more," said Alice.

"Oh thanks so much," said Ida.

"Happy birthday," Alice said, standing, and the two women briefly hugged.

"Good morning," said Elliot, holding out his hand. Alice took it, smiling. "I'm so, so sorry about last night," he said. "I've been taking these new antibiotics and they've totally messed me up. And then it was a friend's party. God knows what happened. I'm mortified. Can I take you all for lunch? Your father and stepmother too? And I'm so sorry about your mother. Really, I know how hard it is."

Alice sat down and nodded at Ida, clearly taken aback. "Yes, that would be lovely," she said.

Tom handed Ida a bunch of freesias. "It's only little, I didn't know it was your birthday until yesterday. I just thought these, well I thought you might like them."

"They're your favourite aren't they Ida? They were Mum's favourite too," Alice said, and Ida nodded. "Sorry, your present from me is going to be late."

Elliot patted Tom on the back. "Well done, I would have had a job to remember that. You need to give me some boyfriend tips mate." Ida winced, Tom was blushing and it was clear everyone felt awkward but no one quite knew why.

"A lucky coincidence I suppose, they were all they had at the corner shop. And, well, lunch would be great, but don't worry I'll pay for me and Ally," said Tom, "it's not cheap round here."

"No, I'm sure it's not," said Elliot, "thank God. It's Ida's birthday after all. I insist."

Tom started to argue, but Alice said, "Let him pay," and Tom looked down at his hands.

They arranged to meet Bryan and Terri on Poole Quay and as they drove Ida tried not to worry. The thing was, as far as she knew Elliot no longer had a bank card or cheque book, and she wasn't at all sure how he was going to make this grand offer a reality. She also worried about what he had been taking to be so 'up' – usually he wasn't even conscious until gone twelve. She tried not to let herself hope that he'd sorted himself out for her sake, made it up with his dad or the gallery, got some cash, and given up the drugs. She tried hard not to hope because she had hoped it before and it hadn't worked out. There was also always the worry she was ashamed of – that if he got too clean and sorted he'd most probably leave her for somebody else.

Elliot was polite and charming as always, asking Tom question after question about his work. They had friends in common (Elliot knew everyone) and the two men walked in front, while Alice and Ida lagged behind. It was a blowy day and they stayed near the shops rather than walking beside the sea. There was a strong smell of salt and something like drains – Ida had forgotten the smell – and ahead of them fishermen were selling their catch to passers-by.

"He's good looking," said Alice. "Very thin though."

"You can talk. He always says I eat too much. Not in a bad way or anything, he just thinks people should eat less in general. And I do eat loads."

"He seems okay, very friendly," said Alice, "and he's getting on with Tom. Turning up pissed wasn't ideal but he is your boyfriend, after all."

"Exactly," said Ida, "what else would you expect?"

Ahead of them Elliot ran over to a boat and started looking at the fish, asking to pick them up and chatting to the other customers. He looked wonderful in his oversized coat and tartan scarf, his hair sticking up at odd angles, so different, Ida thought, to the jeans-and-jumper-wearing families they were surrounded by. He laughed loudly – she loved his laugh – and she smiled to see an old woman jump at the sudden sound of it.

Above them a flock of seagulls was circling the boats and Ida winced despite herself, keeping close to the gift shops, reminding herself that if it all got too much she could always run inside. "I didn't know they were still here," she said, gesturing towards the fishermen. "It all seems so ancient somehow."

"Yes, they're still here. I can't look in their boats though. The poor fish, struggling to breathe. I wish they'd knock them on the head with something, not leave them to die like that."

"You always were a wuss," said Ida.

"And you're not?" Alice asked, looking towards the gulls and laughing.

The waiter greeted them with a wide-eyed expression that Ida knew well. It was the same expression waiters always adopted after her father had complained about their table, or the temperature of the wine, or a crying child. Alice must have noticed the look too because, quite unexpectedly, she squeezed Ida's hand as they were led through the quiet restaurant. It looked the same as it had at least fifteen years before – orange floral carpets and rose shaped up-lighters. She should have known it wouldn't have changed; her father stopped going anywhere as soon as they redid the décor. Bryan stood up as he saw them approach. Terri sat still, her mouth twitching slightly while she fiddled with her napkin.

"Darlings. So good to see you. Happy birthday beautiful girl," he said, reaching for Ida. She hugged him, and he gripped her wrist.

"We had to get the table changed, they put us near the loos, but it's all sorted out now."

"It was that china-man," Terri whispered. "I don't think he realised who your father was."

"Oh God," said Alice, Elliot guffawed, and Tom laughed nervously. Terri beamed up at them.

"Good afternoon, you must be Mrs Irons. I'm Elliot," he leant down and kissed her on both cheeks.

"Well, haven't you got yourself a gentleman here?" said Terri, fanning herself with her menu. Ida felt warm with pride.

They sat down at the round table, boy then girl then boy at Terri's insistence, leaving Ida between Tom and her father. They shook out their peach napkins (folded into enormous swans) and Ida felt ashamed of her father's choice of restaurant. Elliot was sitting almost directly opposite her, flirting wildly and successfully with Terri, but she couldn't meet his eye. His family were so sophisticated, they'd hate it here, and it was lucky he would be far too charming to let Ida's family realise he thought it was anything other than wonderful.

Bryan was talking loudly about someone he used to work with who'd retired and his 'poof of a son' and Ida tried to ignore him, staring instead at the hard line of Elliot's jaw, his mean mouth, his lean, strong arms. It was only when she felt Terri's eyes on her, and noticed her amused expression, that she looked away. She knew that look, the pitying smile that said, *my goodness you love him too much dear*. Not for the first time her supposedly stupid stepmother had got it in one.

Bryan ordered Champagne and, when it came, slipped Ida an envelope with a wink. It would be a cheque, Ida knew, and although she was pleased, it had got to the point that no amount she was given could make a dent in the horrible amount she owed. Terri cleared her throat and lifted a gift bag from under her seat.

"I couldn't stand to see you walking around in all those old-men's things. You look like a blooming tramp!"

Ida tried to keep a straight face as she opened it, careful not to catch Elliot's eye in case she laughed. It was a bright yellow dress, a size too small, made out of some strange, shiny fabric.

"Do you like it? I hope you do. Monica helped me choose it. She's very fashionable."

Monica was Terri's eldest niece, the one, (Ida had it on good authority), who had been part of a live sex show at an Ibiza nightclub. It explained a lot.

Ida laughed. "It's lovely. I better try it on," she said.

After the third bottle of Champagne Ida forgot to be worried about how Elliot would pay the bill and decided to enjoy herself. If people were concerned her drinking was out of hand they didn't say anything – Ida had forgotten this was one of the pluses of birthdays. After a round of tipsy toasts to Bridie they sung *Happy Birthday* three times at Ida's insistence, and the last couple of times the waiters and other guests joined in while Ida stood up and bowed. She forgot to be self-conscious about the very tight dress, instead enjoying the way it clung to her tits, and the way Elliot looked up at her. In fact, Elliot sung the loudest of all, clapping and whooping and shouting 'and many more' at the end. He loved her. Ida was sure he really did.

The food was terrible, as she had known it would be, tiny slices of meat in lukewarm gravy and spongy roast potatoes, but no one was eating much. Even Alice was drinking, and there was a recklessness in all of them, relief that finally, after months of misery, they were allowed to do something that was at least supposed to be fun.

Sudden rain smashed at the windows and they decided to stay where they were. In fact, it was nearly six when Elliot stood up, took the waiter to one side, and handed him a fistful of notes. Only Ida seemed to see.

The rain had died down, although it was still drizzling as they stood in the doorway of the restaurant while Bryan and Terri waited for their cab. Tom offered to drive them home, but Bryan wouldn't hear of it and Ida he knew would hate travelling in Alice's tiny Mini.

She felt very tired and sat down on the doorstep while Tom and Alice went to pick up the car.

Terri made a final trip to the loo and Elliot stood in the rain in front of them, smoking and looking at the choppy sea, while Bryan sat down next to Ida and felt for something in his coat pocket.

"Here, darling, I wasn't sure whether to give it to you, but, I think I should. It's not exactly nice, but it's at least honest – she did love you in her own funny way." He was whispering loudly, his breath hot and boozy.

Ida took the crinkled envelope. On the front it said her name, in writing she knew to be her mother's, although it was far neater, more childish somehow, than Ida remembered.

"You might not want to open it now," said Bryan, but Ida had already taken it out and begun to read.

You are born – May 9th 1969

Well hello Ida!

Welcome.

I'm a little surprised, to tell you the truth. I haven't got over the shock of getting in the family way, let alone having a real life 'you'.

I was never any good at science, but somehow in my womb things I couldn't possibly name have been extracted, divided, multiplied... cell by sparking cell.

Now they've dragged you out, all lagadi, stinking of iron like some rock they've mined. I can hardly speak, and you're lying so still, staring up at me with these coal-chip eyes, knowing all these magic things you'll soon forget.

I'm jealous already. Will we be friends? God help you, dearest girl. I waited so long to have you, I wasn't sure I should. Family scares me, really. I've been so long without one.

Your father's gone for Guinness. I need to go to sleep.

(You don't look like me or her either really. Who are you, I wonder?)

Bridie xx

"I'd forgotten her funny made-up words," said Ida. "Lagadi for dirty. She used to say 'pi' for head, too didn't she?"

"Your mother was a bloody strange woman – bloody strange. I should have had my suspicions even back then that she wasn't a full pound. Anyway, enough of this, it's your birthday after all. Elliot, son, I couldn't borrow a fag?"

Chapter sixteen

~ 1999 ~

Something had shocked Ida in her dream, a dog bite or a fall, but within the split second it took her to open her eyes the memory of it had slipped away. She shut one eye again and tried to work backwards. The curtains were open and outside the light of the street lamp couldn't quite obliterate the moon.

She wondered if it was still her birthday.

Next to her Elliot was snoring loudly and she elbowed him in the ribs. Around her the bed was, thankfully, dry.

"Fuck off," he muttered angrily, shifting in the bed and kicking her accidentally. He was still wearing his shoes – in fact he was still wearing his coat. She looked down. For some reason there was clingy yellow fabric round her waist, and she was still wearing tights and her heavy red boots. Digging into her cheek was the underwire from her bra – it was always coming out. She had period pains as well – bad ones – and moaned to herself.

Piece by piece the day came back to her. Lunch, then a car ride, then a detour to the pub, just her and Elliot. Then home and... attempted sex? Her mouth felt sticky and dry. She got to her feet, awkwardly pulling the dress up over her breasts and kicking off her boots while Elliot groaned at the sound.

"Shut up you baby," she whispered loudly. "I'm getting us some water."

She stepped into the hall. The house was still as she tip-toed towards the kitchen, past the loudly ticking sunburst clock they'd had forever. Although she knew it must be after midnight, it could still be her birthday if she chose not to look.

She filled two pint glasses and carried them back to the room. Opening the door with her hip she found Elliot sitting on the bed, his hair sticking up and his arm extended towards her.

"Fuck, I'm thirsty," he said, yawning. "What time is it?"

"The end of time. It's my birthday forever."

"You'll get bored."

"Never – I'd like it. I had a good day. Maybe this is what getting old is about. Being with your family, all at once... puke."

"Bah, you just liked the food and booze," he said, downing the pint and putting the glass on the carpet. He pulled Ida towards him and slid his hand inside her bra.

"I like you," she said, kissing him on the ear.

"Of course, I'm a handsome chap."

"I love you."

"Love from Ida Irons means next to nothing. As does hate. 'Oh Elliot, I LOVE brie. Oh Elliot, I love dogs.' Next day you'll hate cheese and hate dogs. Day after, won't care either way."

"Well, I love you right now."

"And I love your tits, forever." He kissed her neck.

Automatically she jerked her head away angrily.

Elliot pulled his hand out of her bra. "Bloody hell, you've never done that before. Must be your age. Growing into a real, grumpy old woman," he said.

"I'm tired. And confused. And upset I suppose. You don't 'love' my tits. You can't really love tits. I'm just being stupid when I say I love things normally. But I do love you."

"We've been through this."

"I know. It's fine. Well, it's not fine, but I'm tired." She lay back down and turned away from him.

"Oh God, you nutter. I came all the way to see you, got all clean and nice, and you've gone all frigid. That doesn't seem fair. You were never a fridg'. Well, okay."

He patted her on the thigh, lay down and within seconds Ida could tell from his breathing that he was asleep.

The backs of her eyes hurt and she knew she could cry. She refused to cry. There was no way she could sleep. She reached towards the side table and switched on the light. Elliot didn't stir and she realised she was disappointed, that childishly she wanted him to wake up and apologise or at least see that she was upset. And she knew that if she slept the morning would come, and with it the definite end to her birthday.

On the floor was her bag and she reached inside for her cigarettes and a pill to help with her cramps. Fumbling she found a crumpled note and remembered her father handing it to her. She wanted Elliot out of her bed with a sudden fury and she elbowed him again, hard.

"What the fuck?" he said, turning round to face her.

"If you don't love me sleep on the floor."

"We're practically on the floor. You want me to get off the chair bed onto the floor? So I'll be three inches lower?"

"Yes."

"Fine, you mad bitch." He rolled onto the rug, grabbing two pillows, and went back to sleep, or pretended to sleep, his coat pulled up round his face to shield his eyes from the light.

But still it wasn't enough. Ida felt magical, bad magical, dangerous magical. She wasn't sure what she wanted, to break something or make something new, but she needed to do... something. Her whole life she had seen patterns, waited for signs, for God, the saints, even Satan, to intervene. And she knew this letter, it meant something, but she wasn't quite sure what.

She took the Magical Days Book from behind the bed, found a splintered biro and opened the note. She should copy the most startling phrases – the ones that needed further investigation.

'Stinking of iron.'

Only Bridie would say babies smelled of blood. They must, of course, but Ida had never heard anyone say that before. No clean 'new baby smell' for her ma, just the dirty, stinking facts.

'I waited so long to have you, I wasn't sure I should. Family scares me, really. I've been so long without one.'

She shouldn't have had children. She should have trusted her gut. Not because her own parents had died young or because she'd been an only child, but because she wasn't made for it. She was selfish and bloody insane.

'I'm jealous already. Will we be friends? God help you, dearest girl.'

Ida circled that phrase. Talk about a warning.

'You don't look like her – or me really. Who are you, I wonder?'

'Her.' Ida knew that would be about her namesake, Ida Lupino. Or perhaps she was talking about the 'Ida' in the play. What was it she was meant to look like? Dark haired, beautiful?

She turned to tell Elliot but remembered that she'd shouted at him and it would take a good deal of making up before he'd listen to anything she'd have to say. And who else was there to tell? Alice? Alice hated her, and it would make her father maudlin to talk about it. She stabbed herself in the arm with the biro and bit her lip to fight off the tears. It didn't even bleed and it hurt so much. When she was younger she could cut herself, stub cigarettes out on her legs, and feel nothing at all. Elliot was right, she was turning into a real, normal person in her old age.

She propped herself up and drew circles on the next page of the book. She would spend the rest of the night writing everything she could remember about her strange, horrible mother.

There were footsteps, somewhere in the hall. She held her breath and listened. Alice? No, it was Tom.

She scrambled to her feet, straightened her dress, and found him standing halfway out the front door. He looked at her nervously and smiled. He was smoking.

"Rumbled," he said.

She laughed and reached for a drag.

"I can't sleep. It happens to me sometimes," he said.

"Me neither. Hey, you wouldn't mind looking at something with me would you?"

They sat next to each other on the sofa looking at the letter, a blanket over their knees.

"Perhaps she was spaced out on painkillers," Tom said. "Bet they gave women loads of weird shit when they gave birth back then."

She looked at him, properly. He was wearing a red hand-knitted jumper, the sleeves over his hands, and his Toni and Guy haircut was sticking up around his head. He had lovely eyes – brown with flecks of orange and green. She couldn't tell him that. "I like your jumper," she said. "Did my sister knit it? She seems like she might be a knitter."

"No, my mum," he said. "She's always knitted. Any excuse. If she hears anyone's pregnant down the road she'll knit about five thousand booties before the baby's even born."

"You get on with her?"

"Yeah. She's great. There are four of us, and there was never much money, and my stepdad was a prick, but she's alright. I was the first one of the family to go to uni and she was well proud of me."

"I bet," said Ida, resisting the urge to stroke his head.

Ida woke up with Alice standing over her, holding out a mug of tea. Light poured in through the window and her eyes hurt. As she struggled to sit up her Magical Days Book fell off her chest, and she saw the open pages were covered in a manic biro sprawl.

"Here, I thought you might need this," Alice said.

"Thanks. Where's Elliot. He hasn't left?"

"He went for a walk with Tom, said they wouldn't be back until late. Did you have a fight or something?"

"No, no. Nothing like that. He just likes going out if he has a hangover."

"I hope they'll be okay. The wind's picking up. Right. I've made some lentil soup for lunch. And I've got an appointment with the bank to close Mum's accounts. Don't get excited, think she had about five pence."

"Do you need me to do anything?"

"You could wash? And buy some clothes for the funeral. Terri has given us fifty quid each for a new outfit – she slipped it to me yesterday when Dad wasn't looking. I've got something to wear but she wanted to be fair. Please don't spend it on something mad. Go straight to Beales."

Ida didn't speak but sat blowing on her tea. She remembered the desperation she'd felt in the night, for it to stay her stupid birthday. She really wished it was still her birthday.

"You look so miserable," said Alice. "Post birthday come down eh?"

"I wish."

"I was going to keep it as a surprise but it might get you out of bed – Peter's coming tomorrow."

"Really?" Ida felt such an enormous burst of joy she irrationally suspected it was some kind of trick.

"Yep, he was going to come for Tuesday but managed to change his plans – had some radio ad he was meant to be doing. He said he wants to help us. There's always stuff to do the day before."

"It will be brilliant to see him, it's been years." The last time he'd rescued her from hospital but Alice didn't know about that.

"Well, get to Beales, get some clothes. You could even buy some make-up. You'll need to make a bit of an effort or he'll do you up like a drag queen."

Ida ignored her sister's annoying remark and looked out of the window. Pine needles were blowing everywhere, like weird spiky rain and in the distance the sea looked furious.

"He always comes with the wind, like Mary Poppins," Ida said.

Alice didn't ask what she meant.

"Beales, not the pub. Alright?"

Chapter seventeen

~ 1987 ~

There was a loud creak, then a second or so of silence before the huge, juddering thud of something falling into the square outside.

The wind was whipping its way round the house, rattling the broken sash windows while the other women screamed with delight. It seemed as though they'd been awake for a while, giggling and gasping, while Ida had stayed fast asleep.

She lay as still as she could, her eyes closed while she concentrated on her breathing. The wind quietened slightly and the women walked back across the room chatting or laughing, some pacing and swearing, one of them uselessly clicking the light switch over and over again.

This was it then – the culmination of all Ida's dreams and fears – the thing she supposed she'd always been waiting for.

"Fuck me, fuck me," Nikki repeated from the near corner in her smoker's voice.

"We're all going to die," Adelaide said contentedly to herself in the next bed.

Ida opened her eyes and looked at her. She looked back and winked, her wrinkled hands in her lap, her white cotton nightie done up to her chin, her little walnut face totally serene.

"We're the ones who understand," she whispered, leaning towards Ida, "that this is our time to go. This is Jesus' doing and there's no point working yourself up into a frenzy about it."

It was almost totally dark, the streetlights had gone out as well, but Ida could see the shapes of the eight other women who shared the dorm. Three of them had huddled together, their arms round each other's backs as though about to play some American sport. A few of the less popular ones lay alone on their beds, and Nikki was attempting to listen to her Walkman.

"Is it everywhere or just here?" Ida said loudly to Judy, the massive know-it-all woman who slept in the opposite bed.

"Everywhere I think," said Judy. "Though the phone in the hall's not working so I can't check. Can't find the warden anywhere – reckon she's crapped herself."

Ida reached under her pillow for her fags and lit one. Then she pulled off her blankets, stood up, and walked across to the window wearing her grey knickers, t-shirt and socks.

Outside was pitch black, the usually bright windows of the houses around Soho Square dark and lifeless. Branches and leaves were blowing everywhere, leaping and swooping violently, occasionally hitting the glass and making Ida jump, while on the grass opposite the house lay the old tree that Ida had tried to climb last week when she was pissed. She thought of all the trees in the garden in Bournemouth and wondered if the rickety house had been squashed or blown away.

"It's a twister," she said to herself, wondering if at any moment she'd see her mother flying past on a broomstick. "Please look after Alice," she whispered, closing her eyes.

"Oi, come here."

It was Judy shouting for her, beckoning Ida back over. She had opened a bottle of Scotch and would share with anyone if they'd listen to her gossip and moan. Ida sat on the edge of the bed next to her fat, dimpled leg and took a swig. Perhaps Judy's constant talking would stop Ida worrying. During the week – Terri had told her – Alice stayed in their father's ordered, solid house. It was the early hours of Friday morning and she'd probably still be there.

"Wait, it's not the holidays is it? Half-term or something?" Ida asked.

"No. Are you even listening?" asked Judy.

Ida felt relieved. "Sorry, carry on."

Judy began again, ranting about the staff and the food and the police.

Ida looked towards Adelaide who was muttering to herself as always, laughing and chattering throughout the night. She was alright, not as nuts as they said, just confused sometimes. Who wasn't?

"One sec," Ida said, as she handed Judy the bottle and stood up. She walked over and knelt next to Adelaide. There was a gust and Ida screwed her eyes shut as something cracked above them and someone, somewhere else in the house, screamed. Judy muttered behind them, annoyed that Ida had left her.

"Don't you worry, sweetie," said Adelaide, patting Ida on the top of the head with her firm hands.

"You think this is it?" Ida asked.

"Undoubtedly. You've had the visions, yes?" She twisted Ida's hair and pushed it behind her ear.

Ida nodded. She had been having visions, and although the doctor said they were booze induced, Ida wasn't sure. People did have visions – not only nutters and druggies – they were always having them in the Bible and in things on TV.

"You shouldn't be drinking at a time like this," Adelaide said. "Lie down and pray."

Ida got into bed and lay back, pleased to be told what to do. She felt woozy and it was nice to be in the warm room while chaos reigned outside.

Adelaide began to pray under her breath as the whole house shuddered. Somewhere in the building a window smashed.

Ida shut her eyes. She would tell Jesus what she was grateful for.

Her bed was first – her clean bed – and the house they were in was truly beautiful.

Ida had arrived at the hostel with a note from her doctor, and stood gazing up at the ceiling in the hallway, with its fancy curled plaster, until someone fetched the woman in charge.

Around her the other girls argued and laughed, and even the warden who was showing her round didn't seem that bothered about the plasterwork. Ida knew she sounded manic as she shouted about it enthusiastically into her doughy face.

"Most of the girls who come here, well, they have serious problems. They're not interested in the bloody ceiling," she said, leading Ida up the marble steps to the dorms.

Ida wanted to pull her back down them. "Whatever my circumstances I always try to appreciate nice things," she said. "It's one of my gifts. That and nicking stuff."

There was a garden there as well – a secret garden – the nicest Ida had seen since she'd been living in London. She heard an owl cooing there at night, though the others didn't believe her. Bridie had been able to talk to owls, or at least coo at them until they cooed back, and Ida wished she'd paid more attention to how she'd done it.

In the garden there was a chapel too and Ida liked it best of all, with its gold crucifix and stained glass. Her favourite window was the one with St Barnabas on it, the saint of encouragement and consolation. There were stone seats around the edges of the chapel, originally put there for residents to sit on while other people – clean, normal people – could sit on the pews.

The few of them who went to the chapel sat on the pews too these days, but Ida wouldn't. She liked the cold stone, and the way that she felt hidden, as a big, fragile saint stood above her like her very own patron. She prayed a lot when she was there, shutting her eyes as hard as she could and digging her bitten nails into her knees.

Everything meant something these days. When Bridie had been drunk once – properly drunk, the kind where she started affecting an Irish accent and saying she was a terrible writer – she had told Ida she had once lived in a tiny flat on Greek Street, next door to a fortune teller and above a Chinese launderette.

And now Ida was practically living on Greek Street, and she could see where her mother had lived, the swirly letters that said launderette were still painted onto the building, even though it was a butcher's shop now.

There was the sound of something smashing outside and Ida wished they could make it to the chapel, just her and Adelaide, to sit and pray together, listening to all the destruction without the other women distracting them.

The window shook, harder this time, and Adelaide reached across the gap between their beds for Ida's hand. Ida really hoped the owl was alright.

"Let's pray for forgiveness," she said. "You first darling girl. I've made my peace."

"I'm sorry for all my drinking and drugs and for leaving my family and for sleeping around," Ida said.

"Jesus save her. Jesus save her."

Ida didn't need to speak for a while. Adelaide was off on a tangent, talking to at least three people who Ida couldn't see, smiling and laughing, happy that her misery was going to end.

But Ida didn't feel so happy. She would pray for Alice not to get squashed by a tree. She prayed to St Barnabas for encouragement and consolation, to be rescued, for the money that Bridie had stolen from her savings – a badly forged signature was all that it had taken – to be magically restored so she could go to America after all.

She must have slept because it was light when she opened her eyes and Judy was stumbling to her feet and pulling up her weird green too-short trousers. Adelaide was sitting by the window and reading, not in the least concerned that she hadn't been whisked off to heaven.

"What time is it?" Ida asked. Then, "Did anyone die, down in Bournemouth do you know? Any children?"

"Oh, so you want to talk to me now, now that you need something," said Judy. She hesitated and Ida knew she'd answer anyway. "A couple of people. No children. It's 9.30. Some of us are off down the Square – going to cut up the tree and have a bonfire."

"We allowed to do that?" Ida asked.

"Fuck it, it's Armageddon. We'll do whatever we want. And hardly any of the staff have bothered coming in – they're saying the roads are jammed and the buses aren't running."

They stepped out into Soho Square, the door flying out of Ida's grasp and banging hard behind her, the wind slapping her in the face. Despite the weather there were people everywhere, and roof tiles, branches and rubbish littered the road. Many of the parked cars had been crushed, their windows smashed, and car alarms were going off all over the place. People were cheerful though, talking and laughing as they surveyed the damage.

"Takes a disaster, takes a disaster, a disaster, a disaster, a diiiiis-aster," Judy muttered under her breath. She looked properly mad, ranting to herself, her eyes wandering and her arm jerking strangely as she walked. Ida wondered if she looked like that too. She didn't think she did – not quite – but was pretty sure she could do soon.

They walked through the cast-iron gate and towards the fallen tree. The pain-in-the-arse warden, Lisa, was there with Nikki and some of the others. Someone had spray painted the trunk 'For charity use. KEEP OFF'. Nikki was wielding an axe. God knew where she'd got it.

"Come back inside, girls," Lisa was saying, automatically. "It's not the weather to be out here. Let's go inside, have a coffee and get warm. Nikki, put that axe down."

None of them moved. Ida looked across the square and saw another tree had fallen on top of a house. Part of the roof and top floor was squished and nearly all the front wall missing.

"Fine, fuck it, was trying to do you a favour. Pub?" Nikki asked the crowd and they all laughed.

"You do know that if you return smelling of alcohol we won't be able to admit you?" Lisa said, sounding relieved that without them there she could do her word-search book in peace.

No one answered and some of them began to walk off, as Nikki held the axe in the air and led them like some kind of crazed tour guide before throwing it on the grass and laughing, knowing that she'd get arrested again if she took it into the pub.

Lisa jogged limply to pick it up.

Ida had spent enough time with that lot. There were things to explore. She walked across the square, jumping over branches and scrabbling over some of the bigger trunks, before stepping through the swinging wooden gate outside the destroyed house.

It was an oak tree that had fallen, its roots ripped out of the ground and its leaves and branches sticking out of the roof.

Through a jagged hole on the first floor she could see band posters and an unmade cabin bed and in the bathroom a still-dripping shower, wide open to the street. Downstairs, through a dusty sitting room, was a telly. She should nick it really, but part of her didn't want to change anything. It was like a wonderful set at the theatre. She imagined the family who lived there making their entrances and doing a show just for her. *Normal People,* it could be called.

The wind was starting to pick up again and she turned to see a middle aged woman frantically pulling a black Labrador inside her house while it barked at thousands of flying leaves. The tall pine trees around the square had been swaying before but now they were starting to bend right over, almost down to the ground. She thought of the woods back at home. Perhaps she'd summon up the courage to call Alice later.

Ida began walking back over the square, fighting her way through the fallen trees almost blindly as the wind pushed her backwards and wound her hair round her face. Small things – twigs and plastic bottles – flew at her and she batted them away with her hands and arms.

She was halfway across a large pile of branches when something much harder and bigger hit her face, snapping back her neck and pushing her off balance until with one final gust she flew back onto the grass.

"Fuck," she said out loud as she lay on the ground with her

eyes shut. Everything hurt – her head and her back most of all. She could feel warm blood running down the side of her head, pooling below her ear. Someone should call an ambulance. "Help," she shouted, "hello?" but she couldn't even hear herself over the wind and knew it was useless.

She opened her eyes slowly and looked at the sky. She thought it was birds at first but as her vision cleared she realised it was leaves and sticks, the occasional wing mirror or fence panel, swooping across the silvery sky like some weird junk ballet.

I'm the only one who's seeing this, she thought. It was somehow soothing.

Slowly she wiggled every bit of herself from her ankles upwards to check nothing was broken.

Then, wincing, she inched her way onto her elbows before putting her hands on the ground and beginning to crawl. It reminded her of something firemen or army men would say, 'stay low in a storm'.

Her palms were getting stuck with pine needles and bits of glass but it was too dangerous out here and she knew she wasn't well. All she wanted to do was lie down and sleep. She was beginning to feel sick.

"Hello," someone shouted from across the street, then, "Aggie, call an ambulance."

Ida tried to turn her head to look but it hurt too much. She felt a soft gloved hand on the back of her neck.

"Stop moving. Stop moving. I've done first aid. Don't move! Don't panic," the woman said. She sounded older, at least sixty, with the reassuring, bossy voice of an ex-teacher or hospital matron.

Ida relaxed her arms and fell onto her front, relieved, as the woman knelt down and stroked the back of her head. It was so long since anyone had touched her like that. How wonderful to be stroked.

She asked Ida questions, "What's your name? Where does it

hurt? Do you live nearby?" shouting her awake when it looked like she might pass out.

There was a muffled shout from across the road before, more clearly, "The phone's not working. Janet! The phone's not working." It was an Irish voice, a voice Ida knew but couldn't quite place. Then, "Where's another one? Frith Street? Or I could try the church. Is she okay? What can I do?"

And then there were other fingers on Ida's shoulder and she felt breath on her cooling, blood-soaked ear.

"She's called Ida," the first woman said.

"Ida," said the second in her soft, Irish accent.

It was then that Ida knew who it was. "Ma?" she asked, "Ma? Are you drunk?" Then, when the woman didn't respond she tried, "Bridie, Bridie Adair. It's you."

"Shhhh," said the women together, over and over, as they rubbed Ida's back, letting her finally fall asleep.

Ida found herself in hospital with a bandage tight round her head and a pale, man's hand resting on hers.

"My head," she said idiotically, blinking as she tried to cope with the light.

"Yes your head, darling. They've parcelled you up like something from *Carry On Nurse*. Here."

It wasn't Peter, was it?

"Stay still," the man said and held a mirrored compact up to her face as she struggled to open her eyes. Yes, a white bandage was wrapped ridiculously round her head and below it her right eye was black and almost closed.

"Oh God," she said then, "ow. This really is too tight."

"Let me help."

She saw his face then, his lovely, long face as he fiddled with the bandage.

"Is it you?" she asked.

"Yes, darling. You're not dead, don't worry. Are you getting carried away with this hospital bollocks? How many fingers am I holding up?" He made a V sign in Ida's face and she laughed.

"Now stay still. You better not spring a leak if I do this. Don't want blood all over my new shirt, genuine St Marks. You're bloody lucky they found me to call. One of the girls said you'd mentioned me? They called my agent. She was bloody delighted, thought some work had come in. Rooting for her ten percent, the old slag. Serves her right it was only you getting bonked on the head."

Ida didn't remember mentioning him to anyone but who knew what she said when she was drunk.

She reached up and took his chin in her hand and he looked down into her eyes.

"You're coming home with me sweetheart. You've had your fun playing the poor little match girl." He kissed her on the forehead. "Feel any better?" he asked, loosening the bandage with his thumb.

"Yes, so much," she said.

Peter lived in a mansion flat in Belsize Park. His driver, Pauly, took them there, an old, socialist cockney who had once driven 'Mr O'Shea' between TV shows and theatres and now took him to Waitrose for his weekly shop.

Ida had met Pauly many times before, he had known her mother too, and he gave her the kind of reverent, accepting, all knowing stare that made her think that perhaps he might be God.

The carpet in Peter's house was the deep, brown, unfashionable kind and Ida was so happy to take her shoes off and feel it under her feet. It was how the floor in the woods should feel, but it never did.

"Bed," Peter said. "I'll show you round later." He led her into a small bedroom with a high ceiling, almost filled by an enormous bed. "Queen-sized. Seems fitting. Hand me your clothes. All of them. There are some 'jamas here." He opened a cupboard and handed Ida some silk, stripped pyjamas before closing his eyes and holding out his arms. "I want everything, bra, undies the lot."

Ida did as she was told.

She didn't wake up until the next morning when Peter came into the room with a tray. He was still such a beautiful man, so fragile, his skin almost see-through over his sharp cheekbones and long straight nose.

"Sit up sweetheart. Here's sweet tea for the invalid, croissants, jam and *Hello*. But where are the flowers? Who lays a tray without flowers?"

From the inside of his dressing gown he pulled the big, false flower from all those years ago.

"Great things, remember kid?" he whispered as he brought it to her nose.

Chapter eighteen

~ 1999 ~

Ida left the house without washing. She wanted to bump into Elliot, to check things were okay, but she knew it was unlikely. The men would have gone to the beach or the woods, not along the main road to Bournemouth town centre.

Terri had been sensible enough to give Alice cash for them both – a cheque would have been useless for Ida as it wouldn't clear in time. She rubbed the notes in her pocket and thought of all the things she could buy. There had been a time, not long ago, when she would have found Elliot – or anyone really – and taken them to the pub with it. They would have chosen somewhere cheap and anonymous, The Moon in the Square perhaps, and drunk snakebite-and-black until they'd been thrown out.

Where could she get to with fifty pounds? Back to London certainly, with enough for plenty of wine when she got back. Or even a coach to France. If only she had her passport. It was probably good that she didn't.

Perhaps it would be good to spend the money on clothes. Maybe Alice wouldn't hate her quite so much. To Beales; she should walk straight to Beales.

Most people would have got the bus, especially with the weather, but Ida liked walking and with the strong wind behind her, pushing her along, the whole thing was kind of fun.

She reached the end of the tree-lined road and walked through Westbourne – the O.A.P's paradise on the edge of town – past Oxfam, and the chemist's, and the shop that sold commodes. The Silver Spoon had been renamed Millennium Cafe, in plenty of time for the new year, and Ida felt sorry for all the ninety year olds who went there for ham sandwiches and tepid cups of tea.

It took her twenty minutes to reach the town centre. Girls staggered down the high street, holding desperately onto their hair as though it might fly off. She walked past Topshop, Woolworths, HMV, through the square, and to the Victorian pleasure gardens that led to Bournemouth Beach.

She had spent a lot of time in the gardens when she was young; smoking weed, drinking white cider and snogging ugly boys.

They were still the same really, apart from the hot air balloon Terri had warned her about – a bizarre new tourist attraction that went up on a rope – which today was deflated and tethered firmly to the ground.

Ida imagined releasing it – it wouldn't be that hard – and flying away like Dorothy at the end of the *Wizard of Oz*.

She could remember things as she walked – getting shouted at by groups of girls then jumping in the river to make them think she was mad, drinking whisky by the lions on the war memorial, and snogging Danny the Irish tramp, who'd been fifteen years older than her. Which was gross when she thought about it now.

There was the Peakes stall, where you could win teddy bears. It was closed today. It looked like it had been closed for a while.

That was as far as she would go. Past that point you could see the sea and it would be horrible and angry today. She didn't like it at the best of times.

And the pier. Just before Ida had left home Bridie had taken her to the pier on some strange, angry mission. Ida had forgotten all about that.

She stroked the curly old-fashioned lettering of the Peakes sign and was about to turn to leave when she felt a hand on the small of her back.

Immediately she thought it was Elliot. But instead there was a pale dark-haired man with pockmarked skin, about her height, wearing rectangular glasses.

"It's Ida, isn't it?" He noticed her blank expression, "Martin? From St Lukes?"

He hugged her while Ida stood stock still, her arms by her

sides, very aware that she must smell. From the corner of her eye she noticed a blonde child looking up at her, attached to reins which Martin – or the man who said he was Martin – was holding.

"I heard about your mother, it was in the *Echo*. I am so sorry. She was a wonderful woman," he said as he pulled away.

"Thank you. It's okay. It's odd to see you."

He looked down at the child. "Poppy, this lady was your Daddy's very first girlfriend. Can you believe it?"

Ida looked down at Poppy who was gazing up at both of them with a cross and confused expression.

"Does he always keep you on a lead?" she asked the child.

Martin laughed, nervously. "You haven't changed, you were always funny."

"Oh God, don't," Ida was embarrassed and wanted desperately to get away.

"Not into the whole kids thing? I'm married now – to Tash. We've got Pops here, and we're expecting again."

"Lovely."

"You really want to get away don't you? Sorry. Your mother's just passed away. You must have stuff you need to do."

He looked sad and Ida recognised him then, the keen to please, bullied boy who loved church way too much. But more than that he'd loved her, enough to do stuff that definitely wasn't allowed in the Bible when they were both very much underage.

"It's fine, I'm going to Beales to buy an outfit. I got sidetracked. Are you going that way?"

"Yes! We can do. We normally go to look at books in Waterstones on a Friday. Poppy's into Enid Blyton. I'm a stay-at-home Dad."

He hugged her again. "It's lovely to see you. I always worried. You were such a lost soul."

Ida visibly cringed.

They walked the long way back through the gardens, looking at things with Poppy, pointing out trees and birds. Martin didn't seem to mind that Ida smelled, that her hair was weird. He was looking at her as he had when they were thirteen. And he laughed at everything she said, absolutely everything, even when she made horrible jokes about sleeping with strangers or being a loser.

"Most people don't laugh when I say things like that, they tell me off for having low self-esteem," she said.

"Well, I know you don't mean it. You think you're bloody brilliant, don't you? An ego's never been something you lacked."

She was embarrassed but he was right. Perhaps he was cleverer than she'd given him credit for.

They stopped at Waterstones. It had been bombed once, Ida remembered, by the IRA. There and the pier on the same day.

Ida smiled to herself. What strange places for them to target. What a ridiculous bloody town for them to choose.

"You should come for dinner, with me and Tash. She'd love to see you. It's been years. We don't live far from your mum's – Parkstone Avenue."

"I'm not sure." Ida remembered Tash from church, a short, quiet girl with extremely long blonde hair that she was very proud of. Ida had once pulled a chunk out of it during a fight over some tap shoes at the Christmas jumble sale.

"Don't worry about it," said Martin, embarrassed. "I can't imagine you in our living room to be honest. Not sure it's your scene."

"You'd be surprised – I'd do anything for a comfy sofa and a cup of tea these days. Anyway, I should go."

"Okay, yes, we need to get reading, eh, Poppy?" He looked back at Ida. "Will you be here for long? You wouldn't think about staying now, in the house?"

"I don't think so. My home's in London."

"Try to be happy. Not now, but in time. Remember there'll always be a thirteen-year-old boy who hangs on your every word. Man, I was so gutted when you told me about that actress. I said I didn't believe it but I knew it was true. You were always far too

Hollywood for me."

"No, we were both too Hollywood for Bournemouth," she said, not meaning it, aware that this badly dressed, smiley man and giant, stinking woman – both of them thirty – made a strange and sorry sight.

They hugged again and Ida left them to buy their books, not looking back as she walked away despite knowing they'd be waving at her and hoping that she'd look round.

As she reached Beales she remembered something else, something she'd tried to forget. The day they'd bombed Waterstones, all those years ago, had been the very last time she'd talked to her ma.

Chapter nineteen

~ 1993 ~

Ida got in from college carrying a can of Strongbow and a box of chips and cheese. It was only five thirty but classes hadn't been going well and she'd needed the drink to cheer her up. She couldn't understand the colour wheel – surely there were three shades of blue, max? – and it was making her extremely angry in lessons. Art was meant to be fun, wasn't it? Not all maths-y and anal.

Most of the students had paid to attend but Ida had got on free because she was on benefits and had a letter from the alcohol drop-in centre in Kings Cross. The other people at the drop-in centre were dark yellow and close to death, so Alesha – her support worker – was keen to help Ida as much as she could.

Because she didn't pay, her classmates resented her frequent outbursts even more than they might have done anyway. Or at least she thought they did, which made her even worse.

She'd probably leave, she never finished anything after all.

Her housemate, Kelly, was in the hall, on her way to work. Her hair was crimped, her blusher was alarming, and her hot pants said 'Barbados' right across the arse. "Hi," she said, glancing at the can in Ida's hand. "Your mother called."

"Oh cool, thanks. It was probably my stepmum, Terri?"

"No, she definitely told me she was your mother," Kelly said. "Said you didn't have her number but she'd call back at seven thirty."

"Oh, ok," Ida said. It had to be Terri – of course it would be Terri. But the telephone number thing was odd.

Ida hadn't spoken to her mother for three whole years. It couldn't be Bridie. But still there was a tiny bit of her that was intrigued. There'd never even been the hint of a message like this before.

At ten past eight the phone rang and Ida ran down to the hall.

She took a deep breath and picked up the receiver. "Hello?"

"Darling, they've come for me."

It was Bridie. It was really her. Behaving as though she'd spoken to Ida the week before.

"Where did you get my number? And what do you mean?"

"Peter. And the IRA."

Ida couldn't help but laugh. She'd gone properly mad this time. She'd have to call Bryan. "Sit down, I'm going to call Dad."

"Don't you dare call your bloody father. Haven't you seen the news? They've bombed the pier, or tried to. And Waterstones, of all places."

"In Bournemouth?" Ida asked, unconvinced.

"Yes, bloody Bournemouth. That pier is cursed. Remember I took you there? My last hurrah?"

"I remember. But I don't think they'll have come for you specifically, Ma. Just stay where you are."

"You don't know anything," Bridie said, and put down the phone.

Ida went into the sitting room. Eight of them lived there, shift workers and students, unpopular ones who couldn't get a house-share anywhere else. The room was filthy and unloved – a couple of faded postcards were stuck up above the mantelpiece, two ripped sofas were pushed against the wall, and a film of grime covered everything. She switched on the TV.

It was true. At least the bombing bit was.

She called her father and after an hour he called her back. He hadn't been able to get through to her ma.

Ida lay on her single bed looking up at the lone glow-in-the-dark star some previous tenant had left. Her old room, her room at her mother's, had been covered in them.

Perhaps that was it, really it, and Bridie would be sectioned or top herself – maybe she'd do it tonight. Off the pier if there was still anything left of it.

She closed her eyes and tried to picture her mother's face. Thin, stern with a heavy fringe, that was how she always remembered her. But if she concentrated hard enough, there were other images too.

Bridie brushing Ida's hair when she was small; that time just the two of them had gone to the zoo; her wide, rare smile.

If she was a good, kind daughter she'd go down there tomorrow. She should call Alice, get her number from Terri, but she couldn't quite make herself.

There was too much between them. It had been far too long.

Chapter twenty

Ida was singing badly and loudly when she got back to the house. She hadn't been shopping for years and had enjoyed the experience far more than she'd expected to. And the things you could nick! There wasn't much scope for theft in the corner shops near her bedsit, but a department store was a whole new ball game. She'd hidden make-up in her boots and a new woollen hat in her pocket. And her funeral outfit wasn't bad; a close fitting black dress and three inch heels, a totally un-her look that would surely make Elliot love her, if just for the night.

No one was home and she walked into the kitchen, lifted the lid off the saucepan on the hob and pretended to be sick into the lumpy beige soup. She took some bread from the cupboard and cheese from the fridge, made herself an enormous sandwich and walked towards the study, imagining herself in her new dress and shoes, pretending she was someone different, annoying Alice with her wit and charm.

It was only when she entered the room that she realised what she wanted to do. She found the Magical Days Book behind her bed, ate the last of her sandwich in one big bite and held the book to her face and kissed it. Then she sat on the floor, cross legged, vowing to read it properly, not be embarrassed like last time.

It didn't take her long to find what she'd been looking for.

9th September 1984 – 9.30pm

Ma is out of hospital! Hurrah! Should be pleased but she's harder to look after than Alice really. More tricky – at least you can tell Alice what to do and she'll pretty much do it. As soon as she got home she made me get in the car and drive into Bournemouth with her. I thought we were both going

~ 156 ~

to die. She wouldn't tell me what we were doing but had this weird determined look on her face. We went to the pier, all the way up the pier (she always said she HATED it there) right to the theatre at the end. Bobby Davro is in some show and I honestly thought she'd gone mad and wanted to go to it, but then she got all grumpy and I worried she was going to jump in and top herself. Honestly. It was horrible. And who can I tell? I could tell Ray from pub or Danny (who has made me realise there are different kinds of love. It's not ANNIE love or anything. But he's nice and I like it when he plays me songs on the penny whistle. And he's really kind to his dog who is SO SWEET. I'm MORTIFIED I ever got involved with that square Martin twat. You live and learn...)

Anyway, Ma was doing that annoying twitchy pleased-with-herself face and I couldn't talk to her about it. It was all so annoying – her getting pissed beforehand (despite being told NO BOOZE) and then dragging me out there when Alice was going to be spazzing out at home.

She wanted to stop reading but she knew there were things in here she needed to look at. Things she had forgotten. And after meeting Martin, and remembering she hadn't always been such an unlovable disaster, it was comforting in a way to rediscover her stupid teenage self. She'd been so enthusiastic, was that the word? Changeable and difficult, but perhaps more up than down. She was still like that she supposed, but now her ups were, pretty much always, artificially induced.

There were pages of drawings, some of them not bad, photo after photo of Anna DeCosta cut out from magazines, then postcards, leaflets, things she'd found.

At the back of the book were four blank pages. It seemed a shame for it not to be finished. Ida picked up a pen but had no idea what to write.

There was the noise of someone coming back into the house,

and a knock at Ida's door.

It was Alice, carrying bags of shopping.

"Is everything okay?" Ida asked.

"I'm knackered. The bank were so unhelpful. And we need to look through Mum's stuff properly, we need some kind of ID. I realised I don't even know her real date of birth, I heard her say it was anywhere from '38 to '45. God knows how old she really was. Probably 270 like some kind of vampire. Perhaps we can look tonight? Did you have some soup?"

"It was delicious," Ida said.

Alice closed the door and Ida looked back down at the book. She had no memory of writing any of it. How odd that these things, these bits of herself, only existed in this strange old notebook.

Towards the end, just before the blank pages, were a series of questions, clearly listed in block capitals:

WHY DID MY MOTHER TAKE ME TO THE PIER?

WHAT WAS SHE GOING TO TELL ME?

IS IDA IN THE PLAY REALLY MEANT TO BE HER?
(Same hair, both mean)

Ida picked the pen back up and added:

What was Ma's real birthday?

Four small questions. Perhaps she could try to answer them.

Chapter twenty-one

~ 1984 ~

Ida sat biting her fingernails at Bridie's bedside while their least favourite doctor did some final checks, inexplicably examining her mother's eyes, which were glistening with a combination of anger and barely suppressed laughter. After scribbling a brief note on a clipboard, he perched on the edge of the hard bed and leant towards Ida, his big knobbly hands resting on his knees.

"If we're going to let her go you have to make sure she eats properly. And she has proven she absolutely cannot be trusted around alcohol. There must be none in the house, do you understand me? She needs to be monitored constantly, fed calorific and nutritious food. Can I trust you Miss Irons?"

Behind him Bridie rolled then shut her eyes.

"I'll do everything I possibly can," Ida said, as convincingly as she could, painfully pulling on the safety pin she'd pierced her ear with the night before and was trying to hide with her hair.

He nodded, seemingly satisfied with this not-quite-lie. Ida attempted a grin but she felt sick and nervous, too tired to be amazed by the stupidity of doctors. Surely this man had spent enough time with Bridie over the past few weeks to know the most anyone could do for her was fetch her things and laugh at her mean jokes? And if he'd bothered to ask the fat nurse, Carol, who lived above the pub, she'd be sure to tell him that, despite her height, Bridie Adair's eldest daughter was only fifteen and out washing dishes in a stinking kitchen almost every night of the week.

The doctor smiled briefly at them both and left the room. Ida began to pack her mother's bag according to the strict instructions being barked from the bed. Then she helped her into her coat and down the smelly orange-lit corridor while Bridie swore in a stage whisper about her unfortunate fellow patients as they wheeled along drips or held hushed conversations. The glass double doors loomed closer as they walked, each step another lost chance for someone to call out to them, to carry her frail mother back to bed where she belonged. Ida's red motorcycle boots – a recent charity shop buy – were heavy and uncomfortable as she dragged her feet across the tiles. She was determined to wear them in.

"Thank God for that," said Bridie as she stepped into the sharp air, holding out a shaking arm for a cab. "I'm never, ever, ever going there again. You hear me? You can tell your bloody stepmother to shove it up her tight proddie arse. Where's a bloody cab? Don't they know there are ill people waiting?"

As she often did, Ida tried to take a film to store in her mind; her strange, shaking mother in her smelly camel coat, squinting defiantly at the weak autumn sun.

The cab drove straight to the off-license, and Ida found herself cradling her mother's broken carpetbag while Bridie chose bottle after dusty bottle of cheap red wine. Mrs Dewani even gave her one on the house despite Ida's eye signals. Could she not see Bridie's hospital band, her marbled skin, or notice the rotten smell that seemed to surround her like a force field?

The taxi waited outside for them, the driver chatty and cheerful, and after a stop at home to stroke the cat and drink two of the bottles of wine, Bridie tied a blue silk headscarf over her dirty hair, found her car keys – which had been hidden in the kitchen cupboard – and walked back outside. Ida hesitated briefly before following, grabbing the purple jacket she'd nicked from Miss Selfridge, during a Saturday morning spree with Tina from the pub.

There was really nothing to say as her mother climbed back down the steps towards their ancient Rover so Ida stayed quiet, following, then sliding into the passenger seat and mouthing a quick prayer. Her mother was so low in the broken driver's seat that Ida knew only her eyes and fringe showed over the dashboard. Through a hole in the floor Ida watched as the ground sped by, stone after stone, yellow line after yellow line. She knew that looking up at the swearing fellow motorists and swerving cyclists would only fill her with useless fear. There was no real need to be afraid. If there was one thing her mother had taught her during all the time she'd been 'home-schooled' it was that the Adair women were hard to kill.

"I'm taking you somewhere very important," Bridie said. "Pay attention."

She sounded so lucid that, if Ida hadn't been in similar situations a thousand times before, it would have been easy to believe her, or to at least consider what she had to say. But no, there had been too many times before. The time, aged forty, Bridie had decided she should model again and sent out home-shot snaps of her in her nightdress. The time she sent filthy, threatening letters about Ida's father to almost every publication in *Writers and Artists Year Book 1970* (so many of the addresses had changed that letters marked 'return to sender' plagued them for six months, making that particular mistake a difficult one to forget.)

"I'm not sure I know what you mean," Ida said flatly.

"Of course you don't, that's the point. My last hurrah! You should take notes."

"Alice will be home in an hour or so."

"She has a key."

"Yes, but she's expecting you to be there. She's been excited about you coming home for weeks; she hated seeing you in there. She'll be worried if you're not back."

"She needs to get a backbone, that one. Anyway, we won't be long. Cheer up darling, for God's sake, life's for living, eh?"

Ida snorted at her mother's back-to-front logic and turned towards the window. She didn't need to look to know that her mother was smiling.

Bridie drove through Westbourne, then past the gardens, towards the Royal Bath Hotel.

The road was wide and busy but as they neared the pier Bridie stopped suddenly then made a U-turn, causing cars all around them to brake and honk their horns. Ida put her head in her hands and Bridie laughed, pulling up onto the pavement and coming to a halt.

"You can't stop here, Ma," Ida said but she knew it was useless.

"It's my right to park where I choose," said Bridie. "Traffic wardens are no better than the Nazis."

Ida glanced at the floor of the car which was already strewn with unpaid tickets.

The road was above the promenade and Ida helped her mother down the concrete steps. At the bottom were an empty merry go round and a closed candyfloss stall.

"Have you ever seen anything so depressing?" asked Bridie.

Ida looked at her yellow, shaking mother and thought she definitely had.

"Don't answer that," Bridie said, "come on."

They walked to the booth at the end of the pier, Bridie paid the tattooed old man with exact change, and then they were on the narrow wooden boards, the brown sea visible in the gaps under Ida's boots.

"Let's hope none of them are rotten," Bridie said and cackled.

It was much colder out there and there was hardly anyone else around. It wasn't tourist season or the holidays and even the few teenagers who came in the evenings – to dive-bomb off the pier or smoke fags at the end – weren't out of school yet.

A few angry-looking seagulls stood on the rusty wrought iron railings, watching them intently as they walked and Ida breathed slowly, trying hard to look straight ahead. Right at the end was the theatre with luminous orange letters saying 'Fun, Laffs, Bobby Davro!' Bridie couldn't be taking them there, could she? It was her idea of hell. Ida started to get worried; there was nothing out here for them. It was cold and sad and they were so far away from the man in the booth and the few people walking dogs on the beach.

If she could just concentrate hard enough, have enough belief, she was pretty sure she could bring Bridie back to the car, trancelike and happy, to drive them home. Things like that were always happening in the Bible, and in the new-age healing books her mother sometimes secretly bought. She wished she found it easier to believe.

Bridie walked over to the railing, took a ten pence piece from her pocket and put it into the green telescope. "Here, look," she told Ida.

"I don't want to," said Ida and, with surprising force, Bridie grabbed her hair and manoeuvred her head.

"Look. Don't make me waste 10p. Try to make out our house. I'll never be able to with my eyesight," Bridie said.

Ida opened one eye and angled the telescope towards Branksome Beach.

It seemed alarmingly close.

It was only at the end of her mother's road, but she hadn't been since they had made that stupid film. She imagined seeing them there now, two girls with their arms out as they stood in the sea. One of them pushing the other under the waves...

A gull flew in front of the lens and Ida screamed. "Please, Ma. Please can we go home?"

She hated birds. People thought she was scared, but it wasn't that. They reminded her of that day on the beach, they reminded her how evil she was, deep down.

"No," said Bridie calmly.

Ida was close to tears as her mother led her further along the pier. They didn't speak and soon passed the theatre. So there weren't going in there. There were only the shut-up amusements left ahead of them, the teacup rides and the shooting gallery, before they'd reach the end.

Ida felt scared. "Please Ma, tell me then. Tell me why we're here."

"Hurry up," Bridie said.

Ida followed a few steps behind, unwilling to encourage whatever was happening. She watched her mother's small shape against the sky; such a small body, such a small person, really.

Bridie reached the railing at the end, put her bag down and stepped up onto the bottom rung.

"No!" screamed Ida. She suddenly knew why they were there. She ran towards her mother, grabbed her tiny waist and lifted her down.

"What the hell do you think you're doing? Did you think I was going to top myself? Give me some credit. Suicide from Bournemouth Pier. Do you think that's my style?" Bridie asked.

"I don't know. I thought... "

"Fine. Fine. You don't want to hear. Let's go home. You're just the same as the others. Scared. Stupid. With no imagination."

Ida followed behind as Bridie walked, quickly. She felt miserable as she watched her mother, felt terrible about it all, and her arms were covered in goosebumps.

Bridie didn't speak on the drive home.

Confused, tired and stubborn, Ida pretended to sleep while she tried to make sense of the events of the day and think about what it could possibly mean. There was a poem in all of it somewhere, a real, prize winning poem about the sea. She stroked the sleeve of her new jacket, pleased that she'd stolen it and that her mother didn't know. At least she had secrets too.

"That's it then, you stupid girl," Bridie said as they reached their road, her voice full of glass again. "You missed your chance. You'll regret that, my darling heart, you wait and see."

They pulled into the drive and saw Alice's worried face peering at them through the sitting room window. As they parked she disappeared and Ida knew she would be running to meet them. Then the door opened and there she was in her uniform, her face pink and puffy from crying as Ida had known it would be.

They got out of the car and walked up towards her, Bridie leading, pretending to look at flowers and plants to disguise the fact she found the steps a struggle. To Alice it must have seemed as though she was being deliberately slow, as though she wasn't pleased to see her and her lips trembled. Ida tried to meet her gaze to make her understand, but there was no use. Alice wasn't great at subtlety and began to cry again.

Bridie reached the top, looked down at her sobbing daughter and held on to the doorframe, pulling Alice towards her and grasping the back of her head. "You poor little thing, you poor, pretty little thing," Bridie said over and over again in a strange voice that Ida didn't recognise.

Alice caught Ida's eye and for perhaps the first time, Ida could tell they were both properly scared.

Bridie spent the rest of the afternoon lying on the sofa and drinking ginger wine while Alice sat on a footstool taking an occasional sip. Ginger wine was medicinal in Bridie's book, and allowed however ill or however young you were. They were playing gin rummy – or rather Bridie was attempting to teach her. Ida wasn't allowed to play, Ida was too good. They still didn't talk about the time Bridie had drunkenly bet her last seven pounds and Ida had cleaned her out. Ida had tried to give it back – they hardly had money for food – but Bridie wouldn't take it. She took gambling very seriously indeed.

Ida had used the money to buy her bunk beds from Martin's mother. She'd lugged them, strut by strut, back to the house and spent two days putting them together. She still wasn't entirely sure they weren't going to collapse. Not that they were really dangerous – they were so small compared to her that she was able to put one foot flat on the floor while she lay on the top.

For a while Ida sat in the uncomfortable torn-leather armchair rereading *Jane Eyre*, or trying to, while Bridie changed the rules as she saw fit and Alice didn't notice and asked seemingly endless questions. Eventually it was too annoying and Ida went up to her room.

There were things she needed to think about anyway.

The problem with Bridie though, was that you couldn't just ask. She made things up wildly although she swore she didn't, and was especially likely to if you showed you were interested. If you could get her when she was just drunk enough, three bottles of wine and no spirits, you could sometimes get at what seemed like the truth.

Ida lay on her unmade bed. Her side-lamp was the only light in the room, casting a weak circle onto the flaking ceiling. The sheet had rolled up and an escaped mattress spring scratched her leg. It was all just too uncomfortable.

She gave up, jumped onto the floor, pulled the duvet onto the carpet and lay down there instead. Stretching out her arms she came across fag ends, bits of old sandwich and book after book. At her father and Terri's flat you could eat your supper off the carpet if you chose to. She picked up a few fag ends, chose the longest and lit it with a stray match that lay under the bed – smoking always helped her to think.

Maybe it didn't matter why'd they'd gone to the pier, it was bound to be disappointing anyway.

Ida finished her cigarette, got to her feet and climbed onto the small pine chair that stood by her desk. She had the evening off the pub and would use it to drink and smoke and write. Her fingers were tingling and she needed to do something productive. She reached up to the ceiling tile and pulled out her Magical Days Book. She could start by describing their day, or at least the little she could make of it.

Chapter twenty-two

If she was going to look through her mother's things, properly and without distraction, she needed to do it alone.

Alice wittered on but Ida wouldn't be swayed and shut herself in their mother's bedroom, carrying up all the drawers from the dressing table in the study too. Alice was suspicious, Ida knew, worried she was looking for money or anything she could sell, and brought her cup of tea after cup of tea until Ida, frustrated, put an empty drawer up under the door handle, telling Alice that she should go downstairs and put her feet up. Ida could hear the shrill pitch of her sister's voice as she spoke to Tom in the kitchen. She was obviously annoyed but seemed to have decided this wasn't an argument worth having.

Ida was almost enjoying herself, surrounded by piles of clutter, the radio on, and a mug of strong tea still warm next to her. She was surprised to realise that perhaps it was the fear she would cry that had previously made her unwilling to sort through her mother's possessions. Fuck it, she thought. If she couldn't cry on her own then she was even madder than she'd thought. And she was pretty sure that there was nothing among these theatre programmes, faded photos and old lipsticks that could bring her to tears.

Ida began with the drawers under the bed. There were pink floral sheets in there, gnawed by mice or moths, and Ida removed them, remembering hating them when she was a child. If they hadn't been in such bad nick she would have almost liked them now, at least the fabric for a dress or a shirt. At the back of the drawers were empty bottles, receipts, tissues, and not much else. If there were any notes of her mother's, any interesting things, she didn't keep them there.

She pulled the drawers out and felt the space, shuddering as she found the skeleton of a long dead mouse. Steeling herself she replaced her hand and pulled out what felt like a magazine. She brushed off the dust with her palm and saw it was a catalogue, a Bonhams catalogue – *British and Irish Art Sale, 1989*. Inside was a folded letter and she opened it at the place it marked. On the page was a painting of her mother, the one they'd had when she was young. It had been a long time since she'd seen it and Ida ran her fingers over the shape of her ma, remembering the feel of the layers of paint and how she'd been both fascinated and embarrassed by the naked breasts. There was a caption underneath the image:

> *An important painting by Jacob Collins, 'Untitled' is one of the highlights of the 20th Century British and Irish art sale, taking place on the 16th November at Bonhams New Bond Street.*

Ida opened the letter. It was immaculately typewritten on heavy cream paper, the Bonhams logo raised at the top of the page.

2nd December 1989

Dear Ms Adair

I am writing regarding the recent sale of your painting 'Untitled' by Jacob Collins.

As you are aware, the painting sold for £14,000 to a telephone bidder. Please find a statement attached, detailing our commission and charges, and a cheque enclosed.

The buyer, Mrs A. Simpson, requested that I pass on her telephone number, it is 01 552 439.

Many thanks for doing business with Bonhams.

Yours sincerely,

Joseph Hodder
Specialist – Contemporary British and Irish Art

£14,000. That should have been her bloody cash. She supposed her mother would have lived on it for a year or two, spending it on drink. Ida liked to think that if she'd had the money she would have bought a house or something sensible, but the truth was she may well have done the same. If she couldn't be trusted with fifty quid, what would she do with an amount like that?

Poor old Mrs A Simpson, whatever she'd wanted. She must have been very disappointed to discover that Bridie almost never spoke on the phone.

She felt the carpet behind the other drawer and pulled out a postcard from Peter, 'The Girl with the Pearl Earring'. On the back was his beautiful, looping handwriting – Ida had forgotten his writing – and a message:

Bet she dropped the other pearl down the lav or swapped it for a
G and T.
P x

Her mother had been renowned for losing things, though Ida could hardly imagine how, as Bridie never went anywhere. Ida wondered where all the things were, all those lost earrings and socks, and imagined for a moment that they were under the carpet she was sitting on, filling the gaps under the floor boards and the spaces behind the wallpaper – holding the house up.

She put the sheets and the catalogue back and slid them under the bed. She would leave the mouse there – no need to disturb him. She wiped her dusty hands on her trousers crawled over to the things she'd bought up from her mother's desk.

She would try not to be distracted by all the rubbish, just throw stuff away, and if she did happen to find anything interesting then there would be no need to share it with her sister. Alice had already had first dibs on most things after all.

There was the sound of a man's feet on the landing.

"What you doing in there? Wanking? Or are you dead? Shit, probably shouldn't make jokes." It was Elliot.

Ida opened the door.

Elliot stood there, his hair messy, his face flushed from walking, the collar of his coat up by his cheeks. He looked sweet and eager and so happy to see her. Ida kissed him on the mouth and he stepped into the room, taking off his coat and dropping it on the bed.

"I thought you were going to leave me with those fucking squares talking about fucking chickpeas or some bollocks," he said in a loud whisper.

Ida laughed, closed the door, and put the drawer back. "You can stay here and talk to me while I look through things," she said, sitting on the floor.

"Got you some contraband to cheer you up," Elliot said, sitting on the bed and reaching inside his coat. He bought out a pack of Lambert and Butler and two Peperamis.

"I thought you'd be cross with me after last night," Ida said, and kissed his knee, breathing in his strong smell of tobacco and London air.

He lit a cigarette and Ida carried on making piles of the stuff on the floor. Every so often she would find a photograph and look at it for a second; hoping Elliot would express an interest in her as a child. She caught herself doing it and felt ashamed. No wonder he didn't love her, he could see straight through her. She was an attention-seeking twat.

The theatre programmes were different, as were the photos of her mother's friends; he was interested in them although he'd often take the piss.

"You could sell some of these for a few quid you know," he said.

"That's what Tom was saying when we were out."

"Really?" Ida was surprised. Tom didn't seem the money-motivated type. "He did mention the original Ida script might be worth something. I don't want to sell it though. I told him that." She knew she sounded annoyed and carried on leafing through papers, but couldn't concentrate. "God, he seems so right-on and responsible, but actually he's a fame-hungry, money-grabbing..."

"I know. I told him you wouldn't want to sell anything. Except the painting maybe."

"Maybe." Ida had boasted to him about the painting so many times she couldn't bear to tell him it had already been sold.

"I'd love to see it," he said.

She didn't reply.

"Guess what," he said, "this'll cheer you up – I've got the best bloody gossip ever." He climbed off the bed and sat opposite her on the floor.

"What?"

He put his hands on her arms forcing her to stop sorting through the papers and look at him. "They haven't bloody done it."

"What?" Ida laughed, not quite understanding.

"Shagged! They haven't shagged! We went for a couple of pints over lunch and Tom let on. He says he supposes it's because your mother was so ill."

"Bloody hell," Ida said, laughing.

"He wanted me to talk about you, in the sack, I could tell he did."

Ida wasn't sure that was true, Tom struck her as being far too nice for that. "And did you?" Ida was kind of hoping he had.

"No. Thought you might kill me if I did. Gave the impression you're a goer though."

She punched him on the shoulder, aware that she was blushing.

"You're bright red, you slag!" Elliot said gleefully. "Lucky I came down or Tom would have had his wicked way with you."

Ida sent Elliot down for food, crackers and cheese, and she

could hear Alice's voice as she tried to convince him they should both come downstairs. Ida knew she'd hate them missing supper, she was so fucking controlling.

He brought up the food and closed the door. From his pocket he took out his tin, picked out some pills and swallowed them without water. Ida didn't ask what they were. He didn't offer them to her and she knew it was his way of showing he was trying to be better, that although he needed something small to get by, this wasn't a time for recreational use. There was weed in the tin though, Ida could smell it.

"Skin up, will you?" she said.

"You sure? I suppose we can do it out the window. Your sister can't get too cross about that. Hand me something to roach it with though?"

She handed him a seventies copy of *Vogue*, the last item from her mother's top drawer.

He lit the joint and walked towards the window, struggling to open the stiff metal catch. Ida stood up, and stamped on her right foot. Her legs had gone to sleep and it was agony. She took a moment, and then, realising she was cold, walked to her mother's wardrobe and picked out a pale blue cashmere cardigan, felted from washing and full of holes. She tried it on and laughed. "It's so tight. I feel like the Incredible Hulk."

Elliot turned, holding out the joint. "You look sexy, like some fifties nympho."

She reached for a puff and then handed it back. She didn't need it really, she felt more relaxed about everything with Elliot there, like in some small way he could protect her from the worst of it, and she flicked through her mother's jumpers with the tips of her fingers.

"She had some lovely stuff. Shame she couldn't afford dry cleaning or mothballs. Well, she could have afforded them. The older I get, the less money I have, the more I realise she was pretty well off. Only not as well off as she thought she should be. And she

~ 172 ~

liked the decrepit glamour of it all, Miss Havisham chic."

The sliding door of the wardrobe stuck halfway and Ida nudged it with her elbow. Something was blocking it and she leant down. She pushed the bags and shoes away from the runner but still it wouldn't work.

"Come here and take this, I'll do it. You've always been crap with stuff like that," Elliot said.

Ida knew he was right. She lacked patience and she'd end up breaking it. She stood up, walked to the window and took the joint, holding it out of the window as she turned to watch him struggling with the door.

"There's something stuck," he said.

He leant further into the cupboard, his arm bent awkwardly as he scrabbled at something with his fingernails.

"There," he said, pushing the door, hard. In his hand was a big brown envelope, stuffed full. He opened it and began to flick through the contents.

"It's crap, just bills and receipts but here... a certificate of baptism," he said, pulling it out and holding it up as he tried to read the handwriting. "I thought you always said your grandpa was some fancy engineer?"

Ida reached down for the certificate. It was crumpled and brown at the edges but in pretty good condition, the slanted black fountain pen faded with age.

The Holy Sacrament of Baptism
St Michael's R.C Church
This is to certify:
that: Brigid Catherine Adair
child of: Thomas James John-Paul Adair (TINKER)
and Brigid Theresa Catherine Adair formerly O'Donnell
born in: Tipperary
on: 2ⁿᵈ August 1937
baptized on: 20ᵗʰ September 1937

according to the rites of the Roman Catholic Church
by: Rev. Joseph Lehmann
the sponsors being:
Elizabeth O'Donnell
Fidelma Hogan

"Tinker. It does say tinker, doesn't it?" Ida asked.

"It looks like it," said Elliot.

"And place of birth. She always said London, but Tipperary? Is that a real place?"

"Ha. Your mother the gypsy – explains a lot about you." He stuffed the envelope back in the cupboard.

"And look at her birthday. I always thought she was pretty old when she had me... for back then. But she was even older, thirty-two. She'd been married to Da for years. She really put it off," she said.

"Well she wasn't the most maternal, was she?"

Ida sat on the floor next to him reading and re-reading the certificate in her hand.

"So she was my age, not twenty-five, when she wrote the play."

"Maybe there's hope for you yet, Irons," said Elliot.

It felt like something she should show her sister alone, and Elliot gladly took Tom to the pub.

Alice didn't take the hint at first and tried to protest, but after a few pointed glances realised something was up.

"You can take my car," she said to Tom. "Don't get hammered and smash yourself up."

"I'll look after him, you have my word, we won't get pissed," Elliot said, winking.

"And don't go far, maybe just to the Hogshead?" Alice shouted after them as they walked outside.

"Don't worry, sweetheart," Tom shouted back. "I love you."

Alice closed the door and turned towards Ida. She looked

sweet in a green spotty dress and cardie, like some sort of elf, and her un-brushed hair fell in waves round her face. "What is it then? What do you want to talk to me about? There is something isn't there."

Ida reached into the pocket of her trousers and pulled out the folded certificate. She handed it to her sister. Alice looked confused and as she unfolded it, her eyes glinting with suspicion.

"It's nothing bad," Ida said. "At least I don't think so."

"Let's go into the light," Alice said, peering at it.

They walked into the sitting room and Alice held it under the standard lamp.

Her brow was creased with concentration. She looked somehow too young to be so worried and under the light her gaunt face looked almost transparent.

"A tinker?" Alice said, looking up. She still looked confused and almost angry as though Ida was playing some kind of trick.

"Yep. Well that's what it says. And have you seen the place of birth? She wasn't born in London after all. She is – was – Irish. Properly Irish." Ida walked behind Alice and looked at it over her shoulder, pointing out the place.

Unexpectedly Alice reached up and touched her hand. "I don't know why we're surprised; she always made stuff up. Well, made 'stories better' as she said."

"I know. I get that. But it seems like this is one story she actually made more boring," Ida said. "Shall we sit down?"

The revelation had been a leveller of sorts, which Ida was surprised about. Neither of them knew much more than the other so they couldn't claim superiority and apart from a few minor snaps at each other, had remained relatively calm, drinking cups of tea while they tried to work it all out.

They supposed it made sense that she might have hidden her past, gypsies were far from popular even now, but it was hard to see their mother as someone who would have been ashamed –

shamelessness had always been one of her dominant traits.

"It's odd she ended up with Dad isn't it," said Alice. "Well, she didn't wind up with him in the end, but you know. He's so kind... and simple. That sounds bad. Straightforward."

"You've gone for someone like Dad," said Ida.

"Thanks," Alice said, annoyed. "What, simple?"

"No, Tom is nice. He's really nice. But he suits you. You're not Mum."

They sat in silence for a few moments.

"Elliot's not good for you, you know," Alice said.

"Piss off," Ida said.

"Sorry."

"No, I mean... I'm sorry," Ida said, more quietly. "I do know. A bit. But who else would put up with me?"

Alice didn't reply and they both laughed.

"I've been thinking, about everything. Do you think she was Ida, from the play?" Ida asked. "Not literally, of course. But you know, her hair, and how cruel she could be. And now with the Irish stuff too."

"Perhaps," said Alice. "I always kind of thought it was a version of her. And us... we were both the poor, drowned sister."

"Even me?" asked Ida, surprised. "But I've got her name!"

"You especially," said Alice.

By the time they heard the Mini outside it was nearly midnight, but both women were wide awake from the combination of caffeine, speculation, and the beginnings of shared indignation that the men had stayed out so late.

At the sound of the car they both sat upright. They heard the men's footsteps as they stumbled up the garden steps and Tom fumbled with the spare key.

"Oh God, they're completely wankered aren't they," Alice said, looking very much like she was close to tears.

"It'll be okay," said Ida, standing up and touching Alice on the head. "You stay here."

In the hall the two men were doubled over with laughter, the front door still open.

Without smiling Ida walked past them and slammed it shut.

"Will you two sort it the fuck out?" Ida whispered. "Tom, your fucking girlfriend's lost her mother and she needs you to not be a pissed twat."

"I'm really sorry. He made me," Tom mumbled, straightening up. "He gave me shots."

She turned to Elliot. He didn't look too drunk – he was used to drinking a lot. "You could have looked after him Elliot, he's obviously a lightweight." She couldn't keep the anger out of her voice as she spoke.

"You're right sweet pea," said Elliot, talking as though Tom couldn't hear him. "But he was buying the drinks." He tapped Ida on the nose. "Anyway, don't be arsey with me. I'm sick of your arseyness – you're a bloody hypocrite and a drama queen."

"Oh fuck off. Go and sleep in my room, together, go on." She walked to the study door and opened it. "You can puke on each other. Get yourselves in there. I'll sleep in bed with my sister. And Elliot, get him some water."

She turned to see Alice in the doorway, tears rolling down her face, but she was smiling as well.

"You look almost as mental as me," Ida said. "Did I do the right thing, making them sleep in there?"

"Yes," said Alice. "It would be nice to be with you. And he probably will be sick you know."

Ida walked towards her and hugged her. "We'll be alright, Ally." She heard her mother's voice as she stroked Alice's face. She smelled different, cleaner, but her hair felt the same as it had done when they were young.

"I know," said Alice. Her words were muffled against Ida's jumper.

"Go upstairs and put your pyjamas on, I'll make us a medicinal hot toddy or we'll never get to fucking sleep."

"Yes please," said Alice. "Sorry about all the snot."

They lay together looking up at the ceiling. Hundreds of glow-in-the-dark stars were still stuck up there, Ida had loved those. She wished she had some in the flat.

She was trying to count them but it wasn't working. "I can't sleep," she said.

"Me neither. Concentrate on your breathing," said Alice. "It helps."

"I'll laugh."

"No seriously. I can guide you through some meditation."

"Ha. What are you? A hippy now?" Ida asked.

"No." She paused. "I was in a treatment centre, for my eating. Or my lack of eating. It was a holistic one Terri found. Dad paid."

"Fuck."

"Yeah. I'm better now, mostly. Meditation helps. We're so full of things, you and me. Problems and thoughts and crap. I suppose that's why I starved myself, to feel empty for a bit. And you... I remember why you left, you know. Meditation can make you feel empty. In a good way."

Ida turned towards her sister and tried to make out her profile in the dark. "That sounds horrible. I don't want to be empty."

"Are you sure?" Alice asked. "You seem like you do."

Chapter twenty-three

~ 1984 ~

The kitchen was boiling and sweat was dripping down Ida's arms into the scalding water. She didn't normally show her arms in public, they were scarred and embarrassing, but there wasn't much choice when she was washing up. The chefs weren't interested in her anyway, or at least not the way she looked. They were always stoned or drunk, and now Ray stood humming reggae and staring into space, his dreadlocks swinging as he plated up side salads, not fully aware of where he was let alone Ida standing a few feet away from him.

She'd been doing split shifts, so desperate to get away from the house that even the noise and heat of the pub was better than home. A teacher had 'become concerned' and Alice was staying with their father and Terri. Bridie hadn't taken it well, the intrusion more than anything, but she was too weak to protest. They'd asked Ida to stay too but she knew they didn't mean it. If she went they'd have to employ a nurse or someone for Bridie, and besides that, Ida scared them these days with her pierced nose, home-shorn hair and cut-up arms. Despite having no children of her own Terri prided herself on being a parenting expert and had coached her niece through a teenage pregnancy. But this was something else. What did you do with a fifteen-year-old girl who broke windows, cut herself to pieces, drunk like a sailor and got in endless fights? Bryan talked about reform school and Ida laughed. If they even existed any more she wondered how they thought they'd make her attend.

Jeff, the landlord, walked past. He patted Ida on the arse out of habit rather than affection, and pinned a pink neon notice about the Christmas party on the board near the window.

"Get your tits out again this year I hope," he said.

Ida laughed. She had only recently started at the pub, one shift a week, when they'd held the party the year before. No one had minded that she was fourteen, and had whooped encouragingly when she'd taken off her top.

"If you get me pissed enough maybe you'll be lucky," she said.

There was still a month to Christmas. The last year had been a long one and Bridie was meant to be dead already. It was taking forever. She lay on the sofa most days, watching daytime television and crying at adverts. Ida hated the crying. Her mother had always been so fierce. The crying was one of the very worst bits. And whatever Bridie cried at – *Coronation Street*, the news, *West Side Story* – Ida knew that really, sickeningly, she was crying for herself. And no one came round anymore. Ever since Ida's last birthday when Bridie had passed out in the hall, the few people that they knew had stayed away. Peter phoned them up lots, but he was working usually, in 'all star' cruise ship shows or in seaside farces in places like Margate. Ida had always thought she hated having guests, but life was pretty boring without them.

Ida quite enjoyed washing up. The repetition was comforting and the hot water helped to keep her awake on the longest shifts. A few times she had cut herself accidentally on broken glass or knives and now, during especially slow shifts, she would slice herself on purpose, glorious gashes she wouldn't be able to manage with the razors and blunt knives she had access to at home. Sometimes when she did it she'd go for a break, get sympathy from the chef and patch it up with a roll of sticking plaster. Other times she'd leave it to mix with the washing up water. She liked knowing that despite looking clean the plates and cups were spotted with her blood.

She had some friends at the pub, Tina and Dee, rough girls with bad teeth. Although she liked them she knew she was different around them. Her shoulders would get tense when they went down to the woods to get pissed; however much she drunk she couldn't relax. Their jokes weren't funny and sometimes they were racist, but she forced herself to laugh. And she knew she spoke differently. Not that they thought she was posh, no one ever did these days.

Once she'd bumped into Tina after picking Alice up from school and Tina had raised her eyebrows, assuming Ida was babysitting some 'rich bitch'. Even her name didn't attract much attention among this group. It was an interesting fact to introduce her with, but that was about it. When people asked if she was loaded she'd explain her mother had spent it on drink. They were the kind of people who understood it was entirely possible to spend a fortune on drink.

Despite her efforts to fit in she knew she still didn't. And after Rachel Black had shagged Tina's boyfriend, and Ida had broken Rachel's arm in a fight, Tina and Dee had looked at her with barely hidden fear. No one called the police, no one would have done. Rachel told her mother she'd fallen off her bike and now the local kids crossed the road when they saw Ida. It made little difference to her – she'd never been friends with them anyway and at least they no longer spat.

The bad thing about washing up was the space it left to think. Sometimes it was good, if she could manage to daydream, had come up with the start of a poem or had an idea for something she'd like to paint. But sometimes, if Bridie had been especially annoying or the time Ida's kind of boyfriend Danny got off with Sheila from the bong shop, then the shift could be almost unbearable.

Mostly she thought about Annie, about moving with her to Hollywood, about living in a house in Beverley Hills with a whole load of puppies they'd rescued. They'd have dinner parties for other local stars, but mainly they'd stay in bed, listening to music and smoking an endless supply of weed. Ida would be thin by then, properly thin. She'd wear painting smocks and Annie would be glamorous, with camisoles and kitten heels. And the main thing was that they'd never, ever leave – everything that they needed would get sent to them and nothing bad could ever happen.

Jeff started bringing in the ashtrays and Ida knew it was almost the end of the shift. There was a short stack of plates left and after that the floor to wash. But it was nearly over.

"Staying for the lock-in?" Tina asked.

Her white breasts were almost popping out of her shiny blouse. She was trying to get more tips to save for an ounce of hash and some decent scales to weigh it out with.

"Of course," Ida said. She would stay for the lock-in. There was always the chance her mother would be dead when she returned and she couldn't possibly face that sober.

They shifted the worst of the regulars, the ones most likely to piss themselves and need a taxi home, and Jeff bolted the door. They were left with a mix of locals and staff, middle-aged men mainly and some of their girlfriends and wives.

Jeff emptied the tips jar onto the bar and counted it out. They would have to split it with Ray but the girls didn't mind – Ray was thick as shit but he gave them hash and mix-tapes he'd made. They had nearly three quid each, enough for a couple of pints, and the men would be sure to buy them more. Tina always did the best for tips, she was the one everyone fancied, but she was pretty nice about sharing.

Jeff was in a good mood, smiley and red faced, and he went behind the sticky bar and lined up a long row of vodka shots.

"Ladies first," he said.

They were meant to do as many as they could, each starting at one end and meeting in the middle.

Tina rubbed her hands together. "You don't know what you've let yourself in for with us two Jeff."

Ida stood at one end of the bar and took some deep breaths. She had never been good with spirits and normally mixed them with anything else she had to hand. But she couldn't fail in front of all these men. She imagined herself spitting one over the bar, or even worse, being sick. Behind them the men were clapping and chanting.

"Ti-na, Ti-na, Big Bird, Big Bird..."

The night Big Bird puked on her tits. She could imagine the

stories. She tried to pretend Annie's life was at stake.

"COMMENCE!" screamed Jeff.

Ida picked up the first glass. She pretended she was swallowing a sword and let her throat open up. The first one went down, burning, but okay. She did the same with the second, the third and the fourth, and then, a touch on the bum from Mick or Phil, and she lost her nerve, took the fifth into her mouth and held it there, so scared she would puke. *Jesus, Mary and Joseph,* she prayed and gulped it down, retching, holding her hand up to her mouth to hide the worst of it. A deep breath and she managed a sixth. The end.

"Well, that's six each girls. Very well done," said Jeff.

Tina staggered and everyone roared, including Ida, relieved it wasn't her who was making a twat of herself.

"Don't get excited gentlemen," shrieked Tina. "I just lost my balance. Won't be falling on my back quite yet."

Everyone laughed like it was the funniest thing ever. Ida felt that she was far away, seeing them through a screen, and she sat on the nearest chair as inconspicuously as she could.

Ida knew they were making a lot of noise when they got back. It was pitch black and she kept dropping her keys before she finally unlocked the door. It swung open and she fell through it onto the floor. Ray hauled her up with difficulty. There was no shout of annoyance or even acknowledgement from Bridie.

Despite being terribly drunk, Ray started shivering. "Man, it's colder in here that it was outside, I swear," he said. "We should get up to your room."

"It's always freezing. Welcome to the tomb of the unknown writer," Ida shouted.

Ray chattered on as they walked up the stairs, mainly about the temperature. "This fuck-off fancy house and you ain't got any heating?"

"We've got heating but it's broken down. Come on." She

opened the door to her bedroom and pulled him inside, leaning down to turn on the light.

"This is a shit tip!" he said, sounding genuinely astonished. "You got rats?"

Ida looked around. No one ever came to her room, well Danny, sometimes, but he was pretty much homeless so not inclined to complaining.

It was true the carpet was completely covered with old plates and tissues, mouldy cups and magazines. But the rest of it was nice she thought – the pictures on the walls and the throw over her bunk beds. And you could smoke in there, do whatever you wanted, which she knew made it better than most girls' rooms.

There was a scuttling noise under her desk and Ray stepped backwards.

"You've got rats, I fucking KNEW it."

"They're mice, you can't have rats and mice at the same time. The man from the council said. Mice are nice. People keep mice as pets."

"Fucking hell."

"I've got bunks anyway, see? You won't have to put your precious feet on the floor. No mice will be able to nibble your delicate toes."

He jumped onto the bed and took his tin out of his pocket. "I'll start skinning up, you find us some tunes and some glasses in this bloody hell-hole, then we'll be set."

Ida put on her tape player. It was a brown Fisher Price one she'd had since she was little and Ray shook his head, laughing. She put on a compilation he'd made her, one she didn't much like, but she knew it would shut him up. Then she found two mugs, wiped the mould out of them with the corner of a towel and hopped up next to him, filling them both with rum.

"To health, wealth and incredible happiness," she said, and they both downed the lot in three huge glugs. Then they threw the mugs off the bed, lay back and began to smoke.

"You're so near the ceiling up here – do you ever freak out?"

"Nope."

"You tried sleeping on the bottom?"

"No, never. I wanted them so I'd be up high. My sister's slept on the bottom, a couple of times when she's been scared."

"You had them since you were little?"

"I got them earlier this year."

He turned to face her and kissed her nose. "Big Bird, you crack me up."

They started kissing properly, Ray propping the joint on the edge of the bed, and soon his hands were down her jeans. *Dreadlock Holiday* came on and Ida had to stop herself laughing.

"You okay?" he asked.

"Fine. I'm going to get some water. Want anything?"

"Water, yeah. And, you got any cake? Like... Victoria sponge?"

"Ha. I sincerely doubt it but I'll see what I can do."

She jumped off the bed, buttoned her flies and left the room. She stood just outside for a few seconds so her eyes could adjust to the dark. From her room she could hear Ray humming and smiled. Ray was nice. He was a twat, but a kind twat. If she could overcome him being a moron maybe something more could come of it. He made her feel safe at least.

She turned to walk down the stairs and saw that her mother's bedroom door was ajar, the dim light of her low-wattage lamp showing through the foot-wide gap. She stopped, trying to still her breath so she could hear. A car went by outside and from her room there was the regular thud of the music and Ray tapping his thigh. But from Bridie's room there was nothing, not her normal crackling breath, nor the usual sound of the television. She was probably asleep.

Ida began to walk past and tried to keep her gaze on her floor. But it was no use. With a glance she saw a pale, waxy arm, sprawled on the bedroom carpet at an unnatural angle. She looked back down at her feet, took a deep breath and kept walking. At the bottom of the stairs she stood still and hugged herself, hard.

She entered the kitchen and pulled the cord for the light. It flickered on and off and Ida could see her mother on the table, then not, standing by the fridge, then not – then lying on the floor, all her limbs broken and bent. The light came on properly, buzzing and yellow and Ida took two glasses from the sideboard, rinsed them out and filled them up. She was shivering.

At the back of the fridge was a two-week-old slice of sponge cake Alice had brought home from a party, solid as a brick, still in a pink paper bag. She couldn't believe they actually had cake. She put it under her arm, picked up the two glasses of water, and pulled the light cord with her teeth.

She went back up the stairs half facing the wall, all the while managing to avoid looking towards her mother's bedroom.

The tape player was crackling, it was the end of the side, and Ray lay snoring quietly on her bed. She put down the water and the cake, and climbed up next to him, pulling his arms around her waist and his body towards hers.

"Fucking hell, Big Bird, you're like an ice cube," he mumbled and kissed her ear. She willed herself to sleep.

A beam of light was hitting her face and she thought that she might be dead. She inhaled violently, like someone who had been underwater for too long, and struggled to open her eyes. The light was so strong and so blue-white that she knew it was a very cold day.

She felt someone stir and then draw closer to her, a heavy leg trapping both of hers, the prod of a hard-on against her arse. She concentrated on her breath – in, out, in, out – as she began to remember who she was in bed with and why she felt like someone was dead.

It was Ray next to her, she remembered that now, and he began to kiss her. She didn't look at him although she knew what she would see if she did. He probably hadn't even opened his eyes and his kisses were dry on her neck, an attempt at politeness before he'd begin to undo her jeans. She gulped again, loudly and spontaneously, a high-pitched intake of breath. The kisses stopped.

"You got hiccups?" Ray asked sleepily, squeezing her hip.

Ida said nothing but lay still. The light on her face was warm. She wished he'd fuck off and leave her there alone. She knew she could stay still, lie there forever like someone from Pompeii. She cleared her throat.

"Haven't you got work?" she asked, her voice thin.

"Shit, fuck, Jeff's going to blow his top." He clambered over her roughly, his full weight on her calves as he hopped off the bed. As he scanned the room, picking things up and replacing them, he muttered to himself about his skins, patting his trousers to check for his keys. He kissed her on the forehead, his musty dreadlocks swinging and hitting her face as he turned.

"See you later, you're in later right? Okay, bye."

Ida heard him run down the stairs. She would make herself sleep, she knew she could do it – you just had to keep breathing so slowly you could fool someone you'd died. She let each muscle relax in turn and noticed everything she could feel – the mattress on her arm, the sun on her eyelids, the uncomfortable place where the fly of her jeans dug into her stomach – and prayed to Our Lady to be able to stay like that forever.

At some point she found herself shivering in the darkness, her jeans wet and tight against her skin. She didn't remember needing the loo and was pleased that her body had done as she'd told it – stayed asleep for as long as possible, whatever nature threw at it. But the cold was a problem. She undid her flies and threw her knickers and jeans onto the floor, drying her legs with the duvet, turning it over and pulling it round her. No one could make her leave the bed and there was comfort in that. Each small thing was a comfort and she appreciated every bit of her room. She lay under her damp duvet, breathing slowly for what seemed like hours, the stillness broken by the occasional ring of the phone downstairs, or a noisy sports car outside, until she again managed to fall asleep.

At first she thought an alarm had gone off in a nearby house and was tempted to ignore it and stay asleep. It was only when it came again, loud, desperate and very near, that she knew it was someone screaming. Without quite knowing why she hit herself on the head. There was the sound of someone walking down the stairs, then a car door slamming and more footsteps – two sets of footsteps – coming back up. She hit herself again as hard as she could. She wished she had a hat pin that she could use to pierce her skull – the way she had once seen Bridie kill a pink and cheeping baby bird that had fallen out of its nest.

There were loud noises from her mother's room, shouting, and the sound of her being dragged and lifted perhaps, maybe onto the bed. Ida sat up. She was suddenly desperate to barricade herself in the room and she jumped off the bed. With a sweep of her arm she cleared the top of her chest of drawers and somehow hauled it over tapes and clothes towards the door. With a final push she managed to angle it under the door handle, the best attempt she could make at shutting herself in. She heard sirens in the distance and then her father's voice near her door. "Ida, Ida?"

"She must be at work, Bryan," Terri said calmly.

Ida could imagine her stepmother's manicured hand on her father's arm, reassuring and sensible as he panicked about his beloved ex-wife.

The door handle turned as he tried get inside.

Ida stepped back onto a cassette case, which broke with a crack.

"I can hear someone's in there," he said to Terri, rattling the handle. "Love, are you in there? Are you okay? Your mother's been taken ill. Alice found her when she came home."

"I'll go back in with Bridie," Terri said.

The sirens grew louder. Ida heard muttering and breaths through the door, as though her father's head was resting against it. "Darling, sweetheart... whatever's happened, whatever you've done, it will be okay," Bryan whispered. Ida was amazed that he knew that she had wanted this and she had let it happen.

She heard the ambulance pull into the drive and the doors slam. Her father tapped the door as if reassuring it, and she heard him walk downstairs.

Before they left, Terri got the ambulance men to try Ida's room again, concerned that she may have died or be dying, either of grief or booze. Ida knew they'd have tools to get in if they wanted to so she put on a pair of joggers, pulled away the chest of drawers and opened the door to face them.

"Okay, I'm here. I've been asleep," she said in a flat voice, aware that she was convincing nobody. Her father's relieved face peered round a paramedic's yellow jacket.

"Thank God." Bryan reached out to touch her but she didn't touch him back. "Darling, your mother's ill."

"Is she dead?" Ida asked matter-of-factly. She had no idea why she was behaving so oddly, her voice hard and strong like a bad actress playing a bully in *Grange Hill*.

"No, she's not well though," the paramedic said. He turned to her father. "Mr Irons, we need to leave."

Bryan stepped forwards to hug her.

"We won't be long. It will all be okay. Look after your sister? She's downstairs watching children's programmes."

Ida began to pack her things in the green leather PE bag she hadn't used for years. She looked for knickers under dirty plates and managed to find three pairs. She had no idea how long they'd be. If her mother died, and she was pretty sure she would soon, then she supposed there wouldn't be much reason for them to stay at the hospital.

They'd be able to tell Ida had left her there, they could tell stuff like that on *Columbo*, and the pub would be sure to say she hadn't been in. That was a mistake right there, staying away from work. She should have gone in, blushing about the night before. Not only had she done herself out of an alibi she'd probably got the sack, properly this time. She'd need to find another job.

Of course she could not have spotted her mother, it would be difficult to prove that she had, but the fact of the matter was she was meant to be watching Bridie, keeping a close eye on her, and she evidently hadn't been. She couldn't face the questions, and anyway she'd had it, she'd bloody had it. She wanted to be left in peace to lie in bed, any bed would do.

She gave up looking for clothes and picked up her fags instead. She lit one and looked out of the window at the white sky. Nothing mattered, she realised that now. And no one could touch her. This was a new type of magic, invincible magic, every part of her felt powerful and alive. She wondered what she would do and where she would go. From her bottom drawer she got her post office savings book, Annie's address from a letter and a bottle of whisky and threw them in the bag.

Fuck everything, all her posters and t-shirts – she didn't need anything. She could hear noise from the sitting room as she walked downstairs and saw her sister in front of the television, her hand outstretched, touching the screen like a much younger child. As she turned Ida saw her face was blotchy from crying and her top lip was shiny with snot. Her hair, always messy, was static round her head.

"Is she going to be okay?" Alice asked quietly.

"I don't know. I'm sorry that you found her. I bet she looked gross. You should know, I think you should know, that I left her there on purpose."

Alice began to cry again almost silently. She sat on her hands. Behind her Morph turned into a ball and then back into himself again.

"It's like ill animals, you know, like Ma always taught us. She wanted to die. I thought she should die. She's going to anyway sooner or later. Anyway. I'm sorry I suppose, I am. You should pray for me." She turned away and then back again. "You know, I'd take you with me, I honestly think I would, but I know they'd never let me keep you. I think you're a bit of a nerd but I know I could sort you out. It'll be okay now, you'll be able to live with Dad or whatever. Look I have to go." She blew a kiss and waved. "Bye. Chin up. Hope you'll be okay. You will be. We're magic, you know that? Right."

Ida walked towards the front door, opened it and stepped outside. She was freezing in just a t-shirt but she felt kind of amazing and she didn't look back as she jogged down the steps and away from the house.

Chapter twenty-four

~ 1999 ~

Ida could feel the shape of her sister, her hip bones and tiny breasts, while her thin arm was draped over Ida's middle, resting on her rounded stomach. It felt good to be like this, soft and safe – she hadn't been in bed with someone in a non-sexual way for a very long time indeed. Although her bunk beds were long gone it was nice to be back in her old room, it did still feel like her room even if it looked nothing like it.

Alice was breathing heavily, her nose blocked up from crying, but Ida realised there was another noise in the room, another set of breaths. She opened her eyes and in front of the window, sitting on the chair by the desk, was a tall, grey-haired man holding two bunches of yellow freesias and smiling. His eyes were so kind and so unbelievably sad.

Ida gasped with joy, held out her hand and Peter clutched it.

"Princess of Bournemouth. I had to spend some time looking at you both, to get acclimatized. And sorry if you're fond of them but the men downstairs were being bloody boring. What the hell happened to your lovely hair?"

"Hacked it off. You know I'm still a nut."

"Bah! You love the drama like your ma. And look at Alice. Still looks like something from a Disney cartoon."

"Still behaves like it too," Ida said, sitting up.

Alice stirred next to her and opened her eyes. "What time is it?" she asked in a panicky voice, still more asleep than awake.

"Ten thirty, sweetheart," Peter said, standing up and leaning down to kiss them both.

"Uncle Peter," Alice said. "I'm so sorry, I meant to wake up in time, I knew you were coming."

"Stop it! Don't get your knickers in a twist." He sat back down on the chair. "You poor, funny girls. I'm here to look after you now, don't you worry about a thing. I told them to make you both coffee but neither of your men seem to have a clue how to work the machine. I'm sure they'll get there in the end. Now, tell me everything – especially the horrible bits. Then we can move on to all the nice stuff. Well, there might not be much nice stuff at the moment, but we can always make it up. And I've got lots to tell you. It'll be like intensive rehab. People pay a fortune for this type of thing."

Peter took the coffee when Tom eventually brought it up on a tray but wouldn't let the men in, or the women get out of bed.

Alice told them how she'd met Tom – they both went to the same gym – and about her flat in West Dulwich, her cat – Daisy – and her job in the bank. She worked in personnel and it took her half an hour to explain to Ida what that actually meant. In Ida's world people in banks sat behind glass in Barclays in Westbourne. The rest of it – 'the system' – was as strange and mysterious as angels or the Internet.

Ida spoke about her life in London, the hundreds of places she'd lived, the times she'd hitched round Europe. She tried to make it all sound as good as she could, but there was no fooling Peter.

"Have you been in hospital again? I heard you had been."

"Not really." Ida bit her nails.

"She has, you have. You had that hospital band on when you first arrived," said Alice.

"My tonsils," said Ida, trying to make a joke.

"Bloody hell, darling, we're all friends here. You think we're going to be shocked. What was it? Madness? Abortion? Suicide attempt?"

"All three." Ida laughed but Alice sighed. "Well I've been in a few times. There's been madness – well, depression – and drinking too much. And I was there for a stomach ulcer before I came down here."

"Ow," said Peter.

"Yes. It hurt. Nothing major though."

"You shouldn't be drinking then, should you? Anything at all," Alice said.

"No you shouldn't you naughty girl," said Peter. "That man downstairs, the blonde smart-arsed one, was he around for all this? Is he looking after you?"

"He's got his own problems."

"I bet he has," said Peter. "It seems like there's lots of work to be done here."

"Can't you move in?" asked Alice.

"Too late for that I'm afraid, you two are grown-ups now. But I'll help you as best I can. And you know what? I prayed to St Sharon of Cucumber Sandwiches, and she told me that you're both going be absolutely fine. And St Sharon is known for her accuracy as well as her delicious lunches – "

"There's something else we should talk to you about," Ida said seriously, cutting him off. She reached down to the pocket of her trousers, pulled out the certificate of baptism and handed it to him.

He unfolded it and turned towards the window.

"You didn't know?" asked Alice.

He paused. "Not exactly."

He had never been a particularly good actor and, from the expression on his face, Ida was pretty sure he'd at least known some of it.

He saw her looking and seemed to realise he couldn't pull off a total lie.

"I mean there were lots of things that didn't quite add up," he said. "When we met in rep she didn't know things, how to behave. She'd kill me for saying it. We went to Lyons once for tea and she asked for a slice of the chocolate gateaux – but pronounced it gatoocks."

"Really?" Alice laughed.

"And I had to show her about her knives and forks, stuff like that. And stop her from wearing so much slap."

"Well I never," said Alice.

"You sound about eighty," said Peter.

"I feel it."

"If you're eighty, then I'm at least a hundred," said Ida.

Peter laughed, but his jaw and eyes were tense. There was more to it than he'd said, Ida knew there was. She wouldn't push him to tell her. Not yet.

At two they went downstairs and into the sitting room for lunch. Ida was worried Elliot would be angry but instead he looked miserable, sitting on the sofa watching a James Stewart film, his knees pulled up to his chest, while Tom tidied up.

"Ida, Alice, I'm sorry – we're sorry – for getting drunk and being twats," Tom said as soon as he saw them.

Elliot didn't even look in their direction.

"That's okay," said Ida. "Worse things happen at sea."

Peter wouldn't let the sisters do anything around the house and even persuaded Elliot to help Tom wash up.

"People keep cancelling," said Alice, "and even those who've said they'll try to come; I know most of them won't. The bigger the bunch of flowers they've sent the less likely they'll turn up I reckon. Some people from the church should come at least. She'd been going to Mass again, for the last few years. The old ladies should come, they love an excuse to get their mantillas out. Some of them visited her recently, bought her soup and prayed with her."

"Really? Did they tell her to stop drinking?" Ida asked.

"It was too late by then. And mostly they're practical old birds. That Spanish lady, Isabel, the one with the moustache? Well her husband died of 'thirst' too, she told Ma. Anyway, I've asked them to cater for forty. Not that anyone's going to eat."

"We'll be eating egg sandwiches for bloody weeks. Well, I will – you don't eat eggs."

"That woman you used to work for, after you left home, Mary?

She came a few times too. Look..."

Alice walked over to the mantelpiece and handed Ida a card.

So sorry for your loss. We'll pray for you all.
Love to you girls,
Mary and Willie xxx

"I thought she hated me," Ida said. "I just left you know, walked out of the shop one day."

"She probably doesn't remember," Alice said, putting back the card, "and if she does, well it was bloody years ago. It's weird, you think you're so powerful, like all the stuff you do ruins people's lives. But they just get on with it, you know? It's just you who suffers, really."

Peter appeared in the doorway. "Darling girls, I'm sick of being stuck in the house. Shall we go for a walk to the beach, down through the chine?" He stepped towards them and whispered, "Just us three. We can blow a kiss out to sea, to your ma."

"Ida doesn't like the beach," said Alice.

"It'll be okay," said Ida, standing up.

"But not through the chine," Alice said.

"No, it's okay. I've got you to protect me from everything Uncle Peter. Have you always done that? Blown a kiss for the dead? Ma did it too."

"I think it started when we were in rep," he said, "blew a kiss to Jesus before we went on. One for your ma," he blew a kiss towards the window and the girls copied him, "and one for Jesus." He blew one towards the ceiling and the sisters did the same.

Chapter twenty-five

~ 1984 ~

Ida put the things from the van into piles round the dark, dusty shop while Mary sat on a stool in the corner, a roll-up stuck between her orange-stained fingers as she read through the list.

"Chess set – wooden, box of photographs, bed pan, five men's waistcoats, incomplete *Encyclopaedia Britannica*." She coughed, violently, then looked at Ida. "No, separate the waistcoats too, remember what I said."

Ida immediately complied. Mary was the size of a ten year old, but the deep wrinkles the fags had created gave her the look of an ancient sage, her hooded eyes wise and unshockable beneath her dyed black bob; the white roots at her scalp at least three inches long. Round her shoulders hung a moth-eaten ocelot coat.

How could she have possibly forgotten what Mary had told her? 'You can't put all the things together that came from one person else they'll come back down from where they've gone, God rest their souls.' That's what she'd said. Ida knew exactly what she meant. It was so easy to conjure someone up from their possessions. It was easy to conjure someone up by simply looking at the list Ida had to make when they brought stuff out of a house. Mary insisted on the lists. Ida had to admit Mary was right not to trust her; at least three times a day she noticed some strange thing she'd love to slip under her holey jumper and take back to the flat.

Then, when everything had been mixed up all over the shop – so the person was no longer real, just a collection of junk – they would burn the list out the back, both the women crossing themselves, and Willie too if he was there.

They'd wanted a man for the job, but Willie had seen Ida lifting barrels when he drank in the pub, and two weeks before, when she'd left (after the Ray evening that she tried hard never to think about) he'd bumped into her in town and offered her a trial shift on the spot. Ida was very grateful. She enjoyed it here, they didn't mind if she wore the same smelly clothes every day. It wasn't far from the bedsit either – a short walk down Ashley Road and she was there. And although she hand't yet, she'd promised she would pay Tina half of the rent too.

Willie hadn't only employed her because she was strong. Mary remembered seeing little Ida at Mass years before, and she suspected a Catholic girl would be more prone to understanding her superstitions and the careful way it all had to be done. She was right, Ida did understand, and even added in some superstitions of her own: photographs must be placed face down, clocks must be kept stopped, and a secret kiss had to be blown towards the sky for each dead person whose stuff they picked up.

The special way they did things, the rules and order, made her feel safe. And although Mary was hard as nails, she did odd, kind things, like bring Ida left over shepherd's pie from her dinner the night before.

Mary carried on. "One pair brown brogues, *Sound of Music* LP, collection of local newspapers, wedding certificate, Roberts radio, tweed flat cap." She stopped, looked at the floor and crossed herself. The old men got her the worst, Ida knew, and the fact that it was nearly Christmas made her even more upset.

Ida placed the cap near the window and looked around her. She'd done a good job, his things were indistinguishable from the others, and everything looked dusty and ancient and equally settled in.

Now they would burn the list.

Chapter twenty-six

~ 1999 ~

Ida hadn't been to the chine for years and she started sweating as they turned the corner into the woods.

They'd loved it when they were little, the clear, shallow river leading down to the water, the tall cliffs either side of them, pine trees everywhere and the ground so covered in leaves it didn't matter if you fell off a branch or skidded on your bike.

She'd forgotten the smell of pine and mulch and, as you got nearer to the beach, of salt and seaweed.

And then there were the birds, the bloody huge, scary birds in the sky ahead of them.

The sea came into view and they crossed the road, walked past the tatty café and onto the promenade. Peter put his arms round them both. They stood still, in silence, letting cyclists swerve to avoid them, and staring out at the sea. At the water's edge a Yorkshire terrier ran in circles, uselessly snapping at the gulls.

Alice released herself from Peter's grasp. The wind was blowing her hair into her eyes and she held it back with her hand. "I didn't think I'd miss her you know, I only wanted it to end. But sometimes I really do."

Peter kissed Alice on the cheek. "Of course. Do you Ida?"

She hesitated.

"No. Really I don't. They say you will, don't they, when a parent dies, even if you bloody hate them. But I feel like she died so long ago. I mean, I suppose if I'm honest, I missed her a bit when I first left home. It was miserable living in that bedsit."

Alice's mouth twitched and Ida knew she was thinking about a time, years before, when Ida had almost died. Neither of them ever mentioned it. "I wonder if Dad misses her," said Alice.

"Yes," said Ida. "He loved her."

"We all loved her," said Peter.

"Let's walk on the beach," said Alice.

They jumped down onto the sand.

"We used to come down here when we were little," Alice said.

Ida took a step back.

"You must have done, all summer long I bet," said Peter.

"Not much in the summer," said Alice. "Ma didn't like the sun that much, or the trippers, neither did we. We'd come in the mornings, normally, before school."

"Don't," said Ida.

Alice laughed and turned towards her. "Ida tried to kill me once down here."

"Fuck off Alice, please," said Ida. She knew she should let it go, brave it out, but she couldn't, not with Peter listening.

"She did, she pushed me under the waves. It was after her 'big scene.'"

"Fuck off. It was years ago and you're exaggerating wildly."

"You two are like children," Peter said, sounding flustered but trying to brush it off as a joke. "Look at that seagull, he's flying backwards. The wind's pushing him."

The two women pretended to be interested but Ida couldn't concentrate. She was furious. She wanted to leave the beach, to go back to London, to lie in her dirty bed for the next two days and be bothered by no one. Of all the times to bring it up – they'd been kids when that had happened.

"You see she's never made a mistake in her life, Peter," Ida said as cheerfully as she could, aware that she sounded slightly manic. "She's perfect, flawless, super-fucking-human – she doesn't even have periods, just leaks strawberry sauce once a month. She fucking shits chocolate ice cream."

"Excellent comeback," Alice said, "you really are vile". She was laughing brightly but Ida could tell she was angry as well. She pretended to be so nice, so squeaky clean, when actually, deep down, there was a bitter, vengeful cow, the very sprit of their mother, disguised as a vegan virgin.

"Come on you two, you're both bloody mad." He took their hands and led them back to the steps. Alice had stopped laughing. She didn't want to be mad.

"Embrace it Alice, it's in your genes," Ida said, patting her frowning sister on the head as she climbed back up the steps.

"As much as I loved her, your mother has a lot to answer for," said Peter.

The men had all fallen asleep on the sofa. Alice kissed Tom on the forehead to wake him up.

"Come on Tommy. We need to go and register the death," she said.

Elliot lay snoring and Ida didn't disturb him. She would leave them all to it. The second best thing to bed was a bath; at least you could lock the bathroom door.

Even over the rushing water she could hear voices below and knew Alice would be moaning about how unhelpful Ida was, biting her lip and sighing and getting plenty of sympathy. She sat on the loo seat, chewing her nails, until she heard footsteps coming up the stairs. She turned off the taps.

"Sweet pea." It was Elliot. "Can I come in? I feel like I haven't seen you for the last couple of days."

Ida unlocked the door and he stepped inside. He looked young and sleepy, his hair sticking up in tufts, and she kissed him on the eyelids. It was hot – the extractor fan had broken years ago – and he pushed her against the damp wall.

"I've missed you. I can't believe you made me sleep in bed with that man. His boner was poking into my back this morning. It was wonky like his nose," he said.

Ida felt for his crotch. "You twat," she said and began to rub it playfully.

"Don't you want to talk?" he asked, laughing and pushing his hand into her knickers. He starting kissing her neck, then pulled down her t-shirt and kissed her cleavage, and she began to undo his flies. She lifted her hand to his chin and guided his head back up towards hers, looking him straight in the eye.

"You wouldn't mind whatever I did, would you? If I was a murderer or an embezzler or had sex with dogs."

He laughed. "I think I'd like you more."

"I'm serious. There are things I've never told you. You know, I tried to kill Alice – when we were little."

He guffawed. "Ha! Why didn't you do it? I'd like to kill her now."

"I'm serious! Really, I tried to drown her on the beach," she said, annoyed. There were two things she'd never told him and this was one of them. Now, out loud, she knew it sounded pathetic. But it was true. She had wanted her dead.

"I know you're serious. So am I. It wouldn't matter whatever you did." He wasn't laughing now and she knew he really meant it. He put his mouth to her ear. "That's love isn't it? I don't need to say it all the time for it to be true." He bit her earlobe and pushed his hand further into her pants. She gasped. "And the same goes for you?" he asked.

She nodded and fumbled with the rest of the buttons on his fly. He pushed aside her knickers, lifted her leg over the crook of his elbow and pushed himself into her. Slowly, he ground the small of her back against the hard tiles.

There were footsteps then noises outside the door – Alice and Tom getting ready to go to the registrars' – and Ida pushed her mouth into Elliot's shoulder to stop herself making a sound. He pressed his lips to her cheek then pulled away, panting.

"Sorry."

"What for? I needed that. I get bored when it goes on too long."

She pushed him away from her, pulled her t-shirt over her head and unhooked her bra. He stood watching her, red faced still, his trousers round his ankles.

"Want to get in with me or sit on the loo?" she asked.

"Get in. I probably stink. God knows if we'll fit. At least we can give it a go."

They lay in the bath for over an hour while she told Elliot everything. He pretended to listen at least.

"You were really young. Wasn't it a joke?" he asked as he shaved her legs.

"No, you know it wasn't. I said it was, to Alice, but it wasn't."

"Well, you had a fucked up life. And you were copying what was in the play. And you didn't actually go through with it."

"I would have done, I swear. She bit my hand." Ida laughed, realising it sounded ridiculous.

"She has got some fight in her then. You did her a favour – toughened her up."

"I'm not sure. I could never admit it at Confession. Maybe I should go now."

"You could say sorry – to her."

"But I'm not."

"I think you are." He kissed her on the knee. "Come on you mad bitch. Let's get out before we shrivel up to nothing." He reached behind him and pulled out the plug.

They wrapped themselves in towels and carried their clothes downstairs to the study.

Alice spotted them from the kitchen as she mopped the floor despite Peter's strict instructions to leave the housework to the men. "You two can stay in the study tonight, Tom and I will go in the sitting room and Peter's going to have my room. Oh, and we're making a nut roast for later."

"We're going to have a lie down, before dinner," Ida said.

Elliot lay naked on the bed and put his arm out for her to join him. She rested her head on his almost concave chest.

"I tried to kill myself once," Ida said. There it was, the other terrible thing. She lifted her head and looked at his face, waiting for him to ask.

"Just once?" Elliot said, laughing. "Come on you nutter. Let's go to sleep."

Ida lay back down and closed her eyes. What on earth could she say to that?

Chapter twenty-seven

~ 1985 ~

Willie was in the shop, sorting, when Ida got in. She could see her breath. Mary said it was the coldest February she'd lived through, and she was five hundred years old.

"Where's your Ma?" Ida asked.

"She had a hospital appointment, about her hip. You're late, again," he said, looking up at her.

She quite fancied Willie, though she'd never admit it to anyone. He was about forty or something, with a messy brown beard and pale blue eyes. And he was rough too, she'd seen him fight outside the pub, but he wasn't thuggy like the others. He was alright.

"I'm sorry. I got locked out. Or in." Ida laughed at her lie, realising she made no sense. She wasn't used to explaining herself, they only paid her for the hours she did, and her start time was flexible, wasn't it?

And today she was stoned. Really, unbelievably, insanely stoned. Tina had got some new stuff in and it was strong. They'd been doing bongs all morning and eaten some of it too.

"You're stoned," he said.

"Yes," Ida laughed.

"This has got to stop. You've been taking too many drugs these last couple of months, you look awful."

"Shit," Ida said, surprised.

"Well can you be trusted to wait in here until I get back from the tip? Make a cup of coffee and try to sort yourself out."

"Yes," Ida said again, catching sight of herself in the mirror and realising how tiny and red her eyes had gone.

The door swung as he left and the bell rang. She sat on Mary's stool. It was in the perfect spot, you could see the whole shop – and check no one was on the rob – as well as out of the grubby window that faced the street.

He hates me, Ida thought. *It was some sort of test and I failed. I bet he's got cameras all over the place.* In that case she better look as normal as possible. She tried hard to make her face look casual and non-stoned. What if he got the police involved?

As she sat still she saw people she knew walking past, men from the pub she'd used to work at, or the occasional girl she'd gone to school with – when, briefly, she had gone to school. It was snowing now, and they had on hats or hoods, but when she caught a glimpse of their faces she recognised each one of them. They were people she'd forgotten existed.

A toddler in a red snowsuit pressed her face against the glass and stuck out her tongue before the child's mother pulled her away. She knew the child. It was Alice, was it? It had looked like Alice. But could her sister still be that young? The thought flew away as soon as it had come and when she tried to remember what she'd just been thinking, the thing that had made her scared, she had to accept it had gone for good.

She was hungry. There would be nothing to eat. But if she stayed sitting here she was going to fall asleep or vomit all over her boots.

Ida jumped off the stool and began walking round the room. She'd rummaged here a hundred times, but there was always something new to find and she was never normally left alone.

So many photos, boxes full of them. They were the saddest. The thing that meant the most to the people who'd owned them, but the least to the people who came into the shop.

Underneath the tables were piled-up crates and Ida took one out and started to unpack it. Letters, postcards, a porcelain cat, and a pack of cards with a scribbled-on score sheet. They'd been playing gin rummy, whoever these people had been.

Before she could stop it, she remembered playing with her ma. She looked at the scorecard and realised the big, scratchy writing looked exactly like Bridie's.

Under it was a copy – her copy, surely? – of *Jane Eyre*.

She put it down, shakily, and walked over to a mound of toys: broken Barbies and Action Men, a one-eyed teddy bear, a terrifying gollywog, and a black-haired Sindy doll with a partly rubbed-off nose.

The Sindy she'd had when she was small.

She took deep, slow breaths as she reached the window. Piled up on the sill were ornaments and horse brasses, the things Mary thought passers-by might want. She ran her hands over them and noticed, in between two decanters, an empty wooden box of crystallised ginger and a battered, damp copy of her mother's play.

Ida stood at the bus stop trying to look inconspicuous, shaking her head at drivers when they slowed to stop. Her clothes were icy and she was shaking, rubbing her arms as fast as she could with her white hands.

Now the people who walked past her were wearing Bridie's things. Her blue kimono; her hairpiece; her nightdress; her pearls.

Ida wanted to reach out for them – she'd loved the kimono best of all – but nothing would work properly, not her limbs or her brain.

It wasn't right. None of it was right. Bridie had made her, Bridie had cursed her, and now Bridie had escaped.

Maybe things would be better, or maybe they'd be worse.

She'd walked out of the shop without locking it. People had probably gone in and stolen stuff, all that treasure she'd laid out so carefully. And her mother's things. She had left her mother's things there too.

Terri said Bridie had got a bit better, dried out and started eating. But it hadn't made any difference, had it? Her mother was dead. Ma was dead. Bridie Adair was dead.

They'd left Willie to clean out her house. And no one had thought to tell Ida. It hadn't happened last year – when Ida had left her on the floor – but it had happened now. It was probably still Ida's fault.

She couldn't face the bedsit, her rent was already late. Tina was going to go mad.

Where the fuck was she going to go?

Two doors down from the bus stop there was a dirty-looking locals' pub she'd never been into. The windows were frosted, the light was orange through the glass, and Ida had the feeling it would be ancient inside, that if she dared to go in she'd be offered bread and cheese and a place to feed her horse.

She would make her way to the ladies' loos, stand under the hand driers, then lock herself in a cubicle until she got chucked out. It was the only plan she had.

A small shaven-headed man was going in too, and she squeezed past his round belly.

"Bloody hell, love, you're frozen," he said. "Becky, sweetheart, get this girl a brandy. Put it on my tab."

The bar woman carried on polishing a glass. "She looks about fifteen Dave."

He pointed at Ida's tits. "You're having a laugh Beck! She's at least twenty. Here," he took Ida's arm and a group of men moved away so they could be served.

"New girlfriend?" one of them said and the others laughed. "Carol's not going to be happy about this."

"Pah," he said.

The glass was on the bar and he handed it to Ida. "You sit yourself there and drink that down. Have as many as you want on me. What's your name, love?"

"Annie," Ida said.

The brandy moved right round her body, loosening her joints and heating up her head. She finished it quickly.

The barmaid frowned. "You're not a junkie are you?"

"No."

"Okay. Well, behave yourself. You can use the driers in the toilet to get yourself defrosted."

"Get her another one, the poor girl's thirsty," said Dave, and Becky turned to pour it out. Dave put his hand on Ida's thigh and she moved it away and hopped off her stool.

Ida crouched underneath the drier, the wonderful heat thawing her jumper and warming the back of her neck. People did moan – she was always amazed how much everyone moaned – when brandy and a hand drier were all you needed to make everything okay.

At five thirty Becky stopped serving Ida and asked Dave to take her home.

He'd given up on both Ida and the drinks and was busy at the fruit machine, chain-smoking.

"Lock in!" Ida shouted. She wasn't as drunk as they thought she was, she knew she'd be alright.

"Not time for that yet," said Becky. "The grown-ups have still got a few hours left in us."

"Fuck off," said Ida.

"Dave, will you sort this out?" Becky said.

He'd won forty quid a while before but had pumped it all back in. "Fucking hell." He punched the machine and the group of men to his left went quiet. "What do you want me to do then Beck?"

"Put her in a cab?" she said.

"Well I don't have any cash because of your fucking dickhead machine."

"Fuck it, I'll go and drink in the street," Ida said.

"I'll walk you home." He took her by the hand and dragged her outside while she laughed.

"Hey," Becky shouted. "Look after her now."

Dave held Ida upright as they walked, slagging off his ex-wife and the men who drank at the pub.

Occasionally he'd lunge towards her for kiss, pushing her against shop windows and thrusting his fat tongue into her mouth.

It was only six and there were lots of people about. Ida laughed to think of someone finding her like this, snogging some gross old man against the door of The Silver Spoon.

"Let's go down here," he said, leading her into the narrow alley by the side of the cafe.

He put his hand up her top.

She felt suddenly very sick.

"Don't," she said.

"You've got a fucking boyfriend, haven't you? Same old story, rinse a bloke for all he's worth..."

"I've got a girlfriend. An American girlfriend," Ida said.

"You shitting me?"

"No."

"You pissed away my tab all night when you were a fucking dyke?"

"Yeah, a fifteen-year-old dyke, you stupid prick," she said.

He slapped her, hard, and her head jerked to the left. She'd never been slapped by a man before and the pain was deep and went right through her.

She started to laugh.

"You ugly bitch," he said.

Ida flung back her head and threw it forward into his. The force sent him off balance and he slipped on the ice and onto his back, his head hitting the concrete with a crack. She crouched next to him and pushed her palm into his face.

As she stood up he grabbed her leg. With her free foot she began to kick, her huge red boots meeting his skull again and again. He stopped struggling and started to wail but she kept kicking, her thigh throbbing and the ground around his bald head slick with a halo of blood.

Vomit rose into her mouth and she leant forwards, puking all over Dave's limp left arm.

As she stood outside her mother's house Ida realised she had no idea how she'd got there. Her head was throbbing, her lips were swollen and crusty, and she was clutching a bottle of vodka she had no memory of buying. But at least she knew why she'd come. Her mother was dead. Somehow she had found out her mother was dead. It took all of her effort to remember how she knew. Had someone told her? No. She'd found the things in the shop.

The windows were black and Ida imagined the empty hall, as bare as when they'd first moved in. "It's only the rattssss," she whispered under her breath.

A light appeared in the bathroom window and a woman, who looked like her mother, stood in front of the mirror.

Ida knelt down.

The street lamps came on *one, two, three, four* all down the road and Ida looked at the frosty pavement, sparkling under the electric lights. But she wasn't cold.

She peered over the top of the gate and saw the woman was still there. It was her mother, it really was. Bridie was still alive.

"No," Ida said. "No."

Back in the shop, when Ida had found all those things, she'd thought she was upset. But now she realised it hadn't been that at all. In fact her terrible broken brain was so desperate for her ma to die that it had only taken a few random bits of junk to convince her that she had.

This is what it's like to be mad, she thought. Now I know.

As she looked down at her boots she remembered Dave, how she'd kicked him as hard as she could. She had wanted him dead, too.

Ida walked round the side of the house, down the lane and deep into the woods. She lay on the ground, the frozen twigs cracking beneath her. She would sleep here, among the goblins and the moss. It was a good place for an evil girl to think about things.

There was something wrong with her, something badly wrong.

Because it wasn't only Dave she'd hurt. Once, when she was young, she'd tried to kill her sister in the sea.

There was a tapping on her forehead, something light and soft like fingertips, and she realised it was snow. She thought about *Jane Eyre* on the moors.

Tina was definitely going to chuck her out. She'd said she would if Ida didn't pay the rent.

There was nowhere she could go, nowhere except these woods.

I've got a murderer's name, Ida thought. Her ma must have known what she'd be. It wasn't enough for Bridie to write a girl in a play, she'd had to bring Ida to life. It was a horrible experiment that needed to end.

And Mary. She'd even let wonderful Mary down.

She could die here, couldn't she? People did freeze to death. It wouldn't be like the times before, like cutting your arms, or taking fifteen aspirin. No one could say it was a cry for help.

Fuck cries for help.

Wonder spread through her as she realised that this – a real, quiet death – was exactly what she wanted.

There was a pain in her cheek and she opened her eyes. A teenage boy was poking her face with a stick, while a group of his friends stood round, drinking and smoking and shivering.

"Is she dead?" one of them asked. His teeth were chattering and he sounded scared.

"Boo!" shouted Ida and all the boys screamed.

"Dale, run back to the street. Get someone to call 999," said the one with the stick.

Ida realised that she couldn't move her legs and in her hand, stuck with cold, was an empty bottle. Her clothes were covered in inches of snow.

She closed her eyes and wished to God they'd left her where she was.

They had saved her fingers and toes. Twice a day for a week they'd 'rewarmed them' in a little plastic bowl. It sounded quite nice but it hurt so much she'd scream, and they'd given her Valium to calm her down.

Now each of her digits was separately wrapped like weird sausage rolls. They let her stay on the pills for now.

Tina lied for her and told the hospital they were sisters. They had no reason not to believe her, Ida hadn't been reported missing, but after a few days Ida relented and let Tina call her father; she said that Ida had been mugged and left for dead.

Bryan and Terri piled into the hospital under mounds of grapes and balloons, smiling and tearful, apparently believing the story. It was only Alice – staring, scared, stroking Ida's sore, bound up fingers – who seemed to know that something strange and much worse, something unsayable, had happened.

Terri came in the afternoons and sat by Ida's bed, reading her Agatha Christie books and giving her Coke through a straw. No one suggested telling Bridie and Ida was grateful for that as well.

After a few days it was time to go home. She wished she could stay.

Tina offered to have her back again, but Ida was too dosed up and tired to argue when Terri insisted she came back to theirs.

It wasn't until they arrived at the flat and she saw her room – pink and perfect with teddies on the bed – that she knew she couldn't be there for long. People went their whole lives without saying things, with unspoken horrors, but Ida wasn't one of them. There'd be a time, likely sometime soon, when she'd need to get drunk and tell it all to someone, and it was far too embarrassing for Terri and her father to be there when that happened.

She lay on the bed and found her feet hung off the end. In a month or so she'd get her money from the post office and fuck off to America to see Anna. She reached into her pocket and got another pill, ignoring Terri as she shouted up the stairs about tea. Closing her eyes she tried to imagine she was on a raft, lost at sea somewhere warm and dry, drifting slowly and gently towards her home. Wherever that might be.

Chapter twenty-eight

~ 1999 ~

They'd only meant to lie down for a minute – the sex and the long bath had made them both sleepy – but it was getting dark outside when they were woken by a knock at the study door.

"Shit sorry – let me get dressed," said Ida, confused and shivering, assuming it was her sister.

There was another knock, harder this time.

"What?" Ida asked, annoyed.

"We believe Elliot Hill is in there Miss Irons. It's the police."

"What the fuck?" asked Ida, sitting up and shaking Elliot.

He sat up, blinking, irritated, but far from surprised. "Oh fuck," he said, "I probably should have told you –"

"I'm coming in," the man said. He was wearing a uniform and held his hat under his arm. "Elliot Hill?"

"Yes, that's me."

"Elliot Hill, I am arresting you on suspicion of theft. You do not have to say anything, but it may harm your defence if you do not mention, when questioned, something which you later rely on in court. Anything you do say may be given in evidence."

Elliot laughed, sadly. "Oh shit. Yes, I know the drill. Can I at least get dressed?"

"I'll have to remain in the room, my colleague will wait outside. Miss Irons, can I ask you to leave the room as well."

"Yes, okay, let me get some clothes." She stood up clumsily – she was shaking all over – found the suit trousers, a shirt and a bra and put them under her arm.

"Fucking hell. Fucking hell," she leant down, kissed Elliot on the top of the head, and slapped him lightly on the forehead with her palm. "You total twat."

"'Whatever I've done', right? That was the deal we made in the bathroom?"

"I walked right into that one, didn't I? You're a lucky bastard to have me. I'll meet you at the station, yes?" They kissed briefly on the lips and she left the room.

To the side of the door a young female police officer stood gazing at her shoes, while Alice stood to her right, holding a tea towel and looking totally defeated. Tom was standing behind her with his back against the wall.

"What have you done? What?" Alice asked Ida, quietly.

"What the fuck makes you think I've done anything?" Ida asked.

Tom stepped forwards. "Is there anything I can do to help? Drive you somewhere?"

Peter came out of the sitting room and put his hand to his mouth, his eyes sparkling as he looked at Ida. "It's better than EastEnders round here isn't it?" he whispered.

Ida laughed and hugged him. "Peter, will you drive me to the station in a bit? Tom, you should stay with Ally."

"Of course, of course," Peter said. "Go upstairs and put your kit on or you'll get arrested too – you're practically naked. How do your lot feel about nakedness?" he asked the policewoman who smiled despite herself.

"Bloody hell," said Alice, starting to cry, shaking herself free of Tom and walking quickly across the hall and upstairs.

"Sweetheart," said Tom after her.

Peter shooed him upstairs. "Go up to her darling. This is the last thing she needs."

The policewoman looked embarrassed and examined her fingernails. No one seemed to know quite what to do and Ida was about to go and change when Elliot was led, handcuffed, towards the front door, his head down slightly, smiling sheepishly as though he'd been caught drinking his housemate's wine. The policeman was carrying Elliot's brown bag.

"Really sorry about all this, it's a stupid misunderstanding," Elliot said to no one in particular.

"Worse things happen at sea, as your girlfriend would say," said Peter walking towards him. "Do you need anything? We can try to find you a lawyer?"

Ida touched the back of Elliot's hair as the policeman walked him outside. Peter hugged her, hard.

"I'll be okay, thanks though, both of you," Elliot said behind him as he was led down the stone steps towards the waiting car.

The policewoman followed. "Lovely to meet you all," she said and turned towards Peter. "Saw you in a panto years ago at The Pavillion, Mr O'Shea. My mother was a fan."

"Lovely to meet you too. How kind. I always think police-women look so elegant – you especially. And I'm sure you do a sterling job."

The woman closed the door behind her and Ida buried her head in Peter's neck. "So elegant? Ha."

"Oh my, it never rains but it pours," Peter said.

"Couldn't it stop, for five minutes?" said Ida. "I swear it's been pouring for the last twenty years."

"Sweetheart, you're freezing," said Peter. "Stop feeling sorry for yourself, go into my case and choose yourself a sweater. I imagine you're low on nice things and we can't turn up to the police station with you looking like a rag-and-bone man. Your sister will have to fend for herself for a couple of hours. We've a prison break to arrange."

The man sitting opposite Ida was thin, pale and nervous – nothing like the policemen in films or those she'd met before. It was a small room, brightly lit – the sky through the narrow window was almost black now, and there was a low hum from a tape recorder in the corner. On the table between them, in a clear plastic bag, lay Elliot's leather satchel and next to it was a box file.

"He's a good man, he wouldn't do anything like that," Ida said. It was a formality – both of them knew he would.

"You can see why we might have our suspicions. The gallery are insistent that he coerced a young assistant into providing him with the safe code. Then the cash went missing."

"It's his gallery."

"Not any more – as you well know he sold it to the current owner in 1996. You can see why we might be a little concerned – he has two prior convictions for theft, and many more for drug-related offences. And you have your own convictions, Miss Irons."

"Shoplifting, years ago," she said.

"The gallery have said they had some issues with you at Christmas. Damaging some work?"

"For fuck's sake! I fell on a sculpture at the Christmas party... I was pissed." Ida could hear she was slurring her words. Her cramps were still bad and she'd taken three codeine before leaving the house.

The man's mouth twitched as he tried not to laugh. He composed himself, opened the file and cleared his throat. "I am showing Miss Irons the contents of Mr Hill's bag," he said towards the tape recorder, removing a pile of documents.

"Fuck me," said Ida.

"Miss Irons said 'fuck me' when viewing the first item," the man said. "I am now placing on the table the script for the film *Ida*, signed by Anna DeCosta."

Ida's hand hovered above it.

"Now, a number of pencil sketches by Jacob Collins," he said, laying them down.

Ida looked at the man, confused, hoping this was some kind of trick and knowing that it wasn't. She remembered one of the sketches now though she hadn't seen it for years – it had been Blu-tacked up in the study when she was little – Bridie in two poses side-by-side, naked and sprawled across a bed, a study for the painting Ida guessed.

"A tin believed to contain cannabis and prescription medications," he said putting down Elliot's battered tin and reaching back into the file. "An envelope containing a letter addressed to Miss Irons herself, from her late mother. And a collection of notes, again believed to have belonged to the late Bridie Adair." The man placed a pile of papers near Ida's right hand.

Ida couldn't make anything out, they were scribbled, faded, and upside down. They must have been in the brown envelope they'd found, the one he'd said was 'just full of bills'.

The man looked at her sadly. He pitied her, she could tell. She didn't speak.

"Do you recognise these items?"

"Some of them," she said quietly.

"Did you give these items to Mr Hill?" he asked.

She didn't reply.

"Miss Irons did not respond," the policeman said.

"Well, ummm, he was looking after them I suppose, making sure no one else got them," Ida said, her eyes on the cream envelope and the spidery letters that spelled her name.

The man reached back into the file and removed the last item, another letter, crumpled and without an envelope. He held it up to Ida. It was Elliot's writing.

Dear Jim

Sorry about everything – bit of an emergency. I'm going to pick up some amazing stuff for you (a Jacob Collins painting hopefully) and we'll call it quits?!

E

"Oh God. You stupid bastard," Ida said, as though to herself, feeling like she might be sick.

"Can I ask who you're referring to?"

Ida didn't reply. "What does the letter to me say, the one from my mother?" She pointed at the envelope on the table. "It is mine after all."

"You answer first."

Ida sighed loudly. "Elliot Hill."

"And did you give him these items or did he take them from you?"

She looked at the table.

"Miss Irons?"

She looked him in the eye. "I didn't know he was going to take them but –"

The man shook his head.

She realised what she looked like, a desperate, deluded, ugly girl, defending her horrible boyfriend no matter what. This man saw women like her every single day. Never had she felt so depressingly ordinary, so pathetic or so small. She took a deep breath.

"I didn't give them to him, no, they were my mother's things. My mother recently died."

"And do you know anything about the theft from James Walsh? From the gallery?"

"No. I really, honestly don't."

"Right. I think we can have a break. Do you want some water? Interview ending at 22.26 pm."

"Can I take the letter? And the notes?"

"Not yet, sorry." He looked embarrassed. "We have to photograph it and keep it as evidence. You can have it back eventually though," he hesitated. "I can show it to you, so long as you keep it on the down-low." He opened the wallet containing the letter and removed it. "I'll go and get us a coffee."

"Wait," Ida said, "please. Could you photocopy them? I promise I won't tell anyone. Please."

"Unfortunately not," he said and turned off the tape recorder, then whispered, "Is that Peter O'Shea, outside? He wouldn't sign something for my mother, would he?"

"Of course. He'll probably go round and kiss her," Ida said.

"I'll go and chat to him and see if we can get these photocopied, shall I?"

They drove home in silence. Peter seemed curious about the photocopies, almost anxious, but she wouldn't show him, not until she'd read them all herself.

Peter finally spoke. "It's always the mothers," he said sadly and seriously.

There was a pause before they both started laughing, unable to stop until they were coughing and gasping for breath and Peter had to let Ida get out for a wee.

Ida didn't look at any of it until she got to her room. Had Elliot read these things in the house, locking himself in the bathroom?

It was amazing how cunning he must have been, perhaps he'd sneaked back into the room the time she'd gone to the beach with Peter and Alice. She breathed slowly through her nose as she started with the letter.

April 1999

Dearest,

I wonder where you are, you maddening girl. I do hope you're alright. And I do hope someone's told you I'm really on my way out this time, not playing around like I have done in the past.

I have been thinking that it would be good for you to see me like this for a few reasons:

1. It's always good for creative people to have witnessed death – you can't make any art without it.
2. It would be nice for you to see how terribly fragile and ugly I've become. I'm an insect, a creepy old bug with a few of his legs missing and a nasty broken wing, no longer scary but pitiful, I promise.
3. Perhaps it would stop you going the same way yourself.

I won't say I'm sorry because I can't say that I am. If I started saying sorry, when would it possibly end? We can all only do what we have it in us to do, and I had in me a lot of funny, nasty things. Not the things a mother should have.

You might find some things out about me when I'm dead and I am sorry about those. Yet I'm still so angry. There seems to be anger in the two of us that comes from nowhere. Maybe you're the one who'd understand. I did try to tell you (remember the pier! Ha!), but perhaps it wasn't the time.

Please know that you weren't named for a hard girl in a silly play, but after a real, soft woman. I wish at least I'd told you that.

Goodbye darling, you were always such a good girl.

Your terrible, loving Ma xx

Ida pressed the letter to her cheek. She kissed it before putting it down, laying her hands flat on the table and closing her eyes, expecting to feel shocks and sparks, but there was nothing except the gentle beat of her pulse in her skull.

She remembered the wardrobe upstairs. Maybe, just maybe, he'd left something behind.

As quietly as she could she slid open the door, kneeling down and feeling the space with her hand, pulling out the brown envelope. It was a lot flatter now, and she knew why that was, but there was still something inside.

It was an old theatre programme, it couldn't have meant much to Elliot.

Strippingly Saucy!
(La Revue De La Sauce)
Islington Green Music Hall
Week Commencing May 25th 1959
Monday-Friday – continuous
Saturday – two distinct houses (6.15 and 8.25)
The Boys and Girls Show You Paris
Peachey Keen Petey
The Gypsy Twins
In The Mood for Love (a song and dance spectacular)
"The Case of The Flooded Privyy" – A sketch by Mickey B

She went back downstairs, kicked her clothes and dirty mugs out of the way, and laid out what she had on the study floor.

A programme
Two letters
A pile of notes
A certificate of baptism

The notes were almost illegible and her eyes were tired but a few things were underlined and some written more than once.

Bridie Adair
Bridie Brigid Adair.
Brigid Catherine Adair
Kate and Ida
Agnes Ida
Why can't I remember?
Who is dead? Make list.
Rodas = door
Laicin = girl
Tobar = road
Lagadi = dirty

Get cat put down – won't drink – kidneys' gone.
Judie Dench – good actress.
Agnes
Agnes
Agnes Adair. Still in Soho?

She remembered the lists Mary had insisted she make, all those years before. She remembered thinking she'd found her ma's possessions amongst the junk in the shop.

She had been wrong then, but she knew she wasn't now.

These few things, these few pathetic things, were somehow her real ma. She wouldn't spread them out over the house, or burn them or throw them away. She didn't want her to escape. Instead she'd keep them all together, in one place, and try to conjure her up.

She opened her Magical Days Book and wrote down the list of things she'd found.

Maybe Peter wasn't asleep. She gathered up all the papers and knocked on her old bedroom door.

"Come in," he said.

She stepped inside to see him sitting on the bed in the dark room, pale and crying.

"I know why you've come," he said, looking at the paper under her arm. "I've been waiting for you to ask. I'm glad you're going to. Sit down sweetheart. Let me say sorry, first of all. "

Chapter twenty-nine

Ida sat next to him on the bed without turning on the light. She knew Peter wouldn't want it on, not with him crying and looking so tired.

He put his hand on Ida's and spoke quickly.

"Your mother wasn't exactly who she said she was. She was a traveller, part traveller at least. Her father was from an Irish travelling family. And she had a sister. They were very poor. And unhappy, I think."

He paused for breath and Ida didn't speak for a moment.

"Where is she now? The sister?" she asked slowly. "I don't understand."

"Agnes, well she's in London. I knew her, I still know her. You met her once though you probably don't remember?"

"I don't know. What? When?"

"In London, the day of the storm, she's the one who found you. She never moved out of the flat your mother and she had shared, the little one on Greek Street. The painter bought it for her, Jacob. The only good thing he ever bloody did. It was Agnes who called me up."

"Oh God. That's mad. I wish she had said. Why didn't she say?"

"She and your mother didn't speak. They'd had an... argument, of sorts, in the past. When she phoned me she was sobbing, she hadn't known what to do. She might have told you if you hadn't conked out."

"We should get Alice," Ida said, and went downstairs, to the sitting room, to wake her sister up.

Peter had washed his face, the light was on, and the three of them sat on the double bed.

"Why didn't you tell us?" Alice asked.

"You know your mother would have bloody killed me. I tried,

the other day, on the beach. I mean, of course I should have told you then. But you were having such a horrible fight. Anyway, she says she's going to come, she's booked a train."

"Come where?"

"To the funeral," he said.

"Tomorrow?" said Ida. "Oh, okay."

Ida said it so matter-of-factly that she and Alice looked at each other and started to laugh while Peter looked at them nervously. "I can stop her coming, I am so sorry. God, I was never very good at confrontation," he said.

"No!" said Ida, near hysterical now and gasping for breath, "I mean, the more the merrier, eh?"

Peter tried to laugh too but still looked worried and waited for them to stop before he spoke again. "You haven't still got your mother's projector, have you? I've got something to show you. Something Agnes wants you to see before she comes."

They sat on the floor with cups of tea, their backs against the bed base, while Peter fiddled with the spool of film.

"We shouldn't sleep tonight anyway," he said as he worked. "In Ireland they'd have a wake. They'd have her body right here and sit with it all night long, would have done for three nights. That's what my parents did, and hers too I suppose." He unwound the film and pulled it through the old machine. "This is the next best thing."

"How did you meet, really?" Alice asked.

"We did all work together," he paused. "In the music hall."

"I thought they closed down years ago?" said Ida

"Some of the... less wholesome shows went on until the sixties," said Peter.

"Fuck. 'Surprisingly Saucy'," Ida said under her breath and handed the programme to Alice.

"They were The Gypsy Twins, of course," said Peter.

"Did Da know about Agnes?" Ida asked.

"No. I don't think so. I'm not sure he knows any of it."

A blurred picture appeared on the doors, a jumble of pinks, dark browns and yellows. He adjusted something and it came into focus – two young women wearing garish make-up and tasselled bikinis, smiling broadly, and standing side on to the camera with their hands on their hips. They grainy footage made them look identical, with thick dark hair, wide brown eyes, and skinny legs. They looked so close, so similar, Ida wondered what on earth could have driven them so far apart.

"They were strippers?" asked Alice, climbing off the bed and walking towards the wardrobe doors, the silhouette of her almost obscuring the picture, the shape of her fingers enormous as she tried to touch the image.

"Not quite," said Peter. "But not far off."

Alice turned round – she was covered in the distorted shape of the sisters and the dark hair of one of them quivered behind her. "Who shot the film?"

"We'll get to that in a bit," said Peter, patting the space next to him. "I'll tell you what I know. What your mother told me at least."

The picture stuttered and changed. It was the back of a girl, wearing a pink short-sleeved sweater and straw hat, her arms spread wide towards the distant sea, while walking towards her, smaller and indistinct, was another girl, wearing a pale blue dress, her face cut in half by the edge of the wardrobe door.

Chapter thirty

~ 1960 ~

Rehearsals had finished early and Agnes had gone back to lie down, but Bridie couldn't possibly sleep.

It was opening night tomorrow, which was bad enough, but Jacob was coming later as well, and these two events in combination had sent something like battery acid through her veins. She was certain people could see it, she couldn't keep still, and when she talked she was pretty sure her words were coming out in a garbled stream.

She went through her lines in the mirror for a while, then headed out through the stage door and onto the pier, her new straw hat – a present from Jacob – pulled forwards over her eyes. Men were finishing the gloss work round the entrance, ready for the grand opening of the new theatre, and they nodded as she passed. Miss Collins said Sid James was coming to cut the ribbon but Bridie was certain that couldn't be true.

She had never been on a pier before, and it was so odd to have a theatre at the end of one – suspended over the water. It was dangerous, she was sure. She imagined the theatre falling straight through the wood and into the sea, the two of them – Agnes and herself – drowning in their matching French maids' outfits, of all things.

As she walked she imagined she was Ava Gardner – they had similar hair at least – and tried to avoid the eyes of the tourists that she passed. She was not going to be nervous. The show would be fine. She hoped Agnes wouldn't let them both down.

The sun was hot, but windy out over the water, and Bridie's cotton dress clung to her legs as she walked, while women held down their A-line skirts and men huddled together to light their roll-ups.

In the distance the beach was packed with people, and behind them stood pastel-coloured beach huts and a row of chintzy hotels.

She was going shopping. She knew what she was going to buy. The day before she'd seen a sweater in the department store, a cobwebby pink angora – or at least partly angora – sweater with capped sleeves. She imagined Jacob's long fingers stroking her while she wore it. It was all too much.

Shopping without Agnes was far more fun. Bridie could practice properly. Their friend Peter had taught them how. It didn't matter what you were wearing, or if your hair was badly dyed, you could be anyone you wanted to be if you just believed it with all your heart.

He had taken them to The Ritz. The game was to sit in the foyer without even reading a paper for a full hour with no one who worked there asking what you were doing. The trick was to 'exude class'. That's what he said. Bridie was good at it. Agnes was bloody terrible, as Irish as ever and automatically speaking their own language when anyone in uniform turned up. 'The sheydogue is suni-in at me Brigid,' she'd say, and Peter would whisper, 'what?' before Bridie would angrily translate, 'she says the guards are looking at her,' and then to Agnes, 'they weren't but they bloody well are now.'

Without Agnes, Bridie could forget who she'd been before. She could be Ava Gardner, or a terribly high-class tart, or a minor royal at the drop of a hat. She was a good actress. Sometimes she scared herself.

She reached the start of the pier, the wide beach stretching either side of her, then walked through the pleasure gardens and the little shopping arcade, until there she was, at Beales. The window display was crammed full and in one corner were three headless mannequins dressed in a wedding dress, a cocktail dress, and a black wool suit. Everything you could need from birth to death, Bridie thought.

She checked her reflection in the glass. Today she would be her best possible self.

It had gone well. Her accent had been perfect and the girl had been so convinced by her immaculate vowels and patronising praise that she'd given Bridie a free pair of stockings when she bought the sweater. Bridie smiled but couldn't help but hate the girl, who, when Bridie could have really done with them, would have thrown her straight out of the shop and probably called the police.

People were cruel and people were stupid. She saw these two things every day of her life.

There was still an hour until Jacob's train got in so Bridie decided to go for a drink. The Royal Bath was Bournemouth's best hotel; if Sid James was staying anywhere that's where he'd be. And it was good to get in practice wherever she could.

The bar was in a ballroom with high ceilings and a chandelier, and from her table she could see the sea and the long pier, with the new, square theatre at the end. If she focussed hard she could decipher the banner they'd hung above its entrance with the name of the show and the name of its stars. Their names – hers and Aggie's – probably wouldn't even be in the programme. They were playing twins, twin French maids, whose only job was to be sexy and stupid and set up the jokes. *This isn't forever*, Bridie thought. *This is just the start.*

She wondered what the theatre had been like before they'd rebuilt it, pretty but crumbling she supposed. People were sentimental about that kind of thing but she was all for knocking stuff down. Old things were disgusting.

The waiter brought her a drink and gestured behind him. "If you don't mind, madam, the gentleman over there has asked me to bring you this with his compliments."

Bridie didn't look at the man he was pointing towards. "If he likes. Of course."

The waiter left and she sat and sipped the gin and tonic. She was Ava Gardner, people bought her drinks all the time. She wouldn't give the man a second thought.

She felt someone walking towards her.

"Excuse me, madam, I hope you don't mind me approaching you. I'm Bryan. Bryan Irons. You're an actress, yes?"

She turned to see a small, pretty man with pale blue eyes smiling down at her and holding out his hand.

She took it. "Yes," she said.

"I know an actress anywhere. I'm a critic you see. And a journalist. May I sit down?"

She didn't answer but he sat down anyway. He was blushing. "I'm here to interview Mr James. Sid James. If he shows up. Came down a day earlier to do a restaurant review. My colleague gets to see the show tomorrow night. You're not in it are you?"

"God, no. I work in London mainly. I'm a writer as well."

"Fantastic!" he said.

She wasn't sure what had made her say it, but somehow it seemed to fit.

She gripped Jacob's hand as the receptionist showed them the bedroom he had booked, a large double with a child's single near the window. Three of them, three grown adults, in one small room. The receptionist stood in the doorway, unsure, confused, and more than a little bit shocked.

Jacob took out his wallet – the nice faux leather one that Bridie had bought him – handed the girl a five pound note and winked at her. She ended up doing a clumsy curtsy as she left.

Bridie was close to tears. Perhaps the digs they'd been in for rehearsals were better after all. Jacob noticed her expression and laughed. "Come on Prudie, it'll be fun. At least we'll be cosy and warm, all tucked up together. We couldn't have left poor little Aggie all on her own."

She looked at him, with his haywire blonde hair, his wonderful wonky grin and his lanky, lazy limbs.

It was impossible to say no. She took off her hat and walked across the room. The window seemed impossibly big – its frame held so much sky she felt like she could swim in it. Below them the beach was dotted with tiny people, with the theatre – their theatre – far out over the sea.

Agnes had her forehead pressed against the pane and was blowing shapes on it like a three year old. She still wore too much make-up despite what Peter had told them – they shouldn't dress like they were on the stage all the time. How could it be that they were made of the same stuff, and looked so alike, but that Agnes found it so difficult to learn? She didn't even try. People had noticed their accents of course, Aggie's still Irish, while Bridie's perfect English only slipped when she was drunk.

This was their chance, their first proper show. What would become of her silly little sister?

Jacob was sitting on the bed, bouncing. "Come and sit on my lap baby cakes," he said to Bridie. She smiled and sat next to him, kissed him on the mouth and put her hat on his head.

"One quick sketch of you two before we go and find some chips," he said, taking Aggie's hand.

"Lovely," said Agnes. "We shaved our armpits so we were ready."

"Ag!" said Bridie.

They lay naked on the double bed together while he sat in the armchair near the window, drawing quickly – his long, thin legs drawn up to his chest. The sisters were mirroring each other, knees and palms touching, their breasts inches apart. This is the way he liked them, exactly the same, well almost – there was normally some tiny difference for the clever observer to find. Agnes began plaiting a strand of Bridie's hair.

"Right," said Jacob. "Let's go and get some supper."

They walked down the steep path from the hotel, each holding one of Jacob's arms. He smiled as men eyed the girls, delighted to be between them as he wound up the motor for the little movie camera. It was breezy and Agnes hadn't brought her coat down with her – Bridie knew she regretted it. She had known she would be before they had left the hotel but she was sick of having to tell Agnes what to do. She had to learn some time.

"Okay girls, you two go ahead and look lovely," Jacob said.

Agnes began to run, laughing, reaching for Bridie's hand but Bridie stopped after a few feet. "Just a second," she said, turning towards the camera and flinging out her arms. "'My bounty is as boundless as the sea, my love as deep – the more I give to thee, the more I have, for both are infinite.'" Then, over her shoulder she shouted, "Know who wrote that, Agnes?"

Jacob laughed as he came up beside her. "Very good, Bridie Doolittle, very good indeed. Bow for the camera. We'll make a lady of you yet."

They crossed the promenade, paid the man at the booth and started walking down the pier. People leant against the white wrought iron railings while friends took their photos, a small boy cried as his balloon floated away. Everything was spruced up and new but under her feet, between the cracks in the boards, Bridie could see the sea, still wild and deep. No amount of paint or bloody Sid James could change that.

"It's marvellous here, isn't it? Common as muck, but good fun – a bit like you two girls. And they've been lucky with the weather for this opening," said Jacob.

They were surrounded by families and could hear shrieks as people rode on the clunky little rides.

Seagulls swooped for discarded chips and sandwich crusts, screeching and scrapping with each other for the best bits of food.

She clasped Jacob's hand – God she loved his long fingers against hers – his magical fingers that made her look so beautiful when he drew her. If only he didn't keep asking them to pose together. She had always liked to think that it was a compliment, that he was drawing her twice. But perhaps that wasn't how it was at all.

They reached the end and stood by the railings, looking out to sea, over-arching their backs and saluting the horizon. Bridie laughed and laughed but inside she felt flat and cold. Something was happening – something was wrong – but she couldn't quite work out what.

Jacob filmed them again. The light had nearly gone and the film was almost used up. It was important to make these shots count.

"It's run out," said Jacob. "Good job anyway girls." He put an arm round each of them.

Agnes leant forwards over the railing. "Imagine falling in. It would be awful wouldn't it?"

Bridie clasped Jacob's hand. "Where's this food eh, Jakey? You promised me fish and chips. Then let's all go for a drink."

That night Jacob snored in the single bed, his legs hanging off the end, while the sisters lay awake in the double.

"Are you nervous?" Bridie asked.

"A bit. Are you?"

"No," Bridie lied. "It'll be fine. We're only there to look pretty anyway, and we're good at that."

Agnes didn't reply.

Bridie woke in the middle of the night to the noise of rustling, and the low, hissing sound of a whisper. She turned towards Agnes and saw the shape of a man leaning over her, while Agnes giggled as quietly as she could, her back shaking against Bridie's arm.

She thanked God for all the practice she'd been doing. She was a good actress, she knew she was, and it was almost easy to close her eyes, and slowly, silently, wish herself back to sleep.

Chapter thirty-one

~ 1999 ~

For a moment Ida thought she was in her flat and that everything was normal, but within a second there was a thud in her chest and she wasn't immediately sure why.

There was the sound of birds outside and she knew it was very early. She must only have been asleep for an hour or two. She would lie still until she dozed off again, thinking about the nicest things she could imagine, trying hard to avoid remembering whatever was causing the ache in her chest. As she closed her eyes she noticed that everything slightly hurt, all of her muscles, as though she'd walked up a mountain or been in a fight. There was period pain, certainly, but something else too. The funeral – was that it?

Agnes. Peter had told her about Agnes. They had seen a film of Agnes! Or had that been a dream? She worked through the events of the evening before realising it had really happened. She had a bloody aunt. An aunt she was going to meet today.

And Elliot, of course; she could hardly bear to think about him. That fucking boy.

She knew if she saw him he'd smile and laugh, say he'd been going to tell her all about it, but without him around it was easier to see the truth of things. And the truth of things was horrible.

Since they'd started seeing each other he had cheated on her, stolen from her, called her names behind her back, and every time she had laughed it off. Acknowledging that it made her miserable would have been pointless; she knew she'd never have split up with him.

But something felt like it had changed.

Perhaps it was seeing Alice with Tom that had made things feel different. He did things for Alice, rubbed her back and bought her flowers. He was even properly interested in what she had to say, and boring photos from when she was young. Unless he was planning to sell those too.

She was finding it difficult to get comfortable, there was pain running through her, and her usual trick – lying totally still until she couldn't help but doze off – wasn't working. There was no point trying to sleep. She'd have a bath in a bit but first she needed to write a list and she reached down for her book and pen.

Cons:
Selfish (in general and in bed)
No plans for future
Crap with money and always takes mine
Steals from me
Doesn't love me
Too many drugs

Pros:
He makes me laugh
Alice doesn't like him
He's all I've got.

By the time Ida had finished her bath the others were up for breakfast, sitting round the dining table in their pyjamas. No one talked about Elliot and after downing a full cup of gritty coffee, Ida was the first one to mention their mysterious aunt. "We've got two hours before she gets here, is that right, Peter?"

"Yes," he said shakily. "I'd better get ready I suppose."

It was turning out to be a nice day, possibly even sunny, and Tom had walked for bread and the papers, laying the table with a gingham cloth and proper tea cups, so obviously trying to make things normal, or at least as normal as they could possibly be. Ida pulled out a chair and sat down, reached for three slices of bread and piled them onto her plate. She wasn't hungry but smothered them in butter and began to eat noisily. Alice, picking at muesli with soya milk, didn't comment and carried on reading the headlines.

Peter hummed loudly, lifting breakfast things up and putting them down again, then briefly glancing at page after page of the paper, flicking through it until he came to the end and started again.

There seemed to be so much to talk about that they couldn't talk at all, as though their throats were clogged with thoughts and unsaid words. They were full up, Alice was right. They were all far too full.

"You look very pale," Alice said to Ida as she began to clear the table.

"I've got my period, a real flooding one," Ida said.

Alice winced and Ida just laughed.

They had all got dressed, and Ida had done the best she could manage, wearing the black dress and heels, with a jacket that Peter had leant her. Her hair was clean and round it she'd tied a black scarf, she'd even put on some of the mascara she'd nicked from Boots. She knew she looked sallow and even her ma's ancient foundation wasn't helping. She supposed it was okay to look pale at your mother's funeral.

Tom looked uncomfortable in his cheap suit, borrowed, Ida imagined, from a relative or friend, his hair washed and tucked neatly behind his ears, while Alice looked sweet and pathetic, her miniscule frame swamped in a black woollen dress that had probably fitted her a few years before. Peter, of course, looked immaculate and was being so kind and cheerful and thoughtful that he was making Ida want to cry.

The television was on but they sat round without properly watching it. Ida was relieved, as she imagined they all were, that it meant they didn't need to speak and that they could sit with their own rattling thoughts. She didn't know if Elliot would call her and she wasn't sure she'd talk to him if he did. For the first time in a very long time she had a great deal to think about, and she couldn't relax. She held her reading in her hand – Ecclesiastes chapter three – and went through it, mouthing the words.

Alice was chattering, quickly and constantly. She went over the plans for the day, wondering about the flowers and when the caterers were going to turn up.

"Do you want a Valium?" Ida asked. "Just one. It will help you relax."

Alice nodded. "Please. I've drunk a whole bottle of Rescue Remedy but it's done fuck all."

Ida handed Alice a pill before taking two herself.

She remembered being little, waiting next to the window for Peter to arrive, and realised she felt the same now. Nothing much changed. She was as impatient and nosy as ever.

They heard the noisy growl of an engine growing closer, then the crunch of gravel as it pulled into the drive. Ida stood and walked towards the window followed by all of the others.

A stocky driver got out of a cab, walked round to the passenger's side and opened the door. Someone took his arm with both their hands and he helped them to their feet.

It was a woman, with a pile of greying dark hair and a long black coat, checking and rechecking her bag anxiously until the man felt the floor of the car for her keys or purse or whatever she thought she'd forgotten.

Ida was finding it hard to breath.

The woman by the car held up her hand in greeting as the driver led her towards the steps. She was wearing sunglasses but there was something about the way she was moving, the way she held her head, which made Ida want to lie down on the floor.

Peter came up behind her and patted her hip. "She's here," he whispered before walking out towards the woman and wrapping her in his long arms.

The woman who looked like Ida's mother was standing at the top of the steps now, three feet away from them.

Alice's face had gone slightly grey. Odd things – impossible things – happened to Ida all the time. It's just that they didn't normally happen to people like her sister.

The woman stepped towards them. "I'm so sorry about your ma. About turning up like this."

Her accent was noticeably Irish, but Ida could recognise the tone of her mother's voice. She was smaller and fatter than Bridie had been, and was softer, certainly less scary. Underneath her coat she was wearing a black, silk dress, with a string of pearls brushing her cleavage.

She took off the sunglasses and put them in her coat pocket. "I put these on, thought it might soften the shock. I'm not sure it worked. I had hoped that you knew about me, before yesterday, or at least had a clue. But it doesn't seem as though you did." She looked at Ida. "Come here, if you don't mind. Please, give me a hug."

Ida stepped forwards and the woman rested her face on her lapel, letting out a loud and sudden sob. She smelled of cigarettes and mints and Ida was pleased and surprised. A real woman, who smoked and ate mints to cover it up. Neither a ghost, nor a square like her sister.

They stood in silence for a few moments until the woman lifted her head, wiping the make-up from under her eyes. "I said I wouldn't do this, I didn't think I would. It's been so long – too long." She reached out and touched Peter's face, and he kissed the tip of her fingers.

"Sweetheart," he said.

"You're Agnes," said Alice, as though she was just getting to grips with what was happening.

They all laughed awkwardly.

The woman smiled and turned to Ida. "Yes, I'm Aggie, Agnes Ida Simpson, nee Adair. I'm your aunt. I suppose I'm the other Ida."

Tom stayed out of their way in the kitchen, while the others huddled together in the sitting room, looking at each other, smiling, and touching occasionally.

It was impossible not to stare at this bosomy, sober woman, as though Bridie had not only come back to life but had become a proper mother in the process.

Ida spoke first. "Can you tell us then – all of it?"

"Yes, I should get on with it before I lose my nerve," Agnes said. "I've practised this would you believe it, but I'm still not sure where to start. I'll start at the beginning. I don't know what you know. And I hope you're not easily shocked."

"We don't know anything. And we're not easily shocked," said Alice.

"We do know that she lied about things. And at the weekend we found her certificate of baptism. We know she was born in Ireland, not London. And that your father was a tinker," said Ida.

"She always lied," Agnes said, eating a biscuit. "Ever since she was a little girl. We were treated the same, like twins, really. There was less than a year between us; I was an accident. Bridie always seemed a lot older though. She was so sure of herself. And she wanted to be different, maybe that's why she made things up. Most of her stories were versions of things she'd seen at the pictures, she always loved the pictures. There was a little cinema in town that showed old films – *The Wizard of Oz* was on about every week. But the grown-up ones were the ones she loved – *The 39 Steps* and *From Here to Eternity*. Then there was one called *Road House* with Ida Lupino. She was so jealous I had her name after that. She used to tell people it was hers."

"Right... wow," said Alice.

"Ma didn't know where she'd got her," Agnes said, "always tried to make her own up to her lies. But she seemed to believe her own nonsense, however ridiculous. I don't know what she remembered about the past. Maybe she blocked a lot of it out."

"She made notes. I'll show you," Ida said.

She went to her room and brought back the pile of papers. "Here, look," she showed Agnes the page with her name on it. "This is where I read your name, and there are these funny words. And some stuff about the cat and Judi Dench which I suppose isn't relevant, ha."

Agnes took the notes and started to laugh and cry at the same time. "These words are the Cant – traveller language. Our father spoke it and we did, sometimes. It's a bit like Irish, but not quite. It was our funny, secret language. Jesus, it's so sad to see her trying to remember it here."

"What do you do? Or did you do?" Ida asked.

"I'm not retired," Agnes said. "I was an actress, bit parts in *Crossroads*, things like that. I was never very good. Bridie was far better. And I model – well I'm a life model. At the Slade." She took another biscuit from the tray.

"Fantastic," Ida said, delighted.

Agnes squeezed her knee and carried on. "I still live in Soho. On my own. I was married years ago but I was never very good at picking them. He ran off with a girl who worked in the shoe shop of all things. A stripper, even a waitress, would have been better than that."

Ida and Peter laughed.

"He had money though, thank God," Agnes said. "I just keep working because I like the attention."

"Brilliant," Ida said.

"What happened, between you and Ma?" Alice asked, quietly.

Agnes brushed the crumbs off her lap before meeting Alice's eye. "Firstly, you need to know how bad things were for her. She did everything for me. Our father was God-awful, beat at least two other children out of our mother. Ma was so timid she wasn't much help. Bridie got strong. Too strong really. Something went wrong in her head and she could switch off, from anything. I want you to know I forgive her, totally. And I hope to God she forgave me too."

Chapter thirty-two

Bridie held the thin, rough hotel towel up round Aggie's waist while she changed into her new two-piece swimsuit. It was eight in the morning but it was already hot, and Bridie was impatient to get into the sea. Agnes fussed with her bottoms for ages, but whipped off her bra without a second thought, showing her bosoms to the world.

That was her sister through and through. Shy one minute, and brazen the next. She was an odd girl, really.

There weren't many people on the beach, only a dog walker or two, and a few old couples who, Bridie imagined, swam every day all year round. She watched an ancient woman come out of the water, bent, brown and wrinkled, a pink swimming cap on her small, shrivelled head. Bridie shuddered.

"Finished," Agnes said, throwing her arms into the air.

Bridie looked at her sister's body. It was pale, with a nipped-in waist and full, round breasts. The two of them were similar, but she was shorter and softer than Bridie; less striking certainly, but the type of girl that men liked best.

She thought about Jacob.

She wouldn't ask yet.

They stood side by side looking out to sea. To their right, high above them, was the long pier and in the distance a few small boats floated on the glinting water.

"It's amazing out there," said Agnes. "You always think of just blue, don't you? That's how you colour it in when you're little. But there are so many colours, it's like... I don't know, a dragon's tail."

"Not a dragon's," said Bridie. "That's too overblown. A fish's maybe? Come on, let's go in."

They left their handbags and towels on the sand and held

hands as they ran towards the shore. Shells crunched under their bare feet, before the icy water reached their toes.

"Jesus, Mary and Joseph," said Agnes.

Bridie held her breath. "Come on," she said, pulling her sister's arm. "Let's go out to the theatre, we can look at it from underneath."

The end of the pier was further than it looked and the water got colder as they swam.

"I don't like it," Agnes said, panting and spluttering as she struggled to catch up. "I keep imagining dead bodies and things down at the bottom, God knows how deep it is. Let's go back."

"Come on," said Bridie, treading water as she waited, turning her face to the sun. Why was her sister so slow? If she was on her own she'd have front-crawled there by now. "Don't be a sissy. We're near now. I think there are steps when we get there."

They swam a little further, and Bridie went as slowly as she could, but Agnes was lagging behind.

She sounded panicky. "I'm really cold and tired. Please."

"Let's go over there," Bridie said, pointing at one of the huge steel posts that supported the pier. "We can hold onto it and rest."

The post looked horrible, six feet wide, rusty and covered in barnacles, but Bridie knew Agnes couldn't refuse. They swam through cigarette ends and past a punctured dingy, the sea growing darker as they came under the shadow of the pier.

Agnes reached for the post and grasped it desperately, trying to find a footing. Above them were the wooden planks, the feet of tourists just visible as they stepped onto the gaps.

Bridie looked towards the beach and realised how far they'd come. It was a long way, it really was. No wonder Agnes was scared.

"I want to ask you something," Bridie said.

"What?" Agnes asked, still bobbing uselessly against the post, her hands scrabbling to get a grip.

Without all her make-up she looked like a child.

"Are you sleeping with Jacob?"

"No," Agnes said, but immediately started to cry. A small wave hit her face and she struggled to catch her breath.

"You're lying," Bridie said.

"Yes, I mean. Not sleeping. Slept. I slept with him. Once."

"You're still lying."

"Please," Agnes said.

Bridie looked at her sister, sobbing and spitting as she fought to keep her mouth above the water. She swam round, grabbed Aggie's hair, and pushed her head down, hard.

Bubbles rose to the surface while something thrashed beneath Bridie's hand.

The fingers grabbing at my thighs are fish, she told herself, *and the hair brushing my stomach is seaweed.*

She counted her breaths and looked over at the beach huts and – behind them – the hotel where Jacob was still asleep.

There were small splashes by Bridie's side. Chips hit the water as someone threw them over the railing above, and a flock of gulls, dozens of them, instantly flew down to get them.

She watched them squawk and fight until the last gull was gone, until the thing in her hand was still, and the black strands of seaweed floated slowly to the surface.

It was time to swim back.

On the beach there were more people now, families and couples, but their things lay untouched on the sand and Bridie pulled her dress over her wet swimsuit and picked up her bag.

Next to her a fat man sat with his wife, rubbing oil onto her already sunburnt back.

"Excuse me," she said, flatly. "I saw a girl by the pier, drowning I think, could you call someone please?"

The man opened his mouth.

She didn't wait to hear his response, but turned and walked up the steps to the promenade, leaving the man now hollering behind her, while two young men who heard what he was shouting dropped their towels and ran past Bridie, towards the sea.

It was a lovely day. The sky was enormous. And the sun felt so soothing on her salty cheeks. "The greens and golds of a fish's tail," she said to herself, as she walked through the gardens, up the hill, and back towards the Royal Bath Hotel.

Chapter thirty-three

~ 1999 ~

"So it was true. It actually happened," said Alice.

"Well, she made it simpler and more dramatic of course, with the chorus and all that malarkey. And she swapped our names," said Agnes. "I mean, in the play, Ida's the strong, angry one and Kate – of course your mother's middle name was Catherine – well, she was weak."

"Catherine," said Alice, "of course. I never thought. But why did she swap them?"

"She did always prefer mine," Agnes said, pouring them all another cup of tea.

"You think it was as simple as that? Nothing was simple with Ma," Ida said.

"No," said Agnes, "Not really. I always thought that she really felt like I killed the old her. I mean, she was the one – of the two of us – who was never the same person after what happened that day. She walked straight out of the sea, out of her life, she didn't even take her suitcase. Common old Bridie Catherine was the one who actually drowned."

"Look at this," Ida said, searching for the photocopied letter and handing it to Agnes. "She said she named me after you. I think that's what she meant."

Agnes read it and started to cry.

"So I don't have a murderer's name after all," Ida said.

Alice leant over and touched her cheek.

Chapter thirty-four

~ 1999 ~

The sisters waited on the pavement outside the church for them to bring the coffin, clutching each other's hands so hard it almost hurt.

Although it was sunny they were both shivering and Peter was rubbing them up and down in turn like they were children. His eyes were wet already and Ida felt that she should be the one comforting him.

Ida hadn't been to St. Luke's in years. It was ugly, a green domed roof on the edge of an estate, like some kind of asphalt hill. It was nicer inside if she remembered rightly, pine and candles and lots of space. The area was bleak though – a wide, busy road lined with battered red council houses. Cars were driving past, passengers staring out at them as they waited, and the few pedestrians gawped as they shuffled past.

Agnes had gone inside.

From around the corner Ida saw her father and Terri walking towards them, both neat and perfect in black suits, Terri brushing their father's jacket with the palm of her hand. They came up to the girls and embraced them, Terri's scent stronger than ever, as though she was trying to ward off a plague.

"Shall I go in?" asked Terri.

"No," said Ida. "Wait out here with us – you're our family."

"Where is she?" asked Bryan, looking frail and completely confused. Ida knew he meant Agnes – he'd cried when Ida had told him on the phone. She pointed towards the church.

"She thought it was better for her to wait there. She thought we should be on our own for this bit," Ida said.

Other people started arriving – women Ida vaguely knew from mass years before, Martin and Tash, Claire from Chalk Farm, then some of their mother's local friends who Ida could tell from Alice's expression hadn't been near Bridie for years.

"If they're hoping some celebrities might show up, they'll be sorely disappointed," said Ida.

Alice started to shake with silent laughter.

Then Mrs Dewani from the corner shop grasped them both, then entered the church, sobbing loudly and blowing her nose, leaving the two women unable to contain themselves.

"She should be sobbing," whispered Alice. "She's a bloody Spar murderess! I bet Ma paid for that hat in red wine."

"Ma paid for her bloody house," Ida said.

Peter poked her in the ribs and they all started laughing properly, while Terri coughed and tried to get them to be quiet.

Father Patrick came out in his black vestments and hugged them all, as doddery as he'd always been. He knew better than to be sorry. "She's at peace, thank the Lord she's at peace," he told them. "And well done to you two girls. You are two living miracles. If she wasn't proud of you before she will be when she looks down."

"Thank you," said Ida.

"We'll do a good job for her, I promise you," he said. "Lots of Latin, lots of drama. I stocked up on incense especially. I'm not even joking."

The hearse came round the corner and Ida took a deep breath, realising that she was scared.

As it drew nearer she could see the woven willow coffin in the back. In it lay her mother's body – she hadn't expected it would be so close. She was surprised by the sharp pain in her throat.

Beside her she felt Alice weep, her arm shaking as they held hands. She looked at Peter and saw tears running down his face.

Across the road an old lady crossed herself and Ida bowed her head to show she was grateful.

The car stopped next to them and the men from Hendon's lifted the coffin out, placing it easily onto their shoulders as though it were empty. Father Patrick led them inside and Alice whimpered as they followed into the cool, dim church.

The congregation turned to look, bowing their heads or crossing themselves as the body went past. Ida couldn't stop imagining her mother inside. How light had she been when she died? She wished she could see her, though she wasn't quite sure why – whether it was morbid fascination or a genuine desire to be with her one last time.

Ida and Alice genuflected, followed Peter into a row at the front, knelt down and closed their eyes.

Alice tapped Ida's leg and she knew it was time for her reading. She'd been finding it hard to follow the mass. Father Patrick had spoken beautifully about Bridie – been funny and sad, but lots of the rest of it was in Latin and the pain in her stomach was back. She was feeling woozy as well – a combination, she guessed, of the Valium, incense and everything she'd learnt that morning.

She got up and squeezed her way down the row, bowed and walked past the coffin, brushing it with the hem of her dress as she stepped up to the pulpit.

She cleared her throat.

"To everything there is a season, and a time to every purpose under the heaven, a time to be born, and a time to die; a time to plant, and a time to pluck up that which is planted, a time to kill, and a time to heal; a time to break down, and a time to build up, a time to weep, and a time to laugh; a time to mourn, and a time to dance."

There was a bang as the door at the back of the church opened and a small blonde woman, wearing sunglasses, walked in, saying 'sorry' loudly before finding a place in an empty row. People turned to look at her and Ida noticed two women whispering to each other behind their mass cards about the new arrival.

Ida cleared her throat again, pointedly. "A time to cast away stones, and a time to gather stones together; a time to embrace, and a time to refrain from embracing; a time to get, and a time to lose; a time to keep, and a time to cast away; a time to rend, and a time to sew; a time to keep silence, and a time to speak; a time to love, and a time to hate; a time of war, and a time of peace."

The blonde woman clapped three times, then laughed when no one else joined in.

Ida came down from the pulpit, turned, touched her mother's coffin with her fingers, and squeezed back into her row.

"Who is that? At the back?" Ida asked her sister.

"Fuck – I mean God – I mean fuck knows," said Alice.

The service finished with Ave Maria, then they followed the coffin back outside into the sunlight and the waiting cars. Ida told Alice she was going to the loo, ran round the side of the church and lit a cigarette, leaning against the wall, not sure that she'd ever been so grateful for a fag and five seconds to herself. There were footsteps on the concrete and she peered along the alley, worried it might be Alice. But instead she saw the woman who'd come in late, smiling, with her arms outstretched.

"Ida! It's me. Annie."

Ida peered at her. Surely it couldn't be. Despite her taut face this woman looked old and truly strange, her lips puffy and her skin slightly shiny.

But as she got closer Ida realised it actually could be her. "Fucking hell. What are you doing here?"

They hugged.

"I'm on tour with *Anything Goes*. We're in Bournemouth tonight. I kind of thought it was meant to be. Your mother was so cool." She reached out for Ida's cigarette and took a drag. "You look shocked."

"I am – really, really shocked."

In fact Ida knew she looked ridiculous – gormless, unable to form a sentence in front of her even after all these years. And she knew she was staring, it was impossible not to stare – her face looked like it was made out of wax. All those years

she had desperately wanted to see her and now, here she was –
wobbling on her ridiculous heels and smoking Ida's Lambert
and Butler.

Ida heard her name shouted from the front of the church.
"Annie – I have to go to the burial. You'll come to the house, yes?
Please do. We won't be long."

There were a few of them at the graveside, huddled around the
nondescript plot and listening to Father Patrick as the cars sped
by behind them. Alice was twitching and Ida knew she was upset
about the spot, wished she'd made more of an effort and found
somewhere nicer, underneath a tree or at least further away from
the road.

The coffin was haltingly lowered into the grave and Alice threw
the first handful of earth, sobbing openly, Tom holding her back as
though she might jump in.

Then it was Ida. As she picked up a handful of cool soil she
thought of how her mother had looked when they'd left the
hospital all those years ago, shaking and magnificent in her tattered
camel coat. She closed her eyes and heard the leaves rustling around
them, louder, perhaps, than the noise of the road if you bothered
to listen properly.

Agnes went next, Peter holding her arm as she leant to pick up
the earth, Bryan gazing at her, amazed from the other side of the
grave. "I'm so sorry," she said loudly towards the coffin.

"She was too," said Ida, surprising herself by speaking out loud
and realising that everyone was looking at her. "I know she was.
Trust me. Her whole life was a bloody apology."

They pulled into the drive to find cars were already there – the
caterers had started letting people in. Ida jogged up the steps,
desperate for a drink, relieved that it was finally all over.

The door was on the latch and she walked straight through to
the sitting room. Annie and Elliot were side-by-side on the sofa,

with a glass each and an almost empty bottle of red wine on the coffee table.

Ida winced, confused and annoyed. "What the fuck are you doing here – not you Annie. Elliot?"

He stood up. "Shit, sorry about all of that. I know it sounds crap but I can explain everything, I promise. I was going to show you all of it."

Ida shook her head and walked back out the room and into the kitchen. She realised she was shaking.

"Hey Ida, relax – have a drink," Annie shouted.

There were crates of wine piled up on top of each other and Ida picked the nearest bottle, filled up a huge Christmas mug, and downed it. She did the same thing twice more until the bottle was nearly empty.

More guests were arriving and Ida could hear Alice and the others chatting away to Annie, unaware of what it was, exactly, that Elliot had done.

Peter walked into the kitchen. "Princess – what are you doing? Don't get pissed and make a banana of yourself. I know it's awful – we all feel awful – but this isn't going to make it better. Do you want me to ask him to leave? Is that it? I can do it now, I can be quite scary when I want to be."

"It's fine," she said, hugging him. "I can handle it. Honestly."

She walked back into the room smiling as broadly as she could, carrying two bottles of Chablis, ignoring Elliot who was sitting in a corner, still talking to Annie. Agnes, Bryan and Terri were sitting together, and Terri was coping remarkably well with him having his hand on Agnes' knee. Alice was standing near the food with Father Patrick, piling sandwiches onto his plate. She didn't seem to be eating herself but had a near empty glass of wine which Ida filled up.

More people came into the sitting room – some of the women from church, Martin and Tash, still tiny and simpering – but Ida managed to avoid most of them, drinking glass after glass of wine, talking to Peter mainly. Why wouldn't Elliot leave? The pain was back – somewhere near her womb – and she felt hot and irritated by everything and everyone. She wished she could go to sleep. This should have been a great opportunity to get pissed and relax, but this thing with Elliot was ruining everything. Annie seemed bloody enchanted by him! She'd barely looked Ida's way since she'd arrived.

Alice was on the sofa now, her head resting on Bryan's shoulder.

"She's a little worse for wear," he mouthed up at Ida.

"Oh shit," said Ida, remembering the pill she'd given her that morning, "She'll be okay."

Some flash old drinking friends of Bridie's had crowded round Annie now, their backs to the rest of the room, blow-dried hair bobbing as they laughed, delighted to be meeting someone even a little bit famous and she could hear Elliot telling some anecdote.

She felt sick – she needed to stop this urgently. She walked upstairs.

They'd left a small space around Ida and for the last few minutes had faced her almost silently as she struggled to make the projector work, tutting under her breath at the unhealthy sounding clicks and whirrs which were coming from the machine. The curtains were drawn, it was difficult to see and she stumbled as she fiddled clumsily with the machine, refusing help from Agnes or Peter or anyone else. She was unsteady in heels at the best of times and there was the occasional clink of her glass as she knocked it against the metal box. By Ida's feet were two tins of film.

The chairs and TV had been shoved into the corner and on the bare wall there was a trembling yellow square, splattered with shifting brown shapes.

Someone coughed quietly.

Blues and greens appeared on the wall and Ida fiddled with the knob on the side of the projector, turning it until the image was clear.

There she was, a skinny twelve year old in her ma's blue kimono, flinging her arms out to towards the camera while she mouthed lines from the play and weird, terrible poetry she'd written herself. Above her drifted the blurred shapes of gulls.

"Here we are when we were little," said Ida. "Weren't we bloody magnificent? Well, we thought so at least. I tried to kill her you know, tried to kill Ally that day."

"Princess," Peter whispered. "This isn't the time."

She ignored him.

"Maybe you don't want a film of us on the beach. We were never the interesting ones, were we?" she said to the room, opening the other tin.

She unhooked the beach reel – her teenage self disappearing from the wall – and placed the new one into the machine, drawing the film through the clips and looping it round.

Bridie appeared, frowning beneath her fringe as she leant against the kitchen worktop in their brand new house, the house she had hated from the start.

Then Ida appeared wearing a kilt, her hands in the air, jumping, delighted to be filmed, grasping the tiny Alice and pulling her round the room like a bag full of coal.

Around her people laughed, and it was only when she saw a drop fall into her wine that she realised that she was crying.

Most of the guests had gone, but a few remained huddled around Annie.

The curtains were still closed but the lights were on now – it was dark outside. Tom was hugging the drunken Alice and Ida sat with them for a while, Terri stroking her hair, before pouring herself another glass of wine, walking over and standing with the people in the corner.

Terri beckoned for her to sit back down but Ida shook her head. She stood for a few seconds, listening to them talking, before, pushing her way through the group and standing in front of Annie and Elliot. "Elliot, I mean it now, will you fuck off."

He looked confused and annoyed. "I came down here to help you with stuff – I know you're upset, but..."

"Fuck off!" she shouted more loudly that she'd intended to.

"Jesus, we were only talking," Annie said, looking at her knees.

Ida felt a small hand on her arm.

It was Alice, bleary eyed, pointing towards Annie. "And you can fuck off too, coming in here and flirting with everyone, I've been listening to you for hours. Ma thought you were a shit actress – you are a shit actress by the way – and you never replied to my lovely sister's letters. She loved you, she wrote about it in her secret book, that I read – sorry Ida – and you look like an aging fucking blow-up doll."

"Fuck," said Annie, standing up. "I came here to be supportive." She pushed her way through the crowd of people and out through the hall, shouting something incomprehensible as she left.

"Oh, fuck you," Alice shouted after her at the top of her voice.

Ida laughed.

The rest of the room began to talk again, nervously, while the crowd around the sisters dispersed and people pretended to examine the sandwiches.

"Come on, let's get you to bed," Tom said. "You never should have had that Valium."

Alice shrugged him off. "Stop it, Tom."

Elliot stood up. He was smiling at Ida. "I knew you'd get jealous if I talked to her, didn't know you'd go bloody mental. And her as well," he gestured at Alice. "Didn't know she had it in her. Come here." He winked and held out his arms.

Without stopping to think Ida threw her glass of wine right into his face.

"Fuck Ida, my eyes," he said, wincing and leaning over.

Tom stepped forwards and put his arm out, sensing Ida was about to launch herself at Elliot.

"Oh piss off, you boring wanker," she said to Tom. "Why can't you let me do what I want? I know what you're about, you know. Obsessed with our mother, fame-hungry, grabby..."

"That's not me, Ida. That's him." He looked towards Elliot. "That's all he could talk about when we were in the pub. But I don't give a shit about your mother being famous, or about what you do, not really. I'm here for Alice, who loved her ma. And even, as impossible as it might seem, loves you."

It was dark, but Ida could see the outline of the desk and chair and realised that they were in Alice's room.

She felt the bed and found that it was soaking wet. With a deep breath she reached for the side-light.

At first she thought she'd imagined it, the bright red blood all over the clean white sheets – she'd imagined things before when she'd taken pills. For a few seconds she stared at it but it didn't go away and she froze – convinced that Alice had been murdered, perhaps by her. She checked her sister's back, found that she was breathing, before realising that it was her own dress, not Alice's, that was soaked with blood.

Her breathing was shallow and she felt light-headed. She turned, swung her legs out of the bed and tried to stand, but her skull filled up with light and she felt herself fall onto the carpet.

Chapter thirty-five

It was the morning, she was pretty sure of that, although the pale green curtain was pulled around her bed and she couldn't see a clock. Somewhere an old man was coughing and somewhere else, to her right, there was the scraping sound of a wonky-wheeled trolley being slowly pushed down the hall. Ida knew she was in hospital although she still wasn't quite sure why. She tried to sit up but the sheets were tight around her chest. She was thirsty, but from the fading sound of the trolley, she knew it would be a while before she'd have anything to drink.

No one had been near her yet which wasn't unusual. Normally, a few times a day, people would ask her questions – how does it feel? Does it hurt when I press here? Is there anyone we should call? Different people but always the same questions. She had no confidence in any of them and was almost certain she was going to die there. Apart from anything else the ground was so far away, and she was so unbelievably high up – twenty feet perhaps! – that she wasn't sure how she was ever going to be able to use the loo or stretch her legs.

Despite asking them, no one had brought her a ladder to use to climb down – not that she minded much. She was pleased to discover that, as she'd always suspected, she really didn't mind about death and it felt like it might be easier for Jesus to find her where she was, laid out like an offering on the narrow metal bed.

She slept a lot and occasionally they brought her food. Sometimes it was mashed up, sometimes not, and after a day or two Ida understood that it was because her age was shifting, that sometimes when she lay there, finding it difficult to speak, it was because she'd actually become a child once again. It was a comfort when she realised that and no longer struggled to talk, instead gazing at the yellow outline of the damp on the tiles above her and rubbing the soft place underneath the top of her arm.

Sometimes it hurt inside her and she wouldn't look. But instead of fighting the pain as she would have done in the past she imagined herself inside it. She knew what it looked like – deep and black and red – but at least it was warm and, while she was in there, no one could get to her.

A few times there were people she recognised, and then she wanted to speak. But it had been child-times when they visited so she had no choice but to smile and hope that they could see how much she'd shrunk. Elliot came once or twice, or someone who looked like him. He hadn't been back for a while. Peter came all the time to stroke her hair. And a few times she had been sure her mother had visited, singing Seoithín, Seohó and holding a damp cloth against Ida's forehead.

Above her a television was angled downwards so she could see. You were meant to pay to watch telly, she'd seen other people put coins in theirs, but she couldn't remember putting anything in hers.

Miracles could be small.

She changed the channel.

She knew this film.

Two clasped hands filled the screen before the camera panned back, and she saw Anna DeCosta in the water, her poor, sad future already showing in her eyes.

There was a shot of sky and then the girl again, but instead of Anna it was Ida herself – this Ida, right here! – out in the water, a blue kimono stuck to her skin, while on the beach was grown-up Alice, filming her sister with an ancient Standard 8.

Then it was Alice's turn in the sea.

Ida felt sand under her bare feet and wind on her skin. She was there now, in her hospital gown on Branksome beach, and she laughed as Alice smiled and beckoned her in.

She strode into the sea and reached for her sister's hand. Alice pulled, hard, and they fell together under the gentle waves before clambering out and gasping for breath, the salt scratching their eyes.

"Ha," Alice shouted into the sky as she held Ida's arm aloft. "Haaaaa!"

It was a laugh and a roar, something joyful and victorious, and above them the startled gulls flew upwards, their wings beating the air so hard that Ida was thrown back into her bed.

The curtain clattered around her as someone pulled it open. It was a nurse she recognised. "Here she is, Jan, she's a little confused," she said as she looked at Ida. "Aren't you?"

Ida glared at her. She was trying to watch *Batman* and it only came on once a day.

"That's fine, Denise," said the auburn-haired woman, quietly. "Dr Green filled me in. You can leave us to it."

The nurse didn't reply but looked grumpier than ever and began to walk away.

The woman pulled the curtain back round and sat on the chair next to Ida's bed. "Hi, I'm Dr McRoberts, from the psychiatric team. I'm here to help you, so if there's anything you don't understand please feel free to ask. I have some questions I'd like you to answer. Some of them might seem quite silly, apologies if so, but we need to ask them. Okay."

Ida looked at her. She was beautiful this woman, younger than Ida, and her long hair was so shiny.

The woman laughed nervously. "Okay. Can you tell me your name?"

"Ida Irons," she said. Her voice was hoarse. "I'm thirsty."

"Oh God, okay, yes." The woman looked at the empty water jug on Ida's side table then turned to look round the edge of the curtain, searching for a nurse. "Oh never mind, here," she reached into her bag, pulled out a bottle of Evian, unscrewed the lid and handed it to Ida. "Wait, umm, do you need some help to sit?"

She stood and peeled back the sheets and Ida winced as she hauled herself up. Then the woman lifted the back of the bed, rearranged Ida's pillows, and held her as she slowly leant back and took a sip of water.

"Thank you," Ida said breathlessly.

The woman sat back down. She was pleased with herself, Ida could tell.

"Okay, back to the questions. Can you tell me what the date is?"

Ida finished the water in three gulps. "Ummm, I'm not exactly sure." She tried to remember the last time she'd looked out of the window or at a newspaper. The light where she lay was almost always the same – yellow and buzzing – it was impossible to tell if it was blazing summer or covered in frost outdoors.

Ida could see the woman draw a circle for 'naught' on her clipboard. "You should let me off that one though. All the days are the same in here."

The woman smiled. "How old are you?"

Ida knew what the answer was meant to be – well, kind of. She couldn't tell her about all the age shifting – she'd get excited and think she'd caught Ida out. "Twenty-something."

"Exactly?"

Ida just stared.

"Do you know why you're here?"

"Not really to be honest. No one's told me. I know I have a pain."

"Where's the pain?"

"Inside."

"Where inside?"

"Inside me. Under my skin. All through me."

"All of you hurts? It's important to be specific."

"The core of me hurts. My guts. I'm not sure."

"Do you know who I am?"

"You said you're a psychiatrist."

"You don't believe me?"

"I think you're a trainee. A real psychiatrist would never have given me their water – professional boundaries."

The woman frowned. She looked at her piece of paper and hesitated.

"Let's move on. Do you ever hear voices, Ida?"

"I can hear you now."

The woman smiled weakly. "I mean voices of people who aren't there."

"No."

"Because Dr Green said there had been some mention of religious experience..."

"Yes."

"Could you elaborate?"

"I could but I'd rather not. Just because he's a bloody heathen he shouldn't go round saying I'm mad."

"Who?"

"Dr fucking Green!"

"Okay Ida," the woman lay a hand on Ida's arm. "There's no need to get worked up. I'm here to help you, honestly. Honestly. Sshhhh."

Ida looked the woman in the eye. They had similar eyes, round and brown with huge black pupils. Ida was surprised to realise she would quite like to have told the woman everything but, as always, she knew that she couldn't. She laid her hand on the woman's, who shuddered slightly.

"Dr Mc... Roberts? I don't mean to be a dick. I am trying hard not to be. You have no idea how hard. Could you please tell me what I'm doing here? And am I going to die? If so – do you know when?"

The doctor removed her hand and looked at the questionnaire on her lap. Ida peered over the edge of the bed and made out the words as she wrote them: *refused/unable to answer questions.*

"I'll get Dr Green to come and talk to you. Although he says he has made you aware."

"Well can you please do me a favour – can you make me aware again? And does my sister know I'm here?"

The curtain opened and a shaven-headed, bearded doctor stood at the end of Ida's bed. The woman was with him – the one with the auburn hair.

"Okay, well Ida," he said, looking up at her. "You have had emergency surgery for an ectopic pregnancy."

"Shit. I was pregnant?" She thought about the pain, and the sickness and the blood. All that sex without a condom – it was a miracle it hadn't happened before.

"I'm afraid so. We managed to save your ovary, which is the good news. You've been treated with chlordiazepoxide, which should allay your hallucinations and sickness – common symptoms of alcohol withdrawal – but your condition worsened. I asked Dr McRoberts to determine whether there was an underlying psychiatric disorder."

"I take diazepam normally. Not from the doctor. My boyfriend gets it for me."

"Well that may be part of the problem. Alcohol withdrawal can usually be managed with benzodiazepines. But if you've been abusing diazepam too... this complicates matters. We may need to take things more slowly."

Ida looked up at the television. The credits were rolling – she'd missed another whole episode of *Batman*.

"Miss Irons, we also need to consider the effects of prolonged, excessive alcohol consumption on your physical health. Your liver function tests are still way up. The ultrasound scan shows clear fatty changes. It's not necessarily irreversible, but if you carry on like this..."

"I've got myself in a right state, haven't I?" she said, closing her eyes. "I'm sure I wasn't always like this."

The auburn-haired woman was still by her bed. Ida felt like she'd slept for hours but perhaps it had been a minute or two. She looked at the woman's pale pink shirt from the corner of her eye. Was it a different shirt? She wished she'd paid more attention to what she'd been wearing before – most people, normal people, changed their clothes pretty often and it was a good way to track the days. That was the problem with the nurses, always the same clothes – perhaps uniforms had been invented to keep ill people confused.

On the side was a fresh jug of water and a tray of lunch. If she'd been on her own she would have reached out and touched it – although it was never hot it was normally warmish when they first brought it round – another good way of telling the time.

"What are you thinking?" asked the woman, "You look very serious."

"I was thinking about your shirt."

"What about it?"

Ida didn't answer.

"I'm not here to catch you out," said the woman. "I'm here to help you. I told you everything you asked. You seem to be pretty aware of your problems anyway. Perhaps you can help me find a solution. They're not sure what to do with you when you leave here."

"I've got a flat. I'll go back there."

"That's good to hear. Well, we can help you as an outpatient, if you'd like us too. And can give you details of AA... and NA if you need that too."

"I don't."

"Ida, do you understand that if you keep drinking it's likely that you'll die prematurely? Have you been told that before?"

"Yes."

"We can help you with your drinking," the woman was leaning towards Ida now and talking quickly, warming to her theme. "The more you talk to me the more specialised help we can get you."

Ida didn't reply.

"I've got other patients to see now. Dr Green's going to make some changes to your medication and will see how you respond – it should work pretty rapidly. Perhaps I'll come and see you tomorrow," she tapped the side of the bed, picked up her bag and stood to leave. "There is a way through. And there are people who care about you, believe it or not. Have a think – I'll try to be back tomorrow."

She slipped through the curtain.

Ida immediately put her right hand under the sheet. Her fingers were freezing against her bare skin and she shuddered. She pulled up her thin cotton smock and edged way over her stomach. It felt flatter than usual, and there was a patch of something attached to her, gauze held down with papery tape. She worked her fingers around the thing, feeling its edges, then lifted her hand and poked it right in the middle, quickly and very hard.

A bolt of pain shot down through her legs and straight out of her toes, zipping its way through the bars at the end of the bed. Waves of it flowed through her, right from the top of her head, and she went with them, leaning forwards as they swept down her arms and into her hands. Her fingers began to crackle as the pain came out of their ends – and she opened her hands wide, watching gleefully as sparks shot towards the horrible green curtain, making it twist and turn as they hit. She laughed out loud and wished the woman would come back – one touch from Ida and she'd be on the floor.

The waves subsided gradually and she lay back again in the bed. She stroked the patch on her stomach and pulled back down her smock. Above her Richard and Judy were giggling as they helped a fat chef to make a cake, while all around her other patients were talking to visiting family and friends, unaware of the sparks of pain that were shooting around them and making their curtains flutter.

She pulled the covers back up around her and patted them down, her fingers crackling one last time as they touched the acrylic sheets.

The opening credits of *Neighbours* had begun when the curtain was drawn back again. Alice was there, wheeling a large black suitcase.

Ida reached for her. "Ally. I'm pleased you're here."

She sat down and touched Ida's arm. "Hello. How are you feeling?"

"Less confused – I went a bit mental I think."

"Yeah, you properly did."

"Where is everyone else?"

"You've been here for ages – five days now I think. They've all gone. Peter only went back this morning, he had a voiceover to do. Wants you to call him as soon as you can though."

"What about Tom?"

"He's waiting outside."

"He's good. He's good for you. He's not boring. He's lovely. God, I was horrible to him."

"It's okay. We both went mad."

"No, I'm really horrible. I mean it. Honestly – without self-pity. I thought about making a documentary about Ma you know – when I first heard she'd died. Or writing something for the paper."

"You don't need to tell me this."

"I know. I just… I want to say that I know I've been awful. Seeing how much work you put in for the funeral. Well, I didn't help, even a little bit."

"It's okay."

"And I'm sorry about the beach."

"It's alright. I recovered. No lasting scars."

Ida lifted the palm of her hand and held it out to Alice. "If you look carefully there's a bite mark."

Alice smiled and rested her elbows on the side of Ida's bed. "Are you sad about the pregnancy?"

"It's for the best I suppose. Imagine if I had a bloody child. I would definitely call it Ida if I did, boy or girl. Imagine how fucked up it would be. It would be the most fucked up person who has ever existed. I could probably sell it to… I don't know, Stephen Hawking or someone to do experiments on."

Alice laughed.

"Shit, sorry about your sheets though," Ida said.

"It's okay."

She grabbed Ida's hand and rubbed it hard, like their da used to.

"What happened to Agnes?"

"She came in to see you. She's gone now. Ma left her a share of the house you know – a third to each of us. That's what the solicitor says. A developer will buy it I guess – knock it down please God. Flatten it. There were loads of debts but we'll get a few thousand each."

"What will you do with yours?"

"Go round the world I think. With Tom."

"I might put it down on a house. Or a boat. It would be nice to have someone of my own. I am thirty after all."

"I'll let the local rats know there's a new hotel in town."

"Piss off."

Alice paused and looked at the suitcase.

"I'm leaving – got to go to work. I didn't think you'd want to go back to the house. I brought your clothes in already, they're in the drawers, but here are the rest of your things just in case. There are some other bits I thought you might want too. Something little from Peter... he said you'd understand what it meant."

"Oh, thank you. You heard from Elliot?"

"No. I'm sorry. Look, I don't want you to get angry or upset and I might be wrong –but I think he might have nicked some cash from my purse."

"He probably did. He's a cock."

"You can do better."

Ida didn't reply.

"Perhaps you can make a go of things with Anna DeCosta," Alice said.

They both laughed.

Alice stood up and kissed Ida on the cheek. "I better go –

I've got a train to catch. When you go back to London, well, I'm not far."

"Eat more, eh? Look after yourself."

They hugged and Alice left through the curtain, the sound of her little footsteps fading as she walked away down the tiled hall.

Chapter thirty-six

Ida walked towards the back of the coach, panting and drenched, her suitcase cradled in her arms – she had refused to put it in the luggage hold below. There was a free double-seat near the loos and she slid into it as the driver started the engine and they began to reverse. Her boots and socks were soaking and she unzipped the bulky case hoping that Alice had packed her some dry ones.

There were clean socks inside, a whole unopened pack of them, as well as a brand new pair of blue Adidas Gazelles in a box. There was a card stuck to it with Sellotape:

HAPPY BIRTHDAY
sorry it's so late!
A xx

Ida immediately put them on.

"Goodbye boots," she whispered, and stuffed them under the seat next to her.

There was more inside: her Magical Days Book, her mother's blue kimono, and the red paper flower from Uncle Peter. She held it up to her nose. 'Great things,' she remembered.

At the bottom was a large square parcel wrapped in brown paper.

She tore the corner, saw some thick acrylic paint, and ripped the rest of it open. It was the painting of her mother – the one they'd had on the wall when they were young – and she turned towards the aisle and held it at arm's length. There she was, her beautiful mother, her dark hair on her shoulders, her breasts bare, facing the image of herself. A note was tucked in the wrapping and Ida unfolded it.

Dearest Ida

I bought this a long time ago in the hope I could make peace with your mother. Your sister told me it had been promised to you when you were younger and it seems right for you to have it. Look closely and you can spot the differences.

All my love (I don't think you're the visiting type, but you would always be welcome at ours for a hot bath and a bottle of wine).

How wonderful to be 30.
Agnes xxxxx

Ida propped the painting against the back of the seat in front of her. There were differences between the figures, she could see them now – a wisp of hair, the angle of their index fingers, the slight curve of their mouths; two different women, rather than just one.

She opened the Magical Days Book to the final blank page and put the note inside.

Somewhere nearby there were sirens. The coach slowed as blurred yellow lights flashed through the misty glass and Ida wiped her window with the palm of her hand. There was a car at the side of the road, it had been hit by something, the dashboard pushed against the driver's seat, and the roof half caved in.

"Please let everyone be okay," she whispered, and blew a kiss towards the smashed up car and one towards the roof of the coach.

Acknowledgements

I would like to thank (most of these should also be apologies): The Masons (Martha, Philip, Joe and Ed), my grandparents Eileen and Lionel Jeffries, my lovely friends (especially those who have ever had to live with me and Abigail Algar), Tiffany Murray, Catherine Merriman, Richard Newton, Mrs Banks, Mr Waters, Arts Council England, the Dundee International Book Prize, Cargo Publishing, Sertraline, and Stefan Brugger (unless he dumps me, then please cross this out).

About the Author

Amy Mason is 32 and currently lives in Oxford with her boyfriend. Her autobiographical show *The Islanders* which she wrote and performed in won the 2013 Ideas Tap/Underbelly Edinburgh Fringe Fund, received 5 and 4 star reviews, and was a 'must see' show in *The Stage*. The illustrated script was published by Nasty Little Press. She is currently working on a new show about her relationship with faith. Amy left school at 16 and has had more jobs than she can count. An evening class – which she took aged 25 – was where she started to write. Like Ida, Amy is very tall, but unlike Ida, she won't steal your purse.

www.amymason.co.uk @amycmason